THE PROPHECY OF DANIEL 11 UNSEALED

The Time of the End

by
Harry Riverside

authorHOUSE

AuthorHouse™
1663 Liberty Drive
Bloomington, IN 47403
www.authorhouse.com
Phone: 833-262-8899

Published by AuthorHouse 05/12/2022

ISBN: 978-1-4208-7089-3 (sc)

Print information available on the last page.

Cover design by the author.

This book is printed on acid-free paper.

TABLE OF CONTENTS

Three Charts — Last Days Events

APPENDICES

BIBLIOGRAPHY

ACKNOWLEDGMENTS

Special gratitude is expressed, at this time, to all of the many Christian teachers that I was privileged to receive instruction from during my education at Emmanuel Missionary College, now Andrews University, and at the Seventh-day Adventist Theological Seminary; both located upon the same campus, at Berrien Springs, Michigan.

A very special thank you, to Professor Douglas Waterhouse, for always praying with his students before every class period officially began. Also, to retired Professor Gerald Herdman, a very special thank you, for making history (His-story) a living and vibrant experience.

In memory of the late Arthur Maxwell, author of The Bible Story, the ten volume set, and to his deceased son, Mervyn Maxwell, former Professor of Church History at the Seminary, I wish to express my gratitude for their profound contribution to the Christian way of life. Special thanks, also, to the late Gerhard Hasel, of the Seminary, for his "Christian Witness", and for his excellent book, The Remnant.

KEY TO ABBREVIATIONS OF SPIRIT OF PROPHECY BOOK TITLES BY ELLEN G. WHITE

Key   Book Title

AA.........The Acts of the Apostles

IBC........The Seventh-day Adventist Bible Commentary, Vol. 1 (2BC etc., for Vols. 2–7)

CG.........Child Guidance

DA.........The Desire of Ages

Ev..........Evangelism

EW ....Early Writings

FE..........Fundamentals of Christian Education

GC.........The Great Controversy

PK ....Prophets and Kings

PP ....Patriarchs and Prophets

ISM ....Selected Messages, book 1

2SM.......Selected Messages, book 2

IT...........Testimonies, Vol. 1 (2T etc., for Vols. 2–9)

OTHER ABBREVIATIONS OF SPIRIT OF PROPHECY SOURCES THAT APPEAR IN THIS BOOK ARE THE FOLLOWING:

MS.........Manuscript

RE ....Review & Herald (Magazine)

ST..........Signs of the Times (Magazine)

YI ....Youth Instructor (Magazine)

INTRODUCTION

Over 2500 years ago the prophet Daniel was instructed to "shut up the words, and seal the book, even to the time of the end: many shall run to and fro, and knowledge shall be increased." Daniel 12:4.

Daniel's fourth primary vision is located within chapters 10–12. According to preliminary remarks, in chapter ten, the angel of the Lord, Gabriel, came unto Daniel for the specific purpose of making him to understand what was going to happen to his people, the Jews, in the "latter days: for yet the vision is for many days." Daniel 10:14.

The prophecy of the eleventh chapter of Daniel began its historical fulfillment in 1798, for it was in that very year that the time of the end began (GC 356).

The primary focus of the book that you hold in your hand is the eleventh chapter of Daniel. The foundation for the correct "end time" interpretation of this prophecy is contained within the prophetic visions of chapters 2, 7, and 8 of the book that bears Daniel's name. Therefore, because this is true, these three visions (2, 7, and 8) are presented first, briefly, with that of Daniel eleven following. God takes care to see to it that prophecy and history do agree.

The primary Bible text employed in this book is the KING JAMES VERSION (KJV) of 1611.

Daniel received the vision in chapter 8 while he "was by the river Ulai" (8:2), and that of chapter 11 while he "was by the side of the great river, which is Hiddekel" (10:4).

"The light that Daniel received direct from God was given especially for these last days. The visions he saw by the banks of the Ulai and the Hiddekel, the great rivers of Shinar, are now in process of fulfillment, and all the events foretold will soon have come to pass (Letter 57, 1896)." SEVENTH-DAY ADVENTIST BIBLE COMMENTARY, Volume 4, 1955, page 1166. (4BC 1166).

"The world is stirred with the spirit of war. The prophecy of the eleventh chapter of Daniel has nearly reached its complete fulfillment. Soon the scenes of trouble spoken of in the prophecies will take place....

"Soon the battle will be waged fiercely between those who serve God and those who serve Him not. Soon everything that can be shaken will be shaken, that those things that cannot be shaken may remain.

"Satan is a diligent Bible student. He knows that his time is short, and he seeks at every point to counter-work the work of the Lord upon this earth." White, Ellen G., TESTIMONIES FOR THE CHURCH, Volume 9, 1948, page 14, 15–16. (9 T 14, 15–16).

Chapter 1

NEBUCHADNEZZAR'S DREAM
THE VISION OF DANIEL 2

In 626 B.C. Nabopolassar, Nebuchadnezzar's father, founded the independent Babylonian kingdom, which soon became a great empire. When Nabopolassar died, in 605 B.C., his son, Nebuchadnezzar, whom history declares to be the most famous of the Chaldeans, became king of Babylon.

The Bible says that king Nebuchadnezzar dreamed dreams that troubled him. He called upon the magicians, enchanters, sorcerers, diviners, astrologers; all of the scholars of his kingdom, so that they might tell him about one of his dreams. He wanted them to give him the details of his dream and the interpretation of it, since the thing had departed from his memory. "The Chaldeans answered before the king, and said, There is not a man upon the earth that can show the king's matter: therefore there is no king, lord, nor ruler, that asked such things at any magician, or astrologer, or Chaldean. And it is a rare thing the king requires, and there is none other that can show it before the king, except the gods, whose dwelling is not with flesh." 2:10, 11.

After it became apparent that the wise men of the kingdom could not reveal the king's dream, Daniel was called upon to give the details of it and its meaning. Through the wisdom and grace of God he said to Nebuchadnezzar: "Thou, O king, saw, and beheld a great image... This image's head was of fine gold, his breast and his arms of silver, his belly and his thighs of brass, his legs of iron, his feet part of iron and part of clay. Thou saw till a stone was cut out without hands, which smote the image upon his feet that were of iron and clay, and broke them to pieces." 2:31–34.

Addressing himself to Nebuchadnezzar, Daniel declared, "Thou art this head of gold." 2:38.

HEAD OF GOLD
BABYLON
605–539 B.C.

The head of gold is thus a symbol that represents the kingdom of Babylon. The date for its establishment, as a kingdom, an empire having dominion over the inhabitants of the world, is 605 B.C., for it was in that year that Nebuchadnezzar subjugated Egypt, secured the surrender of Jerusalem, and brought Daniel to Babylon.

Another kingdom was destined to conquer Babylon and have dominion over the earth, for Daniel, continuing his conversation with Nebuchadnezzar, declared: "after thee shall arise another kingdom inferior to thee." 2:39.

BREAST AND ARMS OF SILVER
MEDO-PERSIA
539–331 B.C.

History is very concise and succinct regarding the power that conquered Babylon: "Perhaps Nebuchadnezzar and the Chaldeans spent too much time gardening and star-gazing, and forgot how to fight. All we know is that two tribes, the Medes and the Persians, overthrew Babylon. While Persia was still a small mountain kingdom, a king called Cyrus (SYrus) came to the throne. First he conquered the Medes. Then within five years he had made Persia the leading state of the Eastern world. He gathered his troops of peasants and marched on powerful Babylon. When the vast walls of Babylon fell to his conquering army in 539 B.C., Cyrus was on his way to establishing a great empire." ROGERS, ADAMS, BROWN, STORY OF NATIONS, 1956, page 53.

As silver is inferior to gold, so also was the Medo-Persian kingdom inferior to that of Babylon. It was not inferior in power, however, for it conquered Babylon.

The fall of Babylon to the Medes and Persians "brought comparative peace and prosperity to the people of the Fertile Crescent for almost two hundred years. But later Persian kings were not such good rulers as Cyrus and Darius. Too much luxury brought weakness and decay." ROGERS, etc., (Ibid) page 55. (from now on just ROGERS, with the page number).

It is written that "another third kingdom of brass" was to subdue the Medo-Persian kingdom and "bear rule over all the earth." 2:39.

BELLY AND THIGHS OF BRASS
GREECE
331–167 B.C.

The approximate two hundred years of comparative peace and prosperity ended in 331 B.C. "Perhaps the Persians were too ambitious. They were not satisfied with ruling part of Asia and Africa. They tried to reach into Europe and conquer Greece. Instead, the Greeks under Alexander the Great conquered Persia." ROGERS, page 55.

"To undermine the effectiveness of the Persian fleet, Alexander determined to take its bases. This he accomplished by defeating the Persian army at Issus and, after a seven month's siege, capturing Tyre. These victories gave him possession of the coasts of Asia Minor, Syria, and Phoenicia. Next he added Egypt to his domains, an easy conquest, for the Egyptians had long resented Persian rule. Returning to Asia, Alexander inflicted a crushing defeat on the Persian forces in Babylon in 331 B.C." FERGUSON AND BRUNN, A SURVEY OF EUROPEAN CIVILIZATION, Third Edition, 1958, page 43. (from now on just FERGUSON, and the page number).

Prophecy declared that this third kingdom, Greece, was to "bear rule over all the earth." History, emphatically, declares that "Alexander ruled the known world in 325 B.C." ROGERS, page 95.

Greece held dominion over the earth for 165 years, but, like Babylon and Medo-Persia, another kingdom was destined to conquer and rule, for it is written, a "fourth kingdom shall be strong as iron:

for as much as iron breaks all these, shall it break in pieces and bruise." 2:40.

LEGS OF IRON
ROME
PAGAN ROME
167 B.C. – 476 A.D.

PAPAL ROME
538 – 1798 A.D.

Rome conquered Greece. The leader of the Macedonian Empire in 167 B.C. was Philip V. "When the alliance of Philip V of Macedonia and Antiochus III of Syria threatened to upset the balance of power in the East and destroy the independence of the Greek states, the Senate (of Rome) felt called upon to interfere. After defeating Philip in 197 B.C. and Antiochus in 191, Rome guaranteed the freedom of the Greek states and assumed a benevolent protectorate over them. There was at first no imperialistic intention in Roman policy, but having entered Greek politics she was forced, step by step, into taking stronger measures. After a second Macedonian war (171–167 B.C.) Macedonia was cut into **four republics**, and the Greek states were reduced to the position of dependent allies; and, when even this failed to keep the peace, Rome took over Macedonia as a tribute-paying province (146 B.C.) and tightened her hold on the Greek allies so that they became completely dependent on her. Meanwhile, the growing determination of the Romans to tolerate no rivals in the Mediterranean led Rome into an unprovoked assault on Carthage (149–146 B.C.). The ancient Phoenician city, which had made a remarkable economic recovery since the end of the Punic Wars, was destroyed and the Carthaginian territory became the Roman province of Africa. A few years later, 133 B.C., Rome acquired another province, that of Asia, by the testament of the dying king of Pergamum. The Roman Republic was acquiring an empire." FERGUSON, page 56–57. **Emphasis** supplied.

"In 63 B.C. Judea became formally subject to Rome, being taken by Pompey after he had reduced the Seleucidan kingdom to the level of a province. It was required to pay tribute, but was left for a time under native rulers.…

"It was during the reign of Augustus that Christ was born; during that of his successor Tiberius, that the crucifixion took place. The martyrdom of James the brother of John took place in the reign of the emperor Claudius (Acts 11:28; 12:1, 2). It was to the emperor Nero that Paul appealed (Acts 25:11). The destruction of Jerusalem prophesied by our Lord (Matthew 24; Mark 13; Luke 19:41–44; 21:5–36) was accomplished in the year A.D. 70 by Titus, who afterward became emperor.…

"Weakened by excesses and corruption within, and attacked by enemies without, the empire in course of time began to fail. The last emperor of the whole Roman Empire was Theodosius (A.D. 379–395); at his death it was divided between his 2 sons and was never again united. The W. (western) part disintegrated and finally Rome fell (476 A.D.), when Odoacer, a German leader, became ruler of Italy." DAVIS JOHN D., THE WESTMINISTER DICTIONARY OF

THE BIBLE, 1944, page 519–520. (DAVIS, page 519–520).

The pagan Roman Empire eventually became divided into many smaller and independent kingdoms, with the ten primary ones being the following: (1.) Alamanni, (2.) Anglo-Saxons, (3.) Burgundians, (4.) Franks, (5.) Heruli, (6.) Lombards, (7.) Ostrogoths, (8.) Suevi, (9.) Vandals, and (10.) Visigoths. The division of the pagan Roman Empire into these ten primary and smaller kingdoms became known as the "Holy Roman Empire." Through the Dark Ages, 538–1798 A.D., as well as at the present time, the various popes of Rome have been, and are, selected from among these various nations of Europe.

FEET AND TOES
PART OF POTTERS' CLAY, AND
PART OF IRON

THE "TIME OF THE END"

"We have come to a time when God's sacred work is represented by the feet of the image in which the iron was mixed with miry clay…. The mingling of churchcraft and statecraft is represented by the iron and the clay. This union is weakening all the power of the churches. This investing the church with the power of the state will bring evil results. Men have almost passed the point of God's forbearance. They have invested their strength in politics, and have united with the papacy. But the time will come when God will punish those who have made void His law, and their evil work will recoil upon themselves (MS 63, 1899)." 4 BC 1168–1169.

A STONE CUT OUT WITHOUT HANDS
GOD'S KINGDOM—IT SHALL STAND FOREVER

"Thou saw … that a stone was cut out without hands, which smote the image upon his feet that were of iron and clay, and broke them to pieces. 35 Then was the iron, the clay, the brass, the silver, and the gold, broken to pieces together, and became like the chaff of the summer threshingfloors; and the wind carried them away, that no place was found for them: and the stone that smote the image became a great mountain, and filled the whole earth…. 44 And in the days of these kings shall the God of heaven set up a kingdom, which shall never be destroyed: and the kingdom shall not be left to other people, but it shall break in pieces and consume all these kingdoms, and it shall stand for ever. 45 Forasmuch as thou saw … that the stone was cut out of the mountain without hands, and that it broke in pieces the iron, the brass, the clay, the silver, and the gold; the great God has made known to the king what shall come to pass hereafter: and the dream is certain, and the interpretation thereof sure." 2:34, 35, 44, 45.

God's "kingdom has a superhuman origin. It is to be founded, not by the ingenious hands of man, but by the mighty hand of God." 4 BC 776.

"We here reach the climax of this stupendous prophecy. When Time in his onward flight shall bring us to the sublime scene here predicted, we shall have reached the end of human history. The kingdom of God! Grand provision for a new and glorious dispensation, in which His people shall find a happy terminus of this world's sad, degenerate, and changing career. Transporting change for all the righteous, from gloom to glory, from strife to peace, from a sinful to a holy world, from death to life, from tyranny and oppression to happy freedom and blessed privileges of a heavenly kingdom! Glorious transition, from weakness to strength, from the changing and decaying to the immutable and eternal'" SMITH, URIAH, <u>DANIEL AND THE REVELATION</u>, 1944, page 64. (from now on just SMITH, and the page number)

"The image revealed to Nebuchadnezzar, while representing the deterioration of the kingdoms of the earth in power and glory, also fitly represents the deterioration of religion and morality among the people of these kingdoms. As nations forget God, in like proportion they become weak morally.

"Babylon passed away because in her prosperity she forgot God, and ascribed the glory of her prosperity to human achievement.

"The Medo-Persian kingdom was visited by the wrath of heaven because in this kingdom God's law was trampled under foot. The fear of the Lord found no place in the hearts of the people. The prevailing influences in Medo-Persia were wickedness, blasphemy, and corruption.

"The kingdoms that followed were even more base and corrupt. They deteriorated because they cast off their allegiance to God. As they forgot Him, they sank lower and still lower in the scale of moral value (YI Sept. 22, 1903)." 4 BC 1168.

"Rule over all the earth. History records that the rule of Alexander extended over Macedonia, Greece, and the Persian Empire, including Egypt and extending eastward to India. It was the most extensive empire of the ancient world up to that time. Its dominion was 'over all the earth' in the sense that no power on earth was equal to it, not that it covered the whole world … A 'world power may be defined as the one that stands above all the rest, invincible, not necessarily actually governing the whole known world. Superlative statements were commonly used by ancient rulers.' Cyrus called himself 'king of the world, .. king of the four rims (quarters of the world).' Xerxes styled himself 'the great king, the king of kings, … the king of this big and far (reaching) earth.'" 4 BC 774.

It is recorded, in Luke 2: 1, that a decree went forth, from Caesar Augustus, that "all the world should be taxed." Alexander ruled the "then known world" in like manner as Caesar Augustus taxed the "then known world."

Chapter 2

FOUR GREAT BEASTS
THE VISION OF DANIEL 7

When employed as a symbol, in prophecy, a beast may represent a king. This is evident from verse 17, which says: "These great beasts, which are four, are four kings, which shall arise out of the earth." It is also apparent that kingdoms are designated, and not simply kings, since verse 23 says: "The fourth beast shall be the fourth kingdom upon earth".

Daniel saw in his "vision by night, and, behold, the four winds of the heaven strove upon the great sea. 3 And four great beasts came up from the sea, diverse one from another. 4 The first was like a lion, and had eagle's wings: I beheld (says Daniel) till the wings thereof were plucked, and it was lifted up from the earth, and made stand upon the feet as a man, and a man's heart (mind) was given to it." 7:2–4.

A BEAST LIKE A LION
JEREMIAH 50:17

"Israel is a scattered sheep; the lions have driven him away: first the king of Assyria has devoured him, and last this Nebuchadnezzar king of Babylon has broken his bones."

EAGLE'S WINGS

God declared, through the prophet Habakkuk, that He would "raise up the Chaldeans, that bitter and hasty nation, which shall march through the breadth of the land, to possess the dwellingplaces that are not theirs. 7 They are terrible and dreadful: their judgment and their dignity shall proceed of themselves. 8 Their horses also are swifter than the leopards, and are more fierce than the evening wolves: and their horsemen shall come from far; they shall fly as the eagle that hasteth to eat." Habakkuk 1:6–8.

BABYLON
A BEAST LIKE A LION
WITH EAGLE'S WINGS
605 — 539 B.C.

"An appropriate symbol for Babylon. The winged lion is found on Babylonian objects of art. The combination of lion and eagle was a common motif —more often a lion with eagle's wings, sometimes with claws or a beak; a similar composite was the eagle with a lion's head. The winged lion is one of the forms of the beast often pictured in combat with Marduk, the patron god of the city of Babylon....

"The lion as the king of beasts and the eagle as the king of birds fittingly represented the empire of Babylon at the height of its glory. A lion is noted for its strength, whereas the eagle is famous for the power and the range of its flight. Nebuchadnezzar's power was felt not only in Babylon but from the Mediterranean to the Persian Gulf , and from Asia Minor to Egypt. Thus it is fitting, in order to represent the spread of Babylon's power, that the lion should be provided with eagle's wings." 4 BC 820.

MEDO-PERSIA
A BEAST LIKE TO A BEAR
539 – 331 B.C.

"And behold another beast, a second, like to a bear, and it raised up itself on one side, and it had three ribs in the mouth of it between the teeth of it: and they said thus unto it, Arise, devour much flesh." 7:5.

"The bear is … cruel and rapacious, characteristics that are attributed to the Medes in Isaiah 13:17, 18." 4 BC 821.

"As in the image of Daniel 2, so in this series of symbols a marked deterioration is noticed as we descend from one kingdom to another. The silver of the breast and arms is inferior to the gold of the head. The bear is inferior to the lion. MedoPersia fell short of Babylon in wealth, magnificence, and brilliance. The bear raised itself up on one side.

"The kingdom was composed of two nationalities, the Medes and the Persians. The same fact is represented by the two horns of the ram in Daniel 8. Of these horns it is said that the higher came up last, and of the bear that it raised itself up on one side. This was fulfilled by the Persian division of the kingdom, for although it came up last, it attained the higher eminence, becoming a dominant influence in the nation….

"The Medes and Persians were cruel and rapacious robbers and spoilers of the people.

This MedoPersian kingdom continued from the overthrow of Babylon by Cyrus to the battle of Arbela in 331 B.C., a period of 207 years." Smith, page 107–108.

GREECE
A BEAST LIKE A LEOPARD
331 – 167 B.C.

"After this I beheld, and lo another, like a leopard, which had upon the back of it four wings of a fowl; the beast had also four heads; and dominion was given to it." 7:6.

"The leopard is a fierce, carnivorous animal noted for the swiftness and agility of its movements.

"The power succeeding the Persian Empire is identified in ch. 8:21 as 'Grecia.' This 'Grecia' must not be confused with the Greece of the classical period, inasmuch as that period preceded the fall of Persia. The 'Grecia' of Daniel was the semi-Greek Macedonian Empire of Alexander the Great, which inaugurated what is called the Hellenistic period. Not until Alexander's day could reference be made to the 'first king' (ch. 8:21) of a Greek empire who was 'a mighty king' with 'great dominion' (ch. 11:3).

"In 336 Alexander succeeded to the throne of Macedonia, a semi-Greek state on the northern border of Greece. Alexander's father, Philip, had already united most of the city-states of Greece under his rule by 338 B.C. Alexander proved his mettle by subduing revolts in Greece and Thrace. After order had been restored in his own kingdom, Alexander set himself the task of conquering the Persian Empire, an ambition he had inherited from his father." 4 BC 821.

FOUR WINGS
DENOTE UNPRECEDENTED
SPEED

Since "wings upon the lion signified rapidity of conquest, they ... signify the same here. The leopard itself is a swift-footed beast, but this was not sufficient to represent the career of the nation here symbolized. It must have wings in addition. Two wings, the number the lion had, were not sufficient; the leopard must have four. This would denote unprecedented celerity of movement, which we find to be a historical fact in the Grecian kingdom. The conquests of Grecia under Alexander had no parallel in ancient times for suddenness and rapidity." SMITH, page 108.

"After this I saw (says Daniel) in the night visions, and behold a fourth beast, dreadful and terrible, and strong exceedingly; and it had great iron teeth: it devoured and broke in pieces, and stamped the residue with the feet of it: and it was diverse from all the beasts that were before it; and it had ten horns." 7:7.

A FOURTH BEAST
DREADFUL AND TERRIBLE
PAGAN ROME
167 B.C. – 476 A.D.

TRANSITION TIME:
FROM PAGAN TO PAPAL ROME
476 – 538 A.D.
DIVERSE (*shena* "to be changed")
"DIFFERENT"

THE LITTLE HORN –
DANIEL 7:8–12, 23–25
PAPAL ROME: 538 – 1798 A.D.
ROME IS ROME—2 FORMS:
PAGAN AND PAPAL
167 B.C. – 1798

"It is clear from history that the world power succeeding the third prophetic empire was Rome. However, the transition was gradual so that it is impossible to point to a specific event as marking the change." 4 BC 823.

"Inspiration finds no beast in nature to symbolize the power here illustrated. No addition of hoofs, heads, horns, wings, scales, teeth, or nails to any beast found in nature will answer. This power is diverse from all the others, and the symbol is wholly different from anything found in the animal kingdom....

"This beast corresponds to the fourth division of the great image-the legs of iron.... How accurately Rome answered to the iron portion of the image! How accurately it answers to the beast before us! In the dread and terror which it inspired, and in its great strength, it answered admirably to the prophetic description. The world had never seen its equal. It devoured as with iron teeth, and broke in pieces all that stood in its way. It ground the nations into the dust beneath its brazen feet. It had ten horns, which are explained in verse 24 to be ten kings, or kingdoms, which should arise out of this empire. As already noticed in comments on Daniel 2, Rome was divided into ten kingdoms. These divisions have ever since been spoken of as the ten kingdoms of the Roman Empire." SMITH, page 110.

"The great kingdoms that have ruled the world were presented to the prophet Daniel as beasts of prey, rising when 'the four winds of the heaven strove upon the great sea.' Daniel 7:2. In Revelation 17 an angel explained that waters represent 'peoples, and multitudes, and nations, and tongues.' Revelation 17:15. Winds are a symbol of strife. The four winds of heaven striving upon the great sea represent the terrible scenes of conquest and revolution by which kingdoms have attained to power." WHITE, ELLEN G., THE GREAT CONTROVERSY, 1950, page 439–440. (GC 439–440)

Chapter 3

THE RAM, THE HE-GOAT, AND THE LITTLE HORN THE VISION OF DANIEL 8

Daniel received this vision of chapter 8 while he "was by the river Ulai" (8:2), and that of chapter 11 while he "was by the side of the great river, which is Hiddekel" (10:4), which is today known as the Tigris. "The light that Daniel received <u>direct</u> from God was given especially for these last days. The visions he saw by the banks of the Ulai and the Hiddekel, the great rivers of Shinar, are now in process of fulfillment, and all the events foretold will soon <u>have</u> come to pass (Letter 57, 1896)." 4 BC 1166. **Emphasis** <u>supplied</u>.

Some of the events presented in the vision of Daniel eight and eleven have already come to pass, while others are soon to meet their fulfillment. This vision of Daniel 8, like that of chapter eleven, has no symbol for the literal kingdom of Babylon. Why?

THE TWO-HORNED RAM

Daniel says that he lifted up his eyes, "and saw, and, behold, there stood before the river a ram which had two horns: and the two horns were high; but one was higher than the other, and the higher came up last. 4 I saw the ram pushing westward, and northward, and southward; so that no beasts (kingdoms) might stand before him, neither was there any that could deliver out of his hand; but he did according to his will, and became great." 8:2–4.

THE RAM WITH TWO HORNS MEDO-PERSIA 539–331 B.C.

"In verse 20 an interpretation of this symbol is given in plain language: 'The ram which thou saw … having two horns are the kings of Media and Persia.' We have only therefore to consider how well the power answers to the symbol in question. The two horns represented the two nationalities of which the empire was composed. The higher came up last. This symbolized Persia, which at first was simply an ally of the Medes, but later came to be the leading division of the empire. The directions in which the ram pushed denote the directions in which the Medes and Persians carried their conquests. No earthly powers could stand before them as they marched toward the exalted position to which the providence of God had summoned them. So successful were their conquests that in the days of Ahasuerus (Esther 1:1) the Medo-Persian kingdom, consisting of one hundred twenty-seven provinces, extended from India to Ethiopia, the boundaries of the then-known world." SMITH, page 150–151.

"**Higher than the other**. Although it rose later than Media, Persia became the dominant power when Cyrus defeated Astyages of Media in 553 or 550. The Medes, however, were not treated as inferiors or as a subjugated people, but rather as confederates….

"**Became great**. Literally, 'did great things', 'made himself big', or 'magnified himself'". 4 BC 840.

THE HE-GOAT
GREECE
331 – 167 B.C.

"And as I was considering (Daniel says), behold, an he goat came from the west on the face of the whole earth, and touched not the ground: and the goat had a notable horn between his eyes. 6 And he came to the ram that had two horns, which I had seen standing before the river, and ran unto him in the fury of his power. 7 And I saw him come close unto the ram, and he was moved with choler against him, and smote the ram, and broke his two horns: and there was no power in the ram to stand before him, but he cast him down to the ground, and stamped upon him: and there was none that could deliver the ram out of his hand." 8:5–7.

"T**he 'goat came from the west on the face of the whole earth.**' That is, Greece lay west of Persia and attacked from that direction. The Greek army swept everything on the face of the earth before it….

"The goat 'touched not the ground.' Such was the marvelous celerity of his movements that he seemed to fly from point to point with the swiftness of the wind. The same characteristic of speed is indicated by the four wings of the leopard in the vision of Daniel 7, representing this same nation….

"The notable horn between his eyes is explained in verse 21 to be the first king

of the Macedonian Empire. This king was Alexander the Great." SMITH, page 152.

"**Touched not**". A similar expression occurs in Psalm 105:15, where it is recorded that God says, "Touch not mine anointed, and do My prophets no harm." Furthermore, on page 995, of YOUNG'S CONCORDANCE, we see that the Biblical term employed in both Daniel 8:5 and Psalm 105:15, is "*naga*", which means "To touch, come upon, plague". YOUNG'S ANALYTICAL CONCORDANCE TO THE BIBLE, 1974, page 995.

Alexander's purpose was not to simply destroy and pillage the earth, but, rather, to conquer and govern it for his own glory.

Verse 8 Therefore the he goat waxed very great: and when he was strong, the great horn was broken; and for it came up four notable ones toward the four winds of heaven.

"The conqueror is greater than the conquered. The ram, Medo-Persia, became 'great;' the goat, Greece, became 'very great.' 'When he was strong, the horn was broken.' Human foresight and speculation would have said, When he becomes weak, his kingdom torn by rebellion, or weakened by luxury, then the horn will be broken, and the kingdom shattered. But Daniel saw it broken in the prime of its strength, at the height of its power, when every beholder would have exclaimed, Surely, the kingdom is established, and nothing can overthrow it….

"But he (Alexander) exhausted his energies in rioting and drunkenness, and when he died in 323 B.C., his vain-glorious and ambitious projects went into sudden and total eclipse. The Grecian Empire did not go to Alexander's sons. Within a few years after his death, all his posterity had fallen victims to the jealousy and ambition of his leading generals, who tore the kingdom into four parts. How short is the transit from the highest pinnacle of earthly glory to the lowest depths of oblivion and death! Alexander's four leading generals —Cassander, Lysimachus, Seleucus, and Ptolemy-took possession of the empire." SMITH, page 153, 155, 234.

Verse 9 And out of one of them came forth a little horn, which waxed exceeding great, toward the south, and toward the east, and toward the pleasant land.

"**A little horn**. This little horn represents Rome in both its phases, pagan and papal. Daniel saw Rome first in its pagan, imperial phase, warring against the Jewish people and the early Christians, and then in its papal phase, continuing down to our own day and into the future, warring against the true church." 4 BC 841.

Did this "little horn" power come forth out of one of the four divisions of Alexander's Macedonian Empire, or, does it come to power out of one of the "four winds" mentioned in verse 8?

"**Out of one of them**. In the Hebrew this phrase presents confusion of gender. The word for 'them,' *hem*, is masculine. This indicates that, grammatically, the antecedent is 'winds' (verse 8) and not 'horns,' since 'winds' may be either masculine or feminine, but 'horns,' only feminine. On the

other hand the word for 'one', '*achath*,' is feminine, suggesting 'horns' as the antecedent. '*Achath*' could, of course, refer back to the word for 'winds', which occurs most frequently in the feminine. But it is doubtful (but possible) that the writer would assign two different genders to the same noun in such close contextual relationship. To reach grammatical agreement, either '*achath*' should be changed into a masculine, thus making the entire phrase refer clearly to 'winds', or the word for 'them' should be changed into a feminine, in which case the reference would be ambiguous, since either 'winds' or 'horns' may be the antecedent. A number of Hebrew manuscripts have the word for 'them' in the feminine. If these manuscripts reflect the correct reading, the passage is still ambiguous.

"Commentators who interpret the 'little horn' of verse 9 to refer to Rome have been at a loss to explain satisfactorily how Rome could be said to arise out of one of the divisions of Alexander's empire. If 'them' refers to 'winds', all difficulty vanishes. The passage then simply states that from one of the four points of the compass would come another power."- (Rome). 4 BC 840–841.

In its pagan form, Rome is masculine, but, in its papal form, when it has the church, its form is "feminine." "Winds are a symbol of strife." At the "time of the end", this "little horn" power is to rise to power out of some kind of "strife", or "revolution"!

ROME
PAGAN AND PAPAL
167 B.C. – 1798 A.D.
AND
FUTURE
THE "LITTLE HORN" OF DANIEL 8
THE APPOINTED
"TIME OF THE END"
ROME

In its past history, Rome waxed great toward the "south", and toward the "east", and toward the "pleasant land", but, during the "time of the end", Rome shall wax "exceeding great, toward the south, and toward the east, and toward the pleasant land." During the time of the end, known as the "extremity of the end", Rome shall rise to power out of one of the "four winds", out of "strife", out of a "**REVOLUTION**"!

Gabriel, the angel of the Lord, came near where Daniel was standing and said unto him, "Understand, O son of man: for at the time of the end shall be the vision." 8:17. This does not mean that the entire vision of Daniel 8 is to be fulfilled at the time of the end, but, it does indicate that part of the vision pertains to the time of the end.

In verse 19 Gabriel continues talking to Daniel and says to him, "Behold, I will make thee know what shall be in the last end of the indignation: for at the time appointed the end shall be."

The two key words in verse 19 are right next to each other: the word "last", and the word "end". The word "last", is from the term "*acharith*", which means "last", or "latter end"! The other word, "end", is from the term "*qets*", and means "end", or "extremity"! Gabriel came to Daniel in order that he might understand something very important that is to occur upon the earth during the "extremity" of the "end", for "at the time appointed", by God, "the end shall be."

Another very important word, in verse 19, is the word "indignation", which is from the term "*zaam*", which means "To be indignant", or "insolent". This same term is very important because it also appears in the chronological prophecy of Daniel 11. It also occurs in the twenty-sixth chapter of Isaiah: "Thy dead men shall live, together with my dead body shall they arise. Awake and sing, ye that dwell in the dust: for thy dew is as the dew of herbs, and the earth shall cast out the dead. 20 Come, My people, enter thou into thy chambers, and shut thy doors about thee: hide thyself as it were for a little moment, until the indignation (*zaam*) be overpast. 21 For, behold, the Lord cometh out of His place to punish the inhabitants of the earth for their iniquity: the earth also shall disclose her blood, and shall no more cover her slain." Isaiah 26:19–21.

The period of time known as "the time of the end" began in 1798. The "extremity" of the "end" is a short period of time just prior to Christ's coming. The sealed portion of the book of Daniel, primarily and especially chapter 11, was to remain "sealed up", even until the "time of the end" (1798). "But since 1798 the book of Daniel has been unsealed, knowledge of the prophecies has increased, and many have proclaimed the solemn message of the judgment near." WHITE, GC 356.

The vision of Daniel 2 is a broad outline of events that are to take place upon the earth prior to the coming of Jesus. The visions within chapters 7, 8, and 11 fill in this broad outline and carry us down to the time of the judgment.

In this vision of Daniel 8, the kingdoms of Persia, and Greece are presented, then Daniel takes us past the time of the cross of Christ and carries us all the way down to the time of the "extremity" of the "end"! Notice how verse 20–25 explain the symbols presented and introduces us to a character description of the anti-Christ person whom Daniel saw in vision.

THE RAM WITH TWO HORNS
THE HE-GOAT
WITH A NOTABLE HORN
AND
THE "LITTLE HORN"
DANIEL 8:20–25 (REVISED STANDARD VERSION) (RSV)

Comments appear within the verses in order to save space and time and also to follow a smooth pattern of thought.

20. As for the ram which you saw with the two horns , these are the kings (tribes-kingdoms) of Media and Persia.

21. And the he-goat is the king (kingdom) of Greece; and the great horn between his eyes is the first king (Alexander the Great).

22. As for the horn that was broken, in place of which four others arose, four kingdoms shall arise from his nation, but not with his power.

23. And at the latter end of their rule (during the "extremity" of the "end"), when the transgressors have reached their full measure (when the cup of sin is full), a king (the anti-Christ person) of bold countenance, one who understands riddles, shall arise.

24. His power shall be great, and he shall cause fearful destruction (strife-"revolution"), and shall succeed in what he does, and destroy mighty men and the people of the saints.

25. By his cunning he shall make deceit prosper under his hand, and in his own mind he shall magnify himself. Without warning he shall destroy many; and he shall even rise up against the Prince of princes (Jesus Christ); but, by no human hand (by the brightness of Christ's coming), he shall be broken (destroyed).

(**Emphasis** supplied)

The "little horn" of Daniel 8 is "Babylon" of the apocalypse, that is, of the book of Revelation. So far, in the visions of Daniel 2, 7, and 8, Rome is represented under the symbols of the "legs of iron", the "fourth beast", the "little horn" of Daniel 7 and 8, and, also, under the figure of speech-"a king". In the prophecy of Daniel 11, Rome is represented under two symbols; one being entirely different than any yet encountered.

Chapter 4

PERSIA, GREECE, AND ROME
THE VISION OF DANIEL 11

We now enter upon the purpose for which this volume was written. This vision, like those in chapters 2, 7, and 8, is given to us in plain language and symbols.

The angel of the Lord, Gabriel, informed Daniel that he had come unto him for the purpose of showing him the truth. "Behold, there shall stand up (be in power) yet three kings in Persia; and the fourth shall be far richer than they all: and by his strength through his riches he shall stir up all against the realm of Grecia." 11:2.

"Three kings would yet stand up, or reign, in Persia, doubtless the immediate successors of Cyrus. These were Cambyses, son of Cyrus; Smerdis, an impostor; and Darius Hystaspes.

"**Xerxes Invades Greece**, The fourth king after Cyrus was Xerxes, son of Darius Hystaspes. He was famous for his wealth, a direct fulfillment of the prophecy stating that he should be 'far richer than they all.' He was determined to conquer the Greeks, therefore he set about organizing a mighty army, which Herodotus says numbered 5,283,220 men.

"Xerxes was not content to stir up the East alone. He also enlisted the support of Carthage in the West. The Persian king fought Greece successfully at the famous battle of Thermopylae; but the mighty army was able to overrun the country only when the three hundred brave Spartans who held the pass were betrayed by traitors. Xerxes finally suffered disastrous defeat at the battle of Salamis in the year 480 B.C., and the Persian army made its way back again to its own country." SMITH, page 233–234.

"Xerxes … is Ahasuerus of the book of Esther. Of him it is recorded that he was particularly proud of 'the riches of his glorious kingdom' (see Esther 1:4, 6, 7) ….

"Herodotus enumerates over 40 nations that furnished troops for Xerxes' army. Included in the vast army were soldiers from such widely separated lands as India, Ethiopia, Arabia, and Armenia. Even the Carthaginians seem to have been induced to join in the assault by attacking the Greek colony of Syracuse in Sicily." 4 BC 864, 865.

Verse 3 And a mighty king (Alexander the Great) shall stand up, that shall rule with great dominion, and do according to his will. 4 And when he shall stand up (be in his power), his kingdom shall be broken, and shall be divided (*chatsah*-"To be halved") toward the four winds of heaven; and not to his posterity, nor according to his dominion which he ruled: for his kingdom shall be plucked up (torn up by the roots), even for others beside those.

"After overthrowing the Persian Empire, Alexander became absolute lord of that empire in the utmost extent in which it was ever possessed by any of the Persian kings.' His dominion comprised 'the greater portion of the then-known world.' How well he has been described as 'a mighty king, … that shall rule with great dominion, and do according to his will'!" SMITH, page 234.

A good portion of the focus of Daniel 11 centers around two forces, namely the "king of the south" and the "king of the north." The terminology and language of verse 4 clearly indicates that Daniel is looking beyond the four part division of Alexander's kingdom. As it occurs in the old Testament, the term "*chatsah*" means, predominantly and almost exclusively, "to be halved." Alexander's kingdom was to be "plucked up", that is, "torn up by the roots", and given unto others, even others beside those four generals that ruled after him. Even the dominion, the boundaries, were to be different.

Before presenting the symbol in Daniel 11 that represents the kingdom of Rome, the one that is different than any previously employed to represent it, the structure, the very foundation of the book of Daniel deserves to be emphasized.

The metallic image of Daniel 2 represents the kingdoms of Babylon, Medo-Persia, Greece, and Rome. The four beasts of chapter 7 also represent these same kingdoms: Babylon, Medo-Persia, Greece, and Rome. In the vision of chapter 8, the kingdoms of Medo-Persia and Greece are clearly presented, while that of Rome is symbolized by the "little horn", which is Babylon of the apocalypse —book of Revelation.

In the prophecy of Daniel 11, as presented thus far, we have the kingdoms of Persia, and Greece. After Greece, next comes the kingdom of Rome, which is presented under a symbol. No matter what the symbol may be, it represents the kingdom of Rome.

Verse 5 And the king of the south (Rome) shall be strong, and one of his princes (a Roman prince); and he (the Roman prince) shall be strong above him (stronger than Rome-the "king of the south"), and have dominion; his dominion (that of the Roman prince) shall be a great dominion.

The "king of the south" is Rome! But who is the Roman prince that was destined, according to Scripture, to become stronger than Rome and have a "great dominion"?

THE ISLAND OF CORSICA

Corsica lies just off the southern coast of France in the Mediterranean Sea. There was, according to history, a "special attachment of Corsica to the Papacy, throughout the troubled years of the Dark Ages and the anarchy of the medieval period…. After 455 the Island was invaded in turn by Vandals and Ostrogoths, who exacted tribute from the population, but more widespread pillage and brutality occurred during two centuries of occupation by the Byzantines. In turn the Byzantines were replaced by Lombards who invaded the Island in 725. Their control was short-lived, for in 755 Pepin Le Bref, ruler of the Ostrogothic kingdom of Italy, placed the Island under the protection of the Papacy a decision confirmed by Charlemagne in 774....

"On 15 August (1769) ..., the very day on which Napoleon (Bonaparte) was born, Corsica was proclaimed French." THOMPSON, IAN, CORSICA, 1972, page 56–57, 67–68.

As it was in chapter 8, so it also is here in 11. After presenting the kingdom of Greece, Daniel passes the cross of Christ and comes all the way down to the "time of the end", 1798 and thereafter.

NAPOLEON BONAPARTE THE "ROMAN PRINCE" FROM CORSICA

According to history, "the Buonapartes were of Italian ancestry. They moved from Florence northward to the coastal town of Sarzana, and then to Corsica....

"Napoleon Bonaparte was born at Ajaccio, in Corsica; the original orthography of his name was Buonaparte, but he suppressed the U during his first campaign in Italy. His motives for so doing were ... to render the spelling conformable with the pronunciation, and to abridge his signature." GIMPEL, HERBERT J., NAPOLEON, MAN OF DESTINY, 1968, page 4, 1–2.

"The families of both his (Napoleon's) parents had come centuries earlier from northern Italy.

"Self-conscious about his origins, he hated to be called or thought of as 'the Corsican.' In order to be 'absolutely French', he changed his name from the Italianate 'Buonaparte' to the French 'Bonaparte.'"

WEIDHORN I MANFRED, NAPOLEON, 1986, page 7, 27.

THE ROMAN PRINCE WAS TO BE STRONGER THAN ROME - THE "king OF THE SOUTH" AND HAVE DOMINION OVER HIM HIS DOMINION WAS TO BE A "GREAT DOMINION"

Napoleon personally led two military expeditions into Italy. The following account is in reference to his first campaign of 1796.

"As thorough-going revolutionists, the Directors (heads of government in France) wish to put an end to the temporal power of the pope; for the Papal States are the focus of the religion which Revolutionary France has rejected. The prospect of this moral success, to be gilded by the wealth of the Vatican, charms them more than all Bonaparte's activities in the formation of border states. They insist upon his advancing against Rome.... But he holds his hand. For him, the pope is the only ruler who cannot be dethroned by big guns. He sees the idea behind the papacy, with its millennial influence on France and Europe; ... He moves southward, and, literally, crosses the Rubicon (the river of northern Italy forming part of the boundary between Cisalpine Gaul —France and Italy whose crossing by Julius Caesar in 49 B.C. was regarded by the Senate as an act of war) , but there he stops. Because he is the stronger, he offers a truce; hence-forward this will be his technique. The aged pope accepts the offer, for Bonaparte is wise enough to leave all

"AND THE KING OF THE SOUTH SHALL BE STRONG"

KINGDOM	DANIEL 2	DANIEL 7	DANIEL 8	DANIEL 11
BABYLON 605–539 B.C.	HEAD OF GOLD 2:38	LION 7:5		
MEDO-PERSIA 539–331 B.C.	BREAST AND ARMS OF SILVER 2:32, 39	BEAR 7:5	RAM 8:3, 20	PERSIA (VERSE 2)
GREECE 331–167 B.C.	BELLY AND THIGHS OF BRASS 2:32, 39	LEOPARD 7:6	HE GOAT 8:5, 21	GREECE (VERSES 2–4)
ROME PAGAN ROME 167 B.C.–476 A.D. PAPAL ROME 538–1798 A.D.	LEGS OF IRON 2:33	FOURTH BEAST WITH 10 HORNS PAGAN ROME 7:7, 23 "LITTLE HORN" 7:8, 24, 25	LITTLE HORN 8:9	ROME KING OF THE SOUTH (VERSES 5,6)

"THE WISE SHALL UNDERSTAND" DANIEL 12:10

ecclesiastical questions open. Pius VI promises to pay France several millions; to hand over one hundred pictures, busts, vases, or statues as the French commissioners shall determine. There are only two articles for which the commander-in-chief makes a specific demand; he wants the busts of Janius Brutus and Marcus Brutus from the Capital. He is a Roman from Corsica; he crosses the Rubicon, spares Rome, and does not enter the city; but he requisitions the busts of the two heroes of antiquity." LUDWIG, EMIL, NAPOLEON, 1926, page 84–85.

A SECOND TIME

When Pius VI "fails to pay up, and makes difficulties, Napoleon sets out towards Rome a second time, but does not go to the city. After a trifling skirmish, he is willing to make peace….

"Finally, he sends to the pope, who is on the point of taking flight, an assurance that there is nothing to be afraid of . 'Tell the Holy Father that I am not Attila.' When the nuncio (a papal legate of the highest rank) is slow to sign the new agreement, the polished man of the world is suddenly metamorphosed into a soldier, who tears up the draft and throws it into the fire…. He doubles his demands, and this time he gets what he wants. " LUDWIG, page 85 – 86.

THE TREATY OF TOLENTINO 1797

"By this treaty concluded between Pope Pius VI and Napoleon, the pontiff ceded Avignon, Bologna, Ferrara, the Comtat —Venaissin, the Romagna and Ancona to France. The agreement was signed in February 1797." THE ENCYCLOPEDIA AMERICANA, Volume 21, 1953, page 446.

"Napoleon came very close to uniting Europe briefly." Though only five feet and one inch, or so, in height, he "is most famous as a great military commander. His name was feared by all the monarchs of Europe. The rulers of other nations were eager to punish the French for revolting and for beheading their king, Louis XVI…. He (Napoleon) freed France from invaders. Then he set out to conquer all those who had opposed him: Spain, Austria, and many of the Germanic states, Russia, and Great Britain. His ideal was to bring all of Europe under one emperor —himself." ROGERS, page 309.

Verse 6 And in the end of years they shall join themselves together; for the king's daughter of the south shall come to the king of the north to make an agreement: but she shall not retain the power of the arm; neither shall he stand, nor his arm: but she shall be given up, and they that brought her, and he that begat her, and he that strengthened her in these times.

END OF YEARS

End of what years? In the prophecy of Daniel 7:25, the papacy, under the symbol of the "little horn", was to "speak great words against the most High, and … wear out the saints of the most High, and think to change times and laws: and they shall be given into his hand until a time and times and the dividing of time."

According to the prophecy of Revelation 12, the dragon "sought to destroy Christ at His birth. The dragon is said to be Satan (Revelation 12:9); he it was that moved upon Herod to put the Saviour to death. But the chief agent of Satan in making war upon Christ and His people during the first centuries of the Christian Era was the Roman Empire, in which paganism was the prevailing religion. Thus while the dragon, primarily, represents Satan, it is, in a secondary sense, a symbol of pagan Rome.

"In chapter 13 (verses 1–10) is described another beast, 'like unto a leopard', to which the dragon gave 'his power, and his seat, and great authority.' This symbol, as most protestants have believed, represents the papacy, which succeeded to the power and seat and authority once held by the ancient Roman Empire. Of the leopard-like beast it is declared: 'There was given unto him a mouth speaking great things and blasphemies…. And he opened his mouth in blasphemy against God, to blaspheme His name, and His tabernacle, and them that dwell in heaven. And it was given unto him to make war with the saints, and to overcome them: and power was given him over all kindreds, and tongues, and nations.' This prophecy, which is nearly identical with the description of the little horn of Daniel 7, unquestionably points to the papacy.

"'Power was given unto him to continue forty and two months.' And, says the prophet, 'I saw one of his heads as it were wounded to death.' And again: 'He that leadeth into captivity shall go into captivity: he that killeth with the sword must be killed with the sword.' The forty and two months are the same as the time and times and the dividing of time', three years and a half, or 1260 days, of Daniel 7 – time during which the papal power was to oppress God's people. This period … began with the supremacy of the papacy, A.D.538, and terminated in 1798. At that time the pope (Pius VI) was made captive by the French army, the papal power received its deadly wound, and the prediction was fulfilled, 'He that leadeth into captivity shall go into captivity.'" White, GC 438–439.

The word "end", in verse 6, is from "*qets*", and means "extremity"! In the "end of years", or "extremity of years", that is to say, at the end of the 1260 years, or shortly thereafter, during the beginning of the "time of the end", "they", the Roman prince (Napoleon) and the "king of the south", Rome, were to join themselves together.

FOR THE KING'S DAUGHTER OF THE SOUTH — ROME SHALL COME TO THE KING OF THE NORTH — FRANCE, TO MAKE AN AGREEMENT

When employed as a symbol, in prophecy, the expression, "daughter", represents a religious group, a church. One example of its use, in this manner, occurs in the prophecy of Zephaniah, where the following words appear: "Sing, O daughter (*bath*) of Zion; shout, O Israel; be glad and rejoice with all the heart, O daughter (*bath*) of Jerusalem." This same term (*bath*) occurs in 11:6.

France is, geographically, North of Rome. In the "end of years", 1798, or shortly thereafter, a representative of the "kings daughter of the south", the Roman Catholic Church, the papacy, was to come to the "king of the north", France, for the purpose of entering into an agreement (*mesharim*—"upright things"). Did such a meeting and agreement occur?

Napoleon "Bonaparte had secretly formed a plan of coming to an understanding with the Holy See (the Pope), but he waited until his authority was firmly established before initiating negotiations. The victory at Marengo (1800) supplied his regime with the desired strength. Before returning to France Napoleon stopped at Vercelli in Italy, where he exposed his plan to Cardinal Carlo della Martiniana, whom he delegated to transmit his overtures to the Pope. Pius VII (Pius VI had died in exile, in France, on August 29, 1799 and the new Pope was elected on March 14, 1800) immediately welcomed the First Consul's (Napoleon's) advances.... The First Consul insisted that negotiations be conducted in Paris, where the papal representative would be isolated and more accommodating; he then furnished the envoy with passports for Paris without previously informing the Holy See.

(SPINA)
(A REPRESENTATIVE OF THE CHURCH OF ROME)

"Spina arrived in Paris (Oct. 20, 1800) ... supplied with instructions limiting his power. Thus he was authorized to discuss the French governments proposals, but not to pass final decision on them.... In discussions with the industrious Bernier, who represented the French government, Spina was circumspect and patient. Four successive schemes were studied, modified, and then rejected.... The tenth one proved acceptable to both sides, and it was signed at midnight on July 15, (1801). Pius VII ratified it August 15; Napoleon, September 8 (1801). The French legislature approved the concordat, along with the organic Articles, April 8, 1802." NEW CATHOLIC ENCYCLOPEDIA, Volume 11, 1967, page 115–116.

FRANCE
CONCORDAT OF 1801

CONCORDAT BETWEEN PIUS VII AND NAPOLEON BONAPARTE, WHICH REGULATED CHURCH — STATE RELATIONS IN FRANCE FOR MORE THAN A CENTURY

"**NEGOTIATIONS.** In arranging this agreement Napoleon was inspired solely by political considerations; Pius VII entirely by religious aims." NEW CATHOLIC ENCYCLOPEDIA, Volume 11, page 115.

1801 CONCORDAT PROVISIONS

"Pius VII agreed to renounce all claim to church property confiscated and sold by the revolutionary assemblies, and to permit the French government to nominate French bishops who would in turn appoint the lower clergy. In return the Roman Catholic faith was declared the religion of the great majority of Frenchmen, and the constitutional clergy (i.e., those who had defied the pope and accepted the civil constitution). This settlement

EUROPE

In the "end of years", 1798, or shortly thereafter, the king of the South, Rome, and the Roman prince, Napoleon Bonaparte, were destined to "join themselves together; for the king's daughter of the South", a representative of the church of Rome, was to "come to the king of the North", Napoleon Bonaparte—France, "to make an agreement:" the famous Concodat of 1801. Daniel 11:6.

meant: (1) that the ten-year schism between Rome and the Gallican Church had ended with the spiritual authority of the pope unimpaired; (2) that the purchasers of confiscated church lands might for the first time consider their titles valid; and (3) that the French clergy would prove submissive to the consular (French) government because the selection of bishops and the payment of salaries had become a function of the state (of France)." FERGUSON, page 627.

1804
ROME-THE "KING OF THE SOUTH"
FRANCE-THE "KING OF THE NORTH"
POPE PIUS VII TRAVELS TO PARIS, FRANCE

The year was 1804. The occasion was the coronation of the first Emperor of France.

"At Napoleon's invitation, Pope Pius VII journeyed to Paris to assist at the coronation of the first 'Emperor of the French'. The imposing ceremony took place in the Cathedral of Notre Dame." FERGUSON, page 629.

"Napoleon, robed in an antique mantle, strides to the altar leading the empress by the hand. Josephine's charm helps to divert the great moment of a certain sense of embarrassment. Surrounded by attendant cardinals, the pope is seated, waiting. The organ peals forth.

"Then, when the appointed instant has come, and all are expecting this man who has never bowed the knee to any one, to kneel before the Holy Father, Napoleon, to the amazement of the congregation, seizes the crown, turns his back on the pope and the altar, and standing upright as always, crowns himself in the sight of France. Then he crowns his kneeling wife.

"None but the pope had known his intentions. Informed at the eleventh hour, Pius had lacked courage to threaten immediate departure. Now, all he could do was to anoint and bless the two sinners. Moreover, the crown on the Emperor's head is not a Christian crown at all, but a small circlet of golden laurel leaves.... (similar to the one that Charlemagne was crowned with so many centuries before).

"Thus, in this symbolical hour, Napoleon reduces to mockery the legitimate formalities he is affecting to copy. Furthermore, he makes a laughing-stock of the pope, who will not forget the slight." LUDWIG, page 227–228.

While he was in Paris, the pope made an agreement with Napoleon Bonaparte. In this agreement Napoleon made certain concessions to the pope, which "were limited to assurance of a salary for 25,000 priests (desservants), the foundation of six metropolitan seminaries, the expulsion of married priests from teaching posts, and greater liberty to religious congregations dedicated to education and charity." NEW CATHOLIC ENCYCLOPEDIA, Volume 11, page 402.

Pope Pius VII spent four months in Paris but failed in his attempt to secure the return of the Legations (Bologna, Ferrara, the Romagna) to the Papal States. It also was his hope that Catholicism would be proclaimed as the sole official religion in France; he failed to achieve it. In the contest of wits between the two Italians, the "Prince" had proven himself sharper than the "Holy See."

SHE SHALL NOT RETAIN THE POWER OF THE ARM

The power of the arm is the power of strength. The armed forces of the papacy were not able to stand against the forces of France. Napoleon set up a form of government in Rome known as the "French Republic".

NEITHER SHALL HE STAND, NOR HIS ARM

Napoleon was destined to fail in his attempt to unite all of Europe under one emperor-himself. He, along with the French army under his command, was going to be defeated at the famous Battle of Waterloo.

SHE SHALL BE GIVEN UP

The papacy ceased to function for almost two full years, from 1798 to 1800. The pope, Pius VI, was taken as a prisoner to France, where he died in 1799.

AND THEY THAT BROUGHT HER

The attendants, cardinals, bishops, etc., all ceased to function for almost two full years.

AND HE THAT BEGAT HER

The power that was responsible for the existence of the papacy was also to be given up, cease to function. "In the sixth century the papacy had become firmly established. Its seat of power was fixed in the imperial city, and the bishop of Rome was declared to be the head over the entire church. Paganism had given place to the papacy. The dragon had given to the beast 'his power, and his seat, and great authority.' Revelation 13:2. And now began the 1260 years of papal oppression foretold in the prophecies of Daniel and the Revelation. Daniel 7:25; Revelation 13:5–7." WHITE, GC 54.

"On Napoleon's assertion that he no longer recognized a Holy Roman Emperor, Francis II agreed to abandon that title and style himself Francis I, Emperor of Austria, instead (1806). Such was the ignominious (dishonorable, disgraceful) end of that impressive medieval empire, the rulers of which had traced their authority to Charlemagne and Augustus." FERGUSON, page 634.

AND HE THAT STRENGTHENED HER IN THESE (THOSE) TIMES

He that strengthened her-the papacy-the Roman Catholic Church, in those times, was Pius VII; through the Concordat of 1801, and, also, through his negotiations with Napoleon in 1804. He also was "given up", ceased to function for some years, since Napoleon also took him as a prisoner to France.

1808
MIOLLIS, A FRENCH GENERAL, INVADES ROME

"General Miollis invaded Rome (Feb. 2, 1808). In return the Supreme Pontiff launched an excommunication against the instigators of this aggression, without explicitly designating Napoleon. The non-Roman cardinals were driven from Rome. Pius VII, who had opposed the arrest of Pacca, his Secretary of State, was seized, carried off from Rome (July 10, 1809), and deported to Savona, near Genoa.

(POPE PIUS VII-A PRISONER IN FRANCE)

"CAPTIVITY OF PIUS VII. Deprived of his liberty and his counselors, the Sovereign Pontiff henceforth refused to exercise his papal authority. As a result he would not canonically appoint those nominated to bishoprics by the Emperor (Napoleon) ....

"FONTAINEBLEAU. Napoleon then (June 1812) transferred Pius VII to Fontainebleau, near Paris, to force his capitulation after French victories in Russia. When the Russian campaign turned into a disaster, Napoleon hastened to finish with the pope.... Military reverses in France induced Napoleon to liberate his prisoner, who re-entered Rome on May 24, 1814." NEW CATHOLIC ENCYCLOPEDIA, Volume 11, page 402–403.

So we see that the person who strengthened the papacy, during those time, Pius VII, also was given up, that is, he ceased to function for about 5 years, since Napoleon also took him to France and kept him as a prisoner there.

Verse 7 But out of a branch of her roots shall one stand up in his estate, which shall come with an army, and shall enter into the fortress of the king of the north, and shall deal against them, and shall prevail:

Another, a different power (nation) is here introduced, one that was to share the station of "king of the south" with Rome. This nation was to come with an army and fight against the "king of the north",

Napoleon Bonaparte (of France) and prevail, that is, be victorious.

A BRANCH OF HER ROOTS

Daniel saw that a particular person was destined to come, with an army, and fight against Napoleon Bonaparte, the "king of the north", at his fortress (*maoz*—"stronghold"). This person was to come from a nation designated as "a branch" of "her roots", that is, of the papacy. The word "branch" is from the term *netser*, which means "shoot". The nation here introduced is thus identified as coming from the very roots of the papacy. The church of this particular nation is, in fact, an "offshoot" of the church of Rome. Furthermore, the nation here introduced is one of the ten primary and smaller kingdoms into which the pagan Roman Empire was divided.

A BRANCH-AN OFFSHOOT OF THE ROMAN CATHOLIC CHURCH KING HENRY VIII

"When Henry VIII came to the throne, the Reformation was beginning in Europe. Luther began his attacks against the Church in the early part of the 16th Century (1500's). King Henry, then a devout Roman Catholic, was shocked at Luther's bold criticism of the Church. He wrote a pamphlet against the teachings of the German Monk. The pope was so greatly pleased with Henry VIII that he bestowed on him the title 'Defender of the Faith'.

"All English rulers have since been called 'Defenders of the Faith'. The faith, however, which the English king today promises to defend is that of the Church of England. It may seem surprising that Henry VIII who once defended the Roman Catholic Church was the same king who later established the Church of England…. Because his wife had not given birth to a son, he asked the pope to declare his marriage illegal. When the pope refused, King Henry took matters into his own hands. He brought the Church in England under his control, made himself its head, and proclaimed that the power of the king, and not the pope, was supreme in religion as well as in politics." ROGERS, page 230–231.

THE ANGLO-SAXONS
THE BRITISH
ENGLAND

The people living in England are commonly referred to as the British. The pagan Roman Empire was eventually divided into ten primary and smaller kingdoms and the people living in the geographical area of England were known as the "Anglo-Saxons".

ENGLAND-THE "KING OF THE SOUTH"
FRANCE-THE "KING OF THE NORTH"

We could be really confused if Daniel had mixed everything up, but, fortunately, he did not! He was systematic and very descriptive in explaining to us what he saw in vision. He first presented to us what was to occur between Rome (as the "king of the South") and France (the "king of the North" under Napoleon). Next, he presented what was destined to take place, during those same years, between England (as the "king of the South" sharing that station with Rome) and France ("king of the North"-under the same Napoleon Bonaparte). In verses 20–24 this same systematic method of presentation is very helpful in understanding those verses.

As outlined in verse 7, a particular person from a particular nation (England) was to "stand up" (be in power) in the same station of "king of the south." This person was to come with an army, the English Fleet, and enter into the stronghold of the "king of the north" (Napoleon), and he, this particular person, was to "deal against them", against the French army (under Napoleon), and was to "prevail" — "be victorious" over Napoleon and his army. The particular place where these two armies were to do battle is given in verse 8. The colon (:) at the end of verse 7 indicates that verses 7 and 8 go together and help to explain the famous historical event that took place, in 1798. The last words in verse 7 stipulate that the king of the south "shall prevail:"

Verse 8 And shall also carry captives into Egypt their gods, with their princes, and with their precious vessels of silver and of gold; and he shall continue more years than the king of the north.

THE BATTLE OF THE NILE
ABUKIR BAY, EGYPT
AUGUST 1, 1798

Napoleon once said, "'Egypt's the place, in the footsteps of Alexander; and there we can strike England a shrewd blow.'" LUDWIG, page 115.

Napoleon "planned to conquer Egypt and thence attack the British posts in India…. Though Egypt was easily overrun, Bonaparte's fleet was destroyed by the English Admiral Nelson, who thus severed French naval connections with the homeland." FERGUSON, page 624.

The particular person, who Daniel saw in vision, was none other than the famous Admiral Horatio Nelson.

FRANCE-THEIR GODS
THE FRENCH REVOLUTION
1789–1799

In 1793, France discarded the Bible and denied the existence of the Deity. "The Roman Catholic Church was notoriously corrupt in France … and the people were anxious to break the yoke of ecclesiastical oppression. Their efforts culminated … when France discarded the Bible and denied the existence of the Deity…. Atheists sowed the seeds which bore their logical and baleful fruit. Voltaire, in his pompous but impotent self-conceit, had said, 'I am weary of hearing people repeat that twelve men established the Christian religion. I will prove that one man may suffice to overthrow it.'" SMITH, page 281.

Bibles were gathered and burned and all of the established institutions of the Bible were abolished. The Cathedral of Notre Dame was desecrated and renamed "Temple of Reason". A pyramid was built in the center of the Church and the words — "To Philosophy" —were written thereon. The Goddess of Reason was set up, in the person of a vile female, and it was pub-licly worshipped. The Commune closed all of the churches of Paris, on November 24, 1793, and within twenty days 2,436 French churches had been converted into "Temples of Reason."

WITH THEIR PRINCES AND WITH THEIR PRECIOUS VESSELS OF SILVER AND OF GOLD

"On May 19,1798, at six o'clock in the morning," the French fleet got under way. "The spectacle must have been breath taking. Thirteen ships of the line, carrying 1,026 cannon among them; 42 frigates, brigs, avisos, and other smaller vessels; and 130 transports of every description made up the Armada. Aboard were about 17,000 troops, as many sailors and marines, over a thousand pieces of field artillery, 100,000 rounds of ammunition, 567 vehicles, and 700 horses. Before reaching its destination—known to but a hand full of men-the fleet was to be swelled by three lesser convoys, from Genoa, Ajaccio, and Civita Vecchia, bringing the number of sail (ships) to almost four hundred." CHRISTOPHER, HERALD J., BONAPARTE IN EGYPT, 1962, page 1.

One evening, while enroute to his destination, Napoleon is lying "on deck till a late hour. His intimates (Monge, Desaix, Kleber, Laplace, Berthollet and Berthier) are sitting round him in a circle, and discussion turns on the planets, on the question whether they are inhabited. Pros and cons are voiced by the disputants. This leads to the problem of the creation. The sons of the revolution, disciples of Voltaire, be they generals or be they professors, are agreed upon one point, that the universe and its origin are rationally explicable in terms of natural science, without reference to the idea of God. Napoleon lies there, listening in silence. Then, pointing to the stars, he interjects: 'You may say what you like, but who made all those?'" LUDWIG, page 120.

A UNIVERSITY SAILING TO THE EAST

"On board this fleet there are not only two thousand guns. A whole university is sailing to the East. Astronomers, geometricians, mineralogists, chemists, antiquarians, bridge builders, road engineers, orientalists, political economists, painters, poets —one hundred and seventy-five learned civilians (princes), with hundreds of boxes full of apparatus (instruments of silver and gold) and books. Everything in this land (Egypt) of ancient story is to be meticulously studied…. He (Napoleon) has taken pains in the choice of books for the library with which the flagship is freighted for the voyage to Egypt…. For himself, he has only Werther and Ossian, works of passion, his inseparable companions." LUDWIG, page 119.

ABUKIR BAY-THE BATTLE

The French fleet anchored in Abukir Bay, Egypt. Napoleon left Admiral Brueys in charge of the fleet and went ashore into Egypt. "Brueys had three weeks to rectify his position before Nelson attacked. Perhaps the circumstance that a large part of his crew was ashore at all times on supply details discouraged him from attempting the complex maneuvers that would have been required

(to have the French fleet in the most favorable position when Nelson attacked) ….

"At two o'clock in the afternoon of August 1 (1798), the (French) working parties who were digging wells near Abukir beach were warned by signals from L'Orient to return instantly to their ships…. Besides working parties ashore, several hundred more sailors were absent in Alexandria and Rosetta…. As a result, at this critical moment, the French squadron was short not only many of its sloops and launches but of about 25–30 per cent of its crews (also) ….

"The news of Abukir was brought to Bonaparte on August 13 near Es Saliya, a town at the edge of the Sinai Desert, where he had gone in pursuit of Imbrahim Bey. Imbrahim with his followers had escaped into Syria, and Bonaparte, leaving the occupation of the north-eastern provinces in the hands of his generals, was on his way back to Cairo." CHRISTOPHER, page 110–111, 126.

After 15 months in Egypt, Napoleon, on August 22, 1799, aboard a frigate, one of only four French ships to survive the battle of the Nile, slipped through the English blockade, under cover of night, and sailed back to France. The French army, however, was left behind, in Egypt, for they had become "captives" in Egypt, along with their gods, their princes, and their precious vessels of silver and of gold.

AND HE SHALL CONTINUE MORE YEARS THAN THE KING OF THE NORTH

England was to continue to occupy the station of "king of the south", as a dominant power, for more years than France was to occupy the station of "king of the north".

The last portion of verse 8, in the RSV, is as follows: "and for some years he shall refrain from attacking the king of the north."

England "prevailed" at the battle of the Nile (Abukir Bay, Egypt). That battle was a decisive victory for Admiral Nelson. England and France would not do battle with each other, again, "for some years"; not until 17 years later, at the famous battle of Waterloo, where Napoleon was destined to be, once again, decisively defeated by England.

THE BATTLE OF WATERLOO JUNE 16–18, 1815

On June 16, 1815 Napoleon "hurled back a Prussian corps advancing near Brussels under the command of the Duke of Wellington. 'I tell you Wellington is a poor general, the English are poor soldiers, we will settle the matter by lunch time,' he (Napoleon) insisted to his generals. 'I sincerely hope so', 'responded Soult, who had faced Wellington in Spain and knew better. Throughout the day of June 18 Wellington held his position against the most desperate assaults, the Prussians under the redoubtable Blucher returned in time to aid him, and by nightfall Napoleon's army was completely routed. This was the battle of Waterloo and the end of an era." FERGUSON, page 641.

NAPOLEON SURRENDERED TO ENGLAND

"'I come, like Themistocles,' he wrote the prince regent, 'to claim hospitality at the hearth of the British people.' For the security of Europe, the British government decided, after consulting with other European powers, to imprison him on the lonely island of St. Helena in the South Atlantic. There he beguiled the oppressive days dictating memoirs to explain and justify his career, and there on May 5, 1821, he died." Ibid (FERGUSON, page 641).

Verse 9 So the king of the south shall come into his kingdom, and shall return into his own land.

THE CONGRESS OF VIENNA-1815

"With Napoleon out of the way, representatives of the great powers met at Vienna (650 miles from Paris) to rearrange the boundaries of the European nations.

"The decisions made at Vienna in 1815 gave weary Europe years of peace. The conservatives came back into power everywhere…. As far as France was concerned, all of Napoleon's conquests were lost to her, and her boundaries were fixed at about the same limits as they are today." ROGERS, 311.

Napoleon once said of himself, "'I am the child of destiny.'" Ibid. In all probability he never fully understood the full significance of his own words. More than 2,000 years before his birth, God had portrayed, through His prophetic Word, the very role that he was to play in the history of our world. For history is, in reality, His-story.

"The character of Napoleon Bonaparte was greatly influenced by his training in childhood. Unwise instructors inspired him with a love for conquest, forming mimic armies and placing him at their head as commander. Here was laid the foundation for his career of strife and bloodshed. Had the same care and effort been directed to making him a good man, imbuing his young heart with the spirit of the gospel, how widely different might have been his history." WHITE, ELLEN G., <u>CHILD GUIDANCE</u>, 1954, page 196.

Verse 9 (RSV) Then the latter (France — "king of the north") shall come into the realm of the king of the south (Waterloo) but shall return into his own land.

The French army was defeated and returned home.

REVIEW
DANIEL 11:1–9

Verse 1 Also I (Gabriel) in the first year of Darius the Mede, even I, stood to confirm and to strengthen him.

2 And now will I show thee the truth. Behold, there shall stand up (be in power) yet three kings in Persia (1. Cambyses, 2. Smerdis, 3. Darius Hystaspes); and the fourth (Xerxes) shall be far richer than they all: and by his strength through his riches he shall stir up all against the realm of Grecia (Greece).

3 And a mighty king (Alexander the Great) shall stand up, that shall rule with great dominion, and do according to his will.

4 And when he shall stand up, his kingdom shall be broken, and shall be divided (*chatsah*-"To be halved") toward the four winds of heaven; and not to his posterity, nor according to his dominion which he ruled: for his kingdom shall be plucked up (torn up by the roots), even for others beside those.

5 And the king of the south (Rome) shall be strong, and one of his princes (a Roman prince – Napoleon Bonaparte); and he (the Roman prince) shall be strong above him (stronger than Rome), and have dominion; his dominion (Napoleon Bonaparte's dominion) shall be a great dominion.

6 And in the end of years (1798 or shortly thereafter) they (Rome & Napoleon) shall join themselves together; for the king's daughter of the south (Spina-a representative of the Church of Rome) shall come to the king of the north (Paris, France-1800) to make an agreement: (**Concordat of 1801**) but she (the papacy—the Church of Rome) shall not retain the power of the arm; neither shall he (Napoleon) stand, nor his arm: but she shall be given up (cease to function for a time), and they that brought her (bishops, cardinals, etc.), and he that begat her (the title of Holy Roman Emperor was given up), and he (Pope Pius VII) that strengthened her in these times.

7 But out of a branch (England) of her roots shall one (Admiral Nelson) stand up in his estate (same station of "king of the south"), which shall come with

an army (English fleet), and shall enter into the fortress (stronghold) of the king of the north (Napoleon), and shall deal against them (against the French army), and shall prevail (England was victorious at Abukir Bay):

8 And shall also carry ("cause to go in or on") captives into Egypt (at Abukir Bay) their gods ("with their molten images" —RSV), with their princes (175 of them), and with their precious vessels of silver and of gold (hundreds of boxes of instruments & apparatus); and he (England) shall continue more years than the king of the north (France).

9 So the king of the south (England) shall come into his kingdom (Congress of Vienna), and shall return into his own land (the representatives of the various nations returned home and didn't occupy France).

The last part of verse 8 and all of verse 9, in the RSV: "and for some (17) years he (England) shall refrain from attacking the king of the north (Napoleon). 9 Then the latter (king of the north) shall come into the realm (Brussels-Waterloo) of the king of the south (England) but shall return into his own land.

"In his will, Napoleon had asked to be buried on the banks of the Seine, 'among the French people I have loved so much.' In 1840, the British and French governments cooperated in bringing his remains to Paris. There, at the Eglise du Dome (Church of the Dome), which is part of the Hotel des Invalides (Home for Disabled Soldiers), the body of Napoleon was laid to rest." THE WORLD BOOK ENCYCLOPEDIA, 1992, Volume 14, page 18.

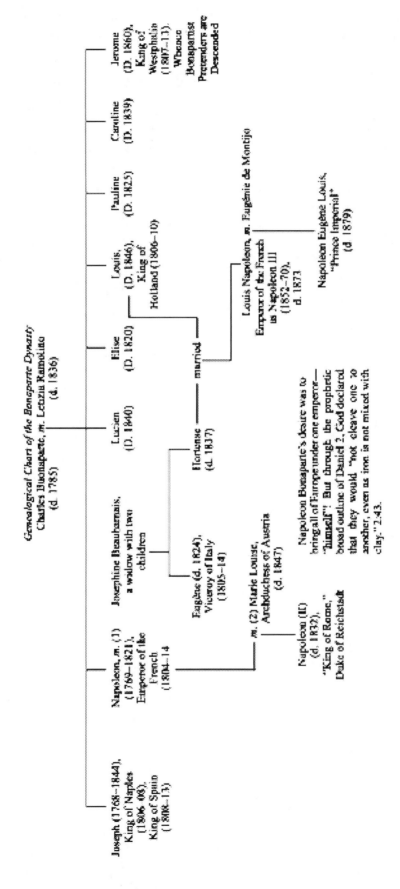

Genealogical Chart of the Bonaparte Dynasty
Charles Buonaparte, *m.* Letizia Ramolino
(d. 1785)   (d. 1836)

Joseph (1768–1844),
King of Naples
(1806–08),
King of Spain
(1808–13)

Napoleon, *m.* (1)
(1769–1821),
Emperor of the
French
(1804–14)

Lucien
(D. 1840)

Elise
(D. 1820)

Louis,
(D. 1846),
King of
Holland (1806–10)

Pauline
(D. 1825)

Caroline
(D. 1839)

Jerome
(D. 1860),
King of
Westphalia
(1807–13).
Whence
Bonapartist
Pretenders are
Descended

Josephine Beauharnais,
a widow with two
children

m. (2) Marie Louise,
Archduchess of Austria
(d. 1847)

Eugène (d. 1824),
Viceroy of Italy
(1805–14)

Hortense
(d. 1837)

married

Napoleon (II)
(d. 1832),
"King of Rome,"
Duke of Reichstadt

Louis Napoleon, *m.* Eugénie de Montijo
Emperor of the French
as Napoleon III
(1852–70),
d. 1873

Napoleon Eugène Louis,
"Prince Imperial"
(d. 1879)

Napoleon Bonaparte's desire was to
bring all of Europe under one emperor—
"himself". But through the prophetic
broad outline of Daniel 2, God declared
that they would "not cleave one to
another, even as iron is not mixed with
clay." 2:43.

32

Chapter 5

EUROPE
THE INTERNAL CONFLICT

Verse 10 But his sons shall be stirred up, and shall assemble a multitude of great forces: and one shall certainly come, and overflow, and pass through: then shall he return, and be stirred up, even to his fortress.

According to the context of this verse, to be "stirred up" is to "wage war"-RSV. The war portrayed in this verse was not fought between the "king of the south" and the "king of the north"! This war was fought between the offspring of Napoleon Bonaparte, within the boundaries of Europe.

In order to achieve his goal of becoming emperor of all Europe, Napoleon had "set up his friends and relatives as kings in the various states of the Empire." ROGERS, page 309. In 1805 he appointed his stepson, Eugene Bonaparte, to the position of Viceroy of Italy. In 1806 he appointed his brother, Joseph Bonaparte, as King of Naples. In this same year he appointed another brother, Louis Bonaparte, King of Holland. Then, in 1807, he appointed his youngest brother, Jerome Bonaparte, to the extremely important position of King of Westphalia. It was Jerome's job to plant the fundamental ideals of the revolution on German soil. He was to transform four million Germans from subjects into citizens. It was to be a great experiment in democracy. In 1808, Joseph Bonaparte, in addition to his appointment as King of Naples, was appointed King of Spain.

By setting up his friends and relatives as heads of the various states of Europe, through intermarriage of royalty, and by means of war, Napoleon aspired to become emperor of all Europe, and, eventually, of all the world.

The word "sons" is from the term "*ben*", which can also be translated as "offspring". Many writers have written about Napoleon Bonaparte. One writer appropriately gave Napoleon the title of "Godfather of Modern Europe". That the words "his sons" is a reference to the "Napoleonic Dynasty", there is no doubt!

By the middle of the 19th Century (1850) the people of France had become sick of kings and revolted. "They formed the Second Republic and elected Louis Napoleon, a nephew of Napoleon I (Napoleon Bonaparte), as president. But Louis Napoleon wanted to follow the career of his uncle. The presidency was only a steppingstone to him. He tried to revive the glory that France had known under Napoleon Bonaparte.

(NAPOLEON III)

"While he was president Louis Napoleon was able to change the Second Republic into the Second Empire with himself as Emperor.

He took the title of Napoleon III. (Napoleon I-Bonaparte had a son who would have become Napoleon II if he had lived). But it was too late to revive the glorious days of the Empire. Napoleon III did not have the ability of his great relative." ROGERS, page 312.

According to verse 10, a "multitude of great forces" was destined to be assembled, and, war was going to be waged between the offspring of Napoleon Bonaparte. Daniel saw that a particular person would carry the battle even as far as his (Napoleon's) fortress-Paris, France. What famous war is recorded in history that meets the specifications of this prophecy?

THE FRANCO-PRUSSIAN WAR KNOWN ALSO AS THE FRANCO-GERMAN WAR 1870–1871

This was "the stupendous conflict between France and Germany in 1870–1871, which resulted in the total defeat of the French, the overthrow of the Napoleonic dynasty, the establishment of the Third Republic in France and the consolidation of Germany into an empire under the leadership of Prussia." THE ENCYCLOPEDIA AMERICANA, 1953, Volume 12, page 1.

A MULTITUDE OF GREAT FORCES

"While the ... French army in the field at the beginning of the war numbered ... about 310,000 men, German troops in the field totaled 477,000 with ample reserves to protect the interior and defend the north coast against naval attack. This gave an agregate (units added together) strength to the Germans of more than 1,000,000 men." Ibid, page 2.

"ONE SHALL CERTAINLY COME" MAN OF "BLOOD AND IRON" OTTO VON BISMARCK

"The man who was to unite Germany and help bring on two world wars became prime minister of Prussia in 1862. He was Otto Von Bismarck (BIHZ mahrk).

"To gain his own ends, Bismarck resorted to some notorious tricks, worst of which was the one that set off the Franco-Prussian War....

"In his own strange way, Bismarck was a religious man. He thought God had picked him to help Prussia unite Germany into one nation. Because he thought God was on his side, he stopped at nothing to carry out his plans. He did not hesitate to lie or cheat or to start wars....

"Bismarck began to work out his plans for war with France. He wanted Alsace-Lorraine for Prussia. He knew that the French emperor, Napoleon III, was having many difficulties and that he might even regard the war as a way out of some of them. In 1870 Bismarck pushed France into a position where she would have to accept an insult or declare war. She (France) did the latter (declared war).

"Bismarck had convinced the other German states that their safety lay in a union with Prussia and in waging war together." ROGERS, page 405–406 .

At Sedan, "Napoleon III was forced to surrender with 86,000 men (September 1,

1870). On October 27, General Bazaine handed over a second French army of 175,000 men which the Prussians had shut up in Metz....

"In the Hall of Mirrors in Louis XIV's stately Versailles palace the German princes hailed William I as 'German Emperor' (January 18, 1871) while the guns of Paris eleven miles away were firing their last despairing volleys." FERGUSON, page 713, 714.

"EVEN TO HIS FORTRESS"

The Germans and Prussians were to "wage war", even to his-Napoleon's fortress (stronghold), which is Paris, France.

"The siege of Paris was longer than was expected.... Paris was near starvation. Three weeks bombardment convinced the government that capitulation was inevitable...."

"On the same day the German troops entered Paris; on 18 January King William, who had taken up his residence at Versailles, had by acclamation been proclaimed Emperor of Germany." THE ENCYCLOPEDIA AMERICANA, Vol. 12, page 2.

"By means of war, Bismarck accomplished his ambition to unite all the German states, except Austria, into an empire. He had the Prussian king proclaimed Kaiser (KI zer), or Emperor, of Germany". ROGERS, page 406.

"It was not with Prussia but with a united German Empire that France concluded peace. The South German states had joined the North German Confederation in the struggle with the hereditary foe, and the common patriotic effort, as Bismarck had predicted, forged the bonds of union." FERGUSON, page 714.

Berlin, Germany superseded Paris, France as the diplomatic capital of Europe, and the new German Empire emerged as the strongest nation of Continental Europe. The designated station of "king of the north" thus passed from France to that of the German Empire. Verse 8 stipulated that the nation occupying the station of "king of the south" would abide therein for more years than would the "king of the north" abide in his station.

"The Franco-Prussian War made Germany an empire and France a republic.... Henceforth, until World War I, five first-class powers, France, Germany, Italy, Austria-Hungary and Russia, were to strain against each other in the narrow confines of Europe while Great Britain looked on and sought to preserve a balance of power among them for her own security." Ibid.

The Franco-Prussian War ended in 1871. This is an important date to remember because "it opened a forty-three-year period of comparative peace." Ibid.

"From 1871 to the beginning of World War I in 1914, the people of the German Empire enjoyed peace and prosperity. More than sixty-seven million people in a country smaller than Texas seemed busy and contented." ROGERS, page 407.

Chapter 6

WORLD WAR I
1914–1918
ENGLAND-THE KING OF THE SOUTH
GERMANY-THE KING OF THE NORTH

Verse 11 And the king of the south (England) shall be moved with choler (anger), and shall come forth and fight with him, even with the king of the north (Germany) : and he (Germany) shall set forth a great multitude; but the multitude shall be given into his (England's) hand.

On August 2, 1914, the German government "demanded permission to march its armies through Belgium to attack France. This permission the Belgian government courageously refused. On August 4, the British government notified the German government that a state of war would commence at midnight unless Germany promised to respect Belgian neutrality. There was no reply, and Britain considered herself at war." FERGUSON, page 807, 808–809.

German aggression, its ruthlessness, caused England, the "king of the south", to come forth and fight with Germany, the "king of the north".

HE SHALL SET FORTH A GREAT MULTITUDE

Germany set forth an army of 11,000,000 men in World War I. The combined forces mobilized by the Central Powers, which consisted of Germany, Austria-Hungary, Turkey and Bulgaria, was 22,850,000.

KAISER WILHELM

"The last Kaiser of Germany, Wilhelm II, discarded Bismarck as his chancellor, and put his faith in the imperial army that had 'forged the German Empire.' Kaiser Wilhelm proceeded to expand the army and the navy. With the help of the General Staff, founded by Frederick, he built the most efficient war machine the world had ever seen." ROGERS, page 408.

BUT THE MULTITUDE SHALL BE GIVEN INTO HIS (ENGLAND'S) HAND

"When World War I started", the German people thought that their army could not be conquered – that they could win a quick and final victory. Instead, defeat came in 1918....

"Kaiser Wilhelm II, the same emperor who had dismissed Bismarck, fled to Holland." Ibid.

Germany was defeated in World War I and its army was given into the hands, into the power, of England.

Verse 12 And when he has taken away the multitude, his heart shall be lifted up; and he shall cast down many ten thousands: but he shall not be strengthened by it.

Verse 12 (RSV) And when the multitude is taken, his heart shall be exalted, and he shall cast down tens of thousands, but he shall not prevail.

THE TREATY OF VERSAILLES

After England, with the aid of the Allied governments, had taken away the multitude, England's heart was "lifted up" – "exalted", through the Treaty of Versailles.

"By May, 1919, the treaty with Germany had been drafted and the Germans were summoned to Versailles to receive it. Stunned by the severity of the terms, Count Brockdorff-Rantzau, head of the delegation, entered an earnest protest at the contradiction between the draft of the treaty and the assurances granted the Central Powers when the armistice was negotiated. The Allied governments, however, were adamant in their hour of victory, making only slight modifications in their original draft. On June 28, in the Hall of Mirrors at Versailles where the German Empire had been proclaimed forty-eight years before, the Germans, yielding to necessity, signed the treaty, acknowledging 'the responsibility of Germany and her allies for causing all the loss and damage to which the Allied and Associated governments and their nationals have been subjected as a consequence of the war imposed upon them by the aggression of Germany and her allies'."

(Article 231 of the Treaty of Versailles). FERGUSON, page 823–824.

The Septuagint (LXX) says that "many thousands" would be cast down, "but he shall not prevail." The reading in the footnote, in the LXX, indicates that "myriads" would be cast down.

Ten million soldiers perished in World War I. Over six-thousand a day for each day the war continued. Twenty-million were wounded and the monetary cost of the war has been computed at $337,980,579,657 dollars. The grand total of mobilized forces was 65,038,810. The conflagration involved approximately 93 percent of the world's population." Ibid.

The Treaty of Versailles also "reduced the area and population of the German Empire by approximately one-tenth." Ibid.

HE SHALL NOT BE STRENGTHENED BY IT HE SHALL NOT "PREVAIL"

In both the LXX and the RSV, the meaning is the same: "he shall not prevail." England could do nothing to prevent Germany from returning in World War II. This is indicated in verse 13, since it clearly says that "the king of the north shall return".

Chapter 7

WORLD WAR II
1939–1945

ENGLAND-THE KING OF THE SOUTH
GERMANY-THE KING OF THE NORTH

Verse 13 For the king of the north shall return, and shall set forth a multitude greater than the former, and shall certainly come after certain years with a great army and with much riches.

A MULTITUDE GREATER THAN THE FORMER

In World War I Germany put forth an army of 11,000,000, but, in World War II it put forth 17,000,000, which was a "multitude greater (by 6,000,000) than the former". In W.W.I Germany and its allies put forth a combined force of 22,850,000, but, in World War II Germany and its allies put forth a combined force of 30,000, 000, which is a combined force in excess of 8,000,000 "greater than the former".

SHALL CERTAINLY COME AFTER CERTAIN YEARS

The margin says "even years". Inclusively, 22 *even years* separate World War I and World War II, since there were 20 "even years" between them. John Garraty informs us that "in the 20 year respite between World War I and World War II, the western democracies might have drawn closer together and become more firm of heart if all had been committed to the League (the League of Nations). What was lost when the treaty failed in the Senate was not peace, but the possibility of peace." GARRATY, JOHN A., THE AMERICAN NATION, 1966, page 697.

WITH MUCH RICHES

Germany's cost for world War II has been computed at 272 billion, 900 million (272,900,000,000) dollars. "Much riches" indeed!

Verse 14 And in those times there shall many stand up against the king of the south: also the robbers of thy people shall exalt themselves to establish the vision; but they shall fall. (The RSV says, "they shall fail")

MANY WERE TO STAND UP AGAINST THE KING OF THE SOUTH-ENGLAND

"By the end of June, 1940, Great Britain (England) stood alone against a continent where Hitler was the master. Not since Napoleon's day had one despot controlled such a wide European empire or commanded such awesome military superiority....

"It had taken the Germans only four weeks to crush Poland, a state of thirty million. They overcame the resistance of Norway, Denmark, the Netherlands, Belgium, and

France, with a combined population exceeding sixty-million, in eight weeks. Could Great Britain, alone and vulnerable, expect to survive? The British themselves didn't know the answer, but they faced the emergency with extraordinary courage and confidence. On the day that the Netherlands and Belgium were attacked (May 10, 1940), the Chamberlain ministry resigned, and the energetic Winston Churchill became minister of a coalition war cabinet. Under his forceful and inspiring leadership the British prepared to fight to the last for their national existence." FERGUSON, page 922–923.

THE ROBBERS OF THY PEOPLE

"Literally, 'the sons of the breakers of thy people.' This expression may be understood subjectively, 'the children of the violent among thy people'." 4 BC 869.

As pointed out in 10:14, the angel (Gabriel) came unto Daniel to make him understand what was going to happen to his people, the Jews, in the "latter days".

"At the beginning of the 20th Century (1900's) a number of prominent Jews founded the Zionist (ZI un ist) movement. (Zion is one of the Hebrew names for Jerusalem). The Zionists wanted to set up a homeland for the Jews. Naturally, they hoped to go back to their ancient home in Palestine. The Turkish Empire had controlled Palestine for centuries. So the Zionists got permission from the Turks to buy some land and make a few Jewish settlements in their ancient homeland.

"By the outbreak of World War I, several thousand Jews had established themselves in Palestine. During the war, Turkey fought on the side of the Germans, and the British conquered Palestine. In the peace treaty the British received a mandate over the territory. While the war was still going on, Lord Balfour, the British Minister of Foreign Affairs, had written in an official letter that 'the British government favors the establishment in Palestine of a national home for the Jewish people and will use their best endeavors to facilitate the achievement of that objective.'…

"The statement became known as the Balfour Declaration. When the British took over control of Palestine, they began to carry out the policy. In the next twenty years thousands of Jews settled in Palestine." ROGERS, page 655–656.

CHRONOLOGICAL TABLE DISPERSION AND GATHERING OF THE JEWS

70 A.D.	The Romans, under Titus, destroyed the Jewish temple and Jerusalem.
135 "	The devastation of Palestine, by the Romans, marks the end of over twelve hundred years of Jewish history in the Holy Land.
636 "	The Moslems, under Omar, occupy Palestine.
1099 "	Jerusalem is captured by the Crusaders, under Godfrey of Bouillon and the Jews are slain without mercy.
1517 "	Palestine is conquered by Selim

I, the Sultan of the Ottoman Turkish Empire and the Jews and Arabs live together under one ruler-Turkey.

1917 " On November 2, before World War I ended, the British government issued the Balfour Declaration declaring that they were in favor of a Jewish National Homeland in Palestine.

1919 " On March 3 President Wilson announced that he was in favor of a Jewish National State in Palestine.

1920 " Turkey ceded Palestine over to the Allied Forces through the Treaty of Sevres. The League of Nations Assembly gave Great Britain a mandate providing for the establishment of a Jewish Homeland.

1922 " The Trans-Jordan area of Palestine is excluded from the mandate by the League of Nations Council (Sept. 16).

1936 " The Peel Commission (established by England) reported to England that she had failed to fulfill her duty under the mandate and recommended that Palestine be partitioned, which was rejected by both Jews and Arabs.

1939 " In a White Paper the British government revoked her promise of a Jewish Homeland. The immigration of Jews into Palestine is limited to 75,000 per year. The League of Nation's Mandate Commission condemned the White Paper declaration upon which the British government revoked her promise of a Jewish Homeland.

1944 " The establishment of a Jewish National Homeland in Palestine is approved by President Franklin D. Roosevelt.

1945 " Each month 1500 Jewish immigrants are admitted into Palestine by Britain. The illegal immigration of Jews into Palestine resulted in clashes with the British government (1946).

1947 " In December, the British government announced that it would terminate her mandate over Palestine on May 15, 1948, and complete her evacuation of British troops by August of that year.

1948 " On May 14, 1948, at midnight, as soon as the British mandate is terminated, the Jewish State was proclaimed. The United States gave, immediately, "de facto" ("exercising power as if legally constituted") recognition to Israel.

JERUSALEM
THE 6-DAY WAR
1967

1967 "   In the 6-Day War the Jews captured Jerusalem.

Jesus said that Jerusalem was to be "trodden down of the Gentiles, until the times (years) of the Gentiles be fulfilled." (completed)

"Thus says the Lord God; Behold, I will take the whole house of Israel out of the midst of the nations, among whom they have gone, and I will gather them from all that are round about them, and I will bring them into the land of Israel. 22 And I will make them a nation in My land, even on the mountains of Israel; and they shall have one prince: and they shall be no more two nations, neither shall they be divided any more at all into two kingdoms." Ezekiel 21:21, 22. (LXX)

In Bible times Israel was divided into two kingdoms; there was the ten northern kingdoms and Judah and Benjamin in the south. Ezekiel looked forward to a time when Israel would be one nation with one leader over it all. We are living in that time!

The prophet Daniel, looking down the ages to the "time of the end", beheld descendants of the Jews, his people, exalting themselves in order to fulfill the vision, but, they shall "fail"!

The parenthetical remarks of verse 14 are followed by a continuation of the narrative begun in verse 13, concerning Germany, the "king of the north."

Verse 15 So the king of the north shall come, and cast up a mount, and take the most fenced cities: and the arms of the south shall not withstand, neither his chosen people, neither shall there be any strength to withstand.

CAST UP A MOUNT

The word "mount" is from "solelah" – "what is raised up, mount, wall", "siege-works"-RSV.

THE GERMAN "WEST WALL"

"Known in Allied circles as the Siegfried Line, the West Wall was a series of fortifications along Germany's western frontier begun in 1938 under an able engineer, Dr. Fritz Todt, who built Germany's superhighways…. The West wall was a band approximately three miles deep of more than 3,000 mutually supporting concrete pill-boxes, troop shelters and command posts…. Touted as impregnable, it contributed to German success in bluffing France and Britain at Munich." THE SIMON AND SCHUSTER ENCYCLOPEDIA OF WORLD WAR II, 1978, page 684–685.

The "most fenced cities" were protected by the famous "Maginot Line." "The most elaborate fortified line of defense ever devised by man—the Maginot Line-stood in Hitler's way…. In 1929, War Minister Andre Maginot (of France) began to construct … a series of gigantic pillboxes stretching from Switzerland to the Belgian border, costing half a billion dollars.

"The Maginot Line was impressive-each pillbox had six underground levels and contained every possible necessity for defense, from power stations and ammunition dumps to hospitals and recreation halls." THE FIVE WORLDS OF OUR LIVES, 1961, page 178–179. The Maginot Line held 300,000 troops underground

"The Germans (King of the North), ensconced behind their newly constructed 'West Wall', the French holding their supposedly impregnable Maginot Line, and the British (King of the South) across the North Sea, measured one another carefully." FERGUSON, page 191.

It was "after a winter lull that cynics called the 'phony war'", that "Hitler loosed his armored divisions against the western powers. Between April 9 and June 22 (1940) he taught the world the awful meaning of Blitzkrieg-lightning war. Denmark, Norway, the Netherlands, Belgium and France were successively battered into submission." GARRATY, page 760.

"Winston Churchill himself, who had taken over as Prime Minister (of England) on the first day of Battle, was dumfounded. He was awakened at half past seven on the morning of May 15 (1940) by a telephone call from Premier Paul Reynaud in Paris, who told him in an excited voice, 'We have been defeated. We are beaten.'" SHIRER, WILLIAM L. THE RISE AND FALL OF THE THIRD REICH, 1960, page 720.

"When the famed Maginot Line was pierced at the Sedan Gap and an army of giant tanks and mechanized infantry raced through the breach to sweep across Belgium and northern France, resistance collapsed. Uncertain which way the German columns would turn, out-fought and out–generaled, and broken in morale, the French and British divisions fell back in disorder. Within ten days (May 11–21) the Germans had sliced through their center, speeding down the Somme Valley to the sea. With Belgium conquered and communications with Paris cut, the British expeditionary force recoiled upon Dunkirk." FERGUSON, page 920.

DUNKIRK
"A WELL-FORTIFIED CITY" (RSV) AND THE FORCES OF THE SOUTH (ENGLAND) SHALL NOT STAND (RSV)

"On the long, flat beaches near Dunkirk, a French city on the English Channel, there occurred the evacuation of Dunkirk. Some eight hundred and fifty ships of all sizes and kinds were rounded up in the British Isles. Tugboats, steamers, river boats, fishing craft, small power boats, many that had never been out in the open sea, came across the English Channel. Long Lines of men waded out to small boats that ferried them over to the larger ships. The fighter pilots of the R.A.F. (British-Royal Air Force) furnished protection against endless bombing by German planes...."

"The Germans actually pushed them into the sea. But British sailors and civilians-even schoolboys and girls-came to rescue their men in every sort of boat they could find...."

"The 'Mosquito Armada' did its work. More than 338,000 soldiers were landed in England in early June, 1940. The British saved their army, but they lost practically all of their equipment-tanks, guns, and supplies. It was then that Prime Minister Churchill rose in the House of Commons and declared:

"'We shall defend our Island, whatever the cost may be, we shall fight on the beaches, we shall fight on the landing grounds, we shall fight in the fields and in the streets, we shall fight in the hills; we shall never surrender.'" ROGERS, page 631.

NEITHER HIS CHOSEN PEOPLE SHALL WITHSTAND

Some Christians believe that this reference to the "chosen people" applies to the Jews. The word "chosen" is from the term "mibchar", which means "chosen", or "choice". This term (mibchar) also occurs in Exodus 15, where it says that "The Lord is a man of war: the Lord is His name. Pharaoh's chariots and his host has He cast into the sea: his chosen (mibchar) captains also are drowned in the Red Sea." Exodus 15:3,4. This same term also occurs in Jeremiah 15:3 and Ezekiel 23:7 with the same meaning, referring to the "strong men of war" of Moab, and to the "chosen men of Assyria". So, the expression in 11:15 (chosen people) is telling us that the best "picked troops" of England would not be able to stand against Hitler and the German army. The RSV says that "even his picked troops" would not be able to stand, "for there shall be no strength to stand." (RSV)

Verse 16 But he that comes against him shall do according to his own will, and none shall stand before him: and he shall stand in the glorious land, which by his hand shall be consumed. ("all of it shall be in his power" RSV).

PALESTINE "THE GLORIOUS LAND"

"Not since Napoleon's day had one despot controlled such a wide European empire or commanded such awesome military superiority." FERGUSON, page 922.

During World War II, and for some centuries before the war, Turkey controlled Palestine, and, because Turkey fought on the side of Adolf Hitler (Germany), during the war, all of Palestine came under Hitler's power.

Verse 17 He shall also set his face to enter with the strength of his whole kingdom, and upright ones with him; thus shall he do: and he shall give him the daughter of women, corrupting her: but she shall not stand on his side, neither be for him.

UPRIGHT ONES - ROMAN CATHOLICS - ITALY ITALY ENTERS WORLD WAR II MUSSOLINI

At precisely the right time, according to prophecy, Italy, under Mussolini (Duce), entered World War II as Hitler's ally.

"Though the generals, as Halder's diary confirms, couldn't have cared less what Italy did—whether it came into the war or not-the Fuehrer (Hitler) for some reason attached importance to Italian intervention. As soon as the Netherlands and Belgium had surrendered and the Anglo–French northern armies had been smashed and the surviving British troops began taking to the boats at

Dunkirk, Mussolini decided to slither into the war. He informed Hitler by letter on May 30 (1940) that the date would be June 5. Hitler replied immediately that he was 'most profoundly moved'.

"'If there could still be anything which would strengthen my unshakable belief in the victorious outcome of this war (Hitler wrote on May 31st) it was your statement … The mere fact of your entering the war is an element calculated to deal the front of our enemies a staggering blow.'" SHIRER, page 739.

During World War II there were three leading men in power in Italy: (1) the Pope, (2) the king—Victor Emmanuel III, and (3) the Prime Minister. When Victor Emmanuel's Prime Minister resigned, "the king asked Mussolini to become head of the government. Although the king kept his crown, Mussolini was the actual ruler and became one of the most powerful men in Europe. Almost at once Mussolini declared himself dictator….

"Fiercely aggressive, greedy for power, dogged in his determination to become the most powerful ruler of a powerful country, he developed the methods of fascism later expanded more ruthlessly by Hitler….

"Although Italy had been the bitter enemy of Germany, Mussolini could not resist the influence of the man who outdid him at his own game, and then led him to his final destruction..

"When the dictator governments of Italy and Germany joined in a mutual assistance treaty, it was called the Rome-Berlin Axis, because Mussolini and Hitler were trying to make the world revolve around them. Germany and Italy very soon became known as 'The Axis Powers.'" ROGERS, page 384, 385, 386.

THE DAUGHTER OF WOMEN THE ROMAN CATHOLIC CHURCH (THE PAPACY)

It is evident from Revelation 17 and other passages of Scripture that a woman, in prophecy, represents a church. "The daughter of women" is an expression which represents the Roman Catholic Church. How did Mussolini give to Hitler the "daughter of women, corrupting her"?

"THE CONCORDAT" BETWEEN GERMANY AND THE CHURCH OF ROME

"On July 20, (1933) the Nazi government concluded a concordat with the Vatican in which the freedom of the Catholic religion and the right of the Church 'to regulate her own affairs (was assured)'. The agreement, signed on behalf of Germany by Papen and of the Holy See by the then Papal Secretary of State, Monsignor Pacelli, later Pope Pius XII, was hardly put to paper before it was being broken by the Nazi government. But coming as it did at a moment when the first excesses of the new regime in Germany had provoked world-wide revulsion, the concordat undoubtedly lent the Hitler government much needed prestige." SHIRER, page 234.

After the Franco-Prussian (or Franco-German) War, of 1870–1871, "each succeeding pope had accepted the precedent set by Pius IX and had regarded himself as the prisoner of the Vatican rather than recognize and come to terms with the Italian government which had taken possession of the papal domains. This papal policy of non-recognition, awkward alike for the Italian government and for the papacy, prevailed for nearly sixty years....

(THE "LATERN TREATY" OF 1929)

"A mutual desire for reconciliation resulted in the Latern Treaty of 1929, which recognized the pope as temporal sovereign of the Vatican City. This minute state of about one hundred (108.7) acres in the heart of Rome was to enjoy complete independence, with its own radio station. As compensation for the loss of that larger patrimony which former popes ruled, the Italian government agreed to make restitution to the extent of 1,750,000,000 lira (about 92 million dollars). The government further consented to declare the Roman Catholic faith the official religion of the state, to provide for religious instruction in the schools, and to enforce the canon law throughout Italy. In return, the Holy See formally recognized the Italian Kingdom with Rome as its capital....

"Thus the papacy brought itself to recognize an authoritarian (Fascist) government in Italy after declining for over half a century to acknowledge the more liberal parliamentary regime that preceded it." FERGUSON, page 879–880.

BUT SHE SHALL NOT STAND ON HIS SIDE—NEITHER BE FOR HIM

"The Catholic hierarch in Germany, which like most of the Protestant clergy, had at first tried to cooperate with the new regime, was thoroughly disillusioned. On March 14, 1939, Pope Pius XI issued an encyclical, 'Mit Brennender Sorge' (With Burning Sorrow), charging the Nazi government with 'evasion' and 'violation' of the concordat and accusing it of sowing 'the tares of suspicion, discord, hatred, calumny, of secret and open fundamental hostility to Christ and His Church.' On 'the horizon of Germany' the Pope saw 'the threatening storm clouds of destructive religious wars ... which have no other aim than ... extermination.'

"In an allocution to the Sacred College on June 2, 1945, Pope Pius XII defended the concordat which he had signed (in 1933 — he was Monsignor Pacelli-Papal Secretary of State), but described National Socialism, as he later came to know it, as 'the arrogant apostasy from Jesus Christ, the denial of His doctrine and of His work for redemption, the cult of violence, the idolatry of race and blood, the overthrow of human liberty and dignity.'" SHIRER, page 235, 234.

Mussolini's wife, Rachelle, says that the Pope eventually dissociated himself from the Fascists and did not hesitate to categorize them with the Nazis when he condemned them.

Verse 18 After this shall he turn his face unto the isles, and shall take many: but a prince for his own behalf shall cause the reproach offered by him to cease; without his own reproach he shall cause it to turn upon him.

THE "ISLES" "COASTLANDS" (RSV) HE "SHALL TAKE MANY OF THEM" (RSV)

By the autumn of 1942, after the "daughter of women" had turned against Hitler and Mussolini, Hitler controlled Korea, Mongolia, Manchuria, most of China, Indo-china, Burma, Siam, Malaya, Indonesia, the Philippine Islands, part of New Guinea and nearly all of the American colonies in the "Pacific."

In Western Europe, Finland, Norway, Denmark, Poland, Czechoslovakia, Belgium, Holland, France, Luxembourg, Albania, Yugoslavia, Hungary, Rumania, Bulgaria, Greece, the "Baltic"-even the "Channel Islands"- all of it was in Hitler's power. The autumn of 1942 was the "high-watermark" for the Axis Powers.

"By the end of June, 1940," after the Pope had turned against Mussolini and Hitler, "Great Britain (king of the south) stood alone against a continent where Hitler (king of the north—Germany) was the master. Not since Napoleon's day had one despot controlled such a wide European empire or commanded such awesome military superiority." FERGUSON, page 922.

"A PRINCE"—QATSIN—"A DECIDER" "A COMMANDER SHALL PUT AN END TO HIS INSOLENCE; INDEED HE SHALL TURN HIS INSOLENCE BACK UPON HIM." (RSV)

"PEARL HARBOR" DECEMBER 7, 1941

FRANKLIN D. ROOSEVELT (F.D.R.) THE "COMMANDER"— "DECIDER"

"On Sunday morning, December 7, 1941, Japanese Planes from aircraft carriers swept down on Pearl Harbor, our great naval base in Hawaii….

"The next day, in his war message to Congress, President Roosevelt said: 'Yesterday, December 7, 1941-a date which will live in infamy-the United States of America was suddenly and deliberately attacked by naval and air forces of the Empire of Japan…. I ask that the Congress declare that since the unprovoked and dastardly attack by Japan, on Sunday, December seventh, a state of war has existed between the United States and the Japanese Empire.'

"Two and a half hours after the attack on Pearl Harbor, Japan declared war on the United States and Great Britain (both occupying the station of king of the south-allies). Germany (king of the north) and Italy also declared war on US. A few days later, the United States declared war on the Axis (Rome-Berlin-Tokyo) and became one of the United Nations." ROGERS, page 634.

"When the year 1944 opened, World War II had already lasted longer than World War I. As in 1918, after successful but exhausting campaigns and conquests, the German armies were facing an encroaching ring of steel, with their enemies multiplying until more than fifty nations had severed diplomatic contact and united against them….

"As signs of German exhaustion increased, the attacks were doubled and redoubled.... In the Balkans the Soviet Russian advance liberated Rumania, Bulgaria, and Yugoslavia from Axis control, and Russian armies also turned north to capture Budapest and Vienna. Through Poland and East Prussia the claws of the Russian offensive closed in upon Berlin. Caught in a vise, with Anglo-American forces (king of the south) driving across the Rhine until they met the Russian spearheads in the Elbe Valley, the German armies split into fragments and disintegrated. Despite the fanatical efforts of suicide battalions and the punitive measures of the secret police, the dreaded Gestapo, many German commanders opened direct negotiations with Soviet, British, and American headquarters. Shattered divisions of the Wehrmacht, herded into pockets, laid down their arms. Mechanized units and tank battalions, lacking gasoline, surrendered impotently. The end came in May, 1945, when the Russians fought their way into Berlin." FERGUSON, 931–932.

Verse 19 Then he shall turn his face toward the fort of his own land: but he shall stumble and fall, and not be found.

The word "fort" is from the term "maoz" and means "stronghold". Adolf Hitler was to meet his death within his own stronghold-Berlin, Germany.

ADOLF HITLER
HIS "BONES WERE NEVER FOUND"

His "bones were never found, and this gave rise to rumors after the war that Hitler had survived. But separate interrogation of several eyewitnesses by the British and American intelligence officers leaves no doubt about the matter. Kempka has a plausible explanation as to why the charred bones were never found. 'Traces were wiped out,' he told his interrogator, 'by the uninterrupted Russian artillery fire.'" SHIRER, page 1134.

"During the afternoon of April 29, (1945) one of the last pieces of news to reach the (German) bunker from the outside world came in. Mussolini, Hitler's fellow fascist dictator partner in aggression, had met his end and it had been shared by his mistress, Clara Petacci.

"They had been caught by Italian partisans on April 26 while trying to escape from Como into Switzerland, and executed two days later. On the Saturday night of April 28 the bodies were brought to Milan in a truck and dumped on the piazza. The next day they were strung up by the heels from lamp-posts....

"It is not known how many of the details of the Duce's (Mussolini's nickname) shabby end were communicated to the Fuehrer. One can only speculate that if he heard many of them he was only strengthened in his resolve not to allow himself or his bride to be made a spectacle, presented by the Jews, to divert their hysterical masses', as he had just written in his Testament — 'not their live selves or their bodies.'

"Shortly after receiving the news of Mussolini's death Hitler began to make the final preparations for his. He had his favorite Alsatian dog, Blondi, poisoned and two other dogs in the household shot....

"They (Hitler and Eva Braun) finished their farewells and retired to their rooms. Outside in the passageway, Dr. Goebbels, Bormann and a few others waited. In a few moments a revolver shot was heard. They waited for a second one, but there was only silence. After a decent interval they quietly entered the Fuehrer's quarters. They found the body of Adolf Hitler sprawled on the sofa dripping blood. He had shot himself in the mouth. At his side lay Eva Braun. Two revolvers had tumbled to the floor, but the bride had not used hers. She had swallowed poison.

"It was 3:30 P.M. on Monday, April 30, 1945, ten days after Adolf Hitler's fifty-sixth birthday, and twelve years three months to a day since he had become Chancellor of Germany and had instituted the Third Reich. It would survive him but a week.

"The Viking funeral followed. There were no words spoken; the only sound was the roar of Russian shells exploding in the garden of the Chancellery and on the shattered walls around it....

"The corpses were carried up to the garden during a lull in the bombardment, placed in a shell hole and ignited with gasoline. The mourners, headed by Goebbels and Bormann, withdrew to the shelter of the emergency exit and as the flames mounted stood at attention and raised their right hands in a farewell Nazi salute." SHIRER, page 1131, 1133, 1134.

Verse 20 Then shall stand up in his estate a raiser of taxes in the glory of the kingdom: but within few days he shall be destroyed, neither in anger, nor in battle.

With the defeat of Germany in World War II, the station of "king of the North" passed to another atheistic nation. "At the end of World War II, Germany was occupied by the victors. Russia controlled East Germany (Berlin included), while the democracies occupied West and South Germany." ROGERS, page 649.

A RAISER OF TAXES IN THE GLORY OF THE KINGDOM

This can be a reference to but one man, and only one man. He instituted his Five-Year-Plans in Russia and was in power when World War II ended.

JOSEPH STALIN
RUSSIA -THE "KING OF THE NORTH"

Joseph Stalin was the undisputed dictator of Russia. He "tried to make an industrial nation out of Russia with his Five-Year plans. Stalin was as determined and ruthless in making Russia into a strong nation as he was in building his own power. In the First Five-Year Plan...Russia developed her heavy industries such as steel mills, railways, and power plants....Those who were responsible for any part were ruthlessly liquidated if they failed.

(COLLECTIVISM)

"At the same time Stalin was developing heavy industries, he decided to turn the small individual farms into big collective farms. He wanted them run like factories. But the Russian peasants who owned a little land fought collectivism, as did the larger landowners.

"Stalin sent in his secret police. Those who opposed the new farm policy were arrested. Thousands died; many more were exiled to labor camps in Siberia. The entire class of landowning farmers were wiped out. It was as if all the landowning farmers in the United States were to disappear. They are the chief producers of our food, and without them we would starve. And that is just what happened in Russia. From two to three million people died of starvation during the years when the Communists took the land away from the owners and organized collective farms." ROGERS, page 496.

THE GLORY OF THE KINGDOM

Communism is "a theory advocating elimination of private property". It is "a system in which goods are owned in common and are available to all as needed". It is "a doctrine based on revolutionary Marxian socialism and Marxism —Leninism that is the official ideology of the U.S.S.R." (Russia). It is, furthermore, defined in the dictionary as "a totalitarian system of government in which a single authoritarian party controls state owned means of production with the professed aim of establishing a stateless society". "A final stage of society in Marxist theory in which the state has withered away and economic goods are distributed equitably." WEBSTER'S NEW COLLEGIATE DICTIONARY, 1981, page 226.

WITHIN FEW DAYS HE SHALL BE DESTROYED

In 1945 Russia, under the dictatorship of Joseph Stalin, occupied the station of "king of the north". Stalin didn't die until 1953,

therefore, how can it be true that he was destroyed (died) "within few days"? The word "few" is from "achadim", and means "single ones". This term occurs very few times in the old Testament, with one of its occurrences being Genesis 29:20,21, where it is recorded that "Jacob served (Laban) seven years for Rachel; and they (the 7 years) seemed unto him but a few (achadim) days for the love he had to her. And Jacob said unto Laban, give me my wife, for the days (7 years) are fulfilled".

From the time that Russia began to occupy the station of "king of the north", in 1945, until Stalin's death in 1953, just 8 single years had passed. The remainder of verse 20 describes the manner in which he was to die:

NEITHER IN ANGER, NOR IN BATTLE

"Four times a day, at 9:00 A.M., 1:00 P.M., 7:00 P.M., and 10:00 P.M., food and drink came to Stalin through a slit in the armor-plated door of his chambers (Stalin secluded himself behind barred doors for his own protection). He would telephone the guards and give them his orders for food.

"The captain of the guard testified that Stalin had rung for his dinner at 7:00 P.M., but he had failed to ring for his tea at 10:00 P.M. Nothing of this nature had ever happened before. When the captain called Stalin on the phone, there was no answer. He finally called the members of the Presidium. He did nothing during the interval, for he had been given strict orders that he was to never break into any of Stalin's three rooms under penalty of death."

The members of the Presidium soon arrived and Molotov ordered that the door be broken down, which took nearly an hour. The captain of the guard entered the room first and froze in his tracks, Beria (the head of the KGB) passed by him. Khrushchev gives his personal testimony in regard to what happened next: "I was just behind Beria when I saw Stalin in his marshal's uniform stretched out on his back on the wooden floor. My comrades crowded forward, for they too wanted to see what had happened. Suddenly there came the voice of Beria, piercing, strident, triumphant: 'The tyrant is dead, dead, dead.'

"I don't know what obscure peasant instinct made me kneel down beside Stalin's head. And then I saw his eyes, wide open, staring at me — not the eyes of a dead man, but the eyes of the living Stalin.

"I jumped up and backed away, my arms spread out. The others behind me understood (the penalty for entering Stalin's room, uninvited, was death) . And then I saw that they too were backing away toward the corridor. I fled with them. Only one man stayed behind. This was Beria." PAYNE, ROBERT, THE RISE AND FALL OF STALIN, 1965, page 700.

Within a few days, at about 8:30 A.M., all the radios in Moscow suddenly stopped. Then, after a pause, the announcement was made: "'During the night, between the first and second of March, Comrade Stalin, while in his apartment in Moscow, was struck by a cerebral hemorrhage which attacked the vital areas of the brain. Comrade Stalin has lost consciousness. His right arm and leg are paralyzed. He has lost his power of speech. Serious cardiac and respiratory complications have set in.'" BORTOLI, GEORGE, THE DEATH OF STALIN, 1975, page 147.

On March 5, 1953, 800 million Communists were informed that Stalin was dead. He had been destroyed (shabar-"to be broken, shivered"), neither in anger, nor in battle." The footnote, in the LXX, reads - "not in faces"! Joseph Stalin was not destroyed "in anger, nor in battle", but, rather, he died in private, behind closed doors.

Verse 21 And in his estate shall stand up a vile person, to whom they shall not give the honour of the kingdom: but he shall come in peaceably, and obtain the kingdom by flatteries.

At this point in the chronological prophecy of Daniel 11, Russia still occupies the station of "king of the north." Daniel beheld, and saw in vision, the very person who was to replace Stalin. His replacement was indeed "a vile person" ("a contemptible person"-RSV), a direct fulfillment of the prophecy. He was drunken and coarse and alternately savage and jolly. He was the disciple of Stalin and employed his methods and tactics of intrigue to bring himself to power. He was conditioned by thirty-five years of Stalinism in sweeping away all opposition. Through the purge of the Kulaks, in the Ukraine, he earned himself the unenviable nickname of the "Bloody Widower." Because of the part which he played in putting down the 1956 Hungarian revolt, he was called "The Butcher of Hungary." In September, 1959, he came to America and wanted to go to Disney-world. His name: NIKITA KHRUSHCHEV.

"Stalin died in March 1953, and after a period of internal conflict within the Kremlin, Nikita Khrushchev emerged as the new master of Russia. Khrushchev cleverly set out to obtain Communist objectives by indirection rather than by arms." GARRATY, page 793.

Khrushchev "was never to be the supreme autocrat... This is not hindsight: during the whole of his period of ascendance, in a continuous running commentary on his extraordinary and multifarious activity, it was my own persistent contention (says Edward Crankshaw) that the men who had raised him up could, and one day might, pull him down. In the end they (the members of the Russian Presidium) did just that. They did more; by the timing of his fall and by their subsequent actions they demonstrated which aspects of the policies enunciated by Khrushchev had been in fact collectively agreed on, and which had been imposed on them by Khrushchev. The most important were then seen to have been agreed on; they continued after Khrushchev's eclipse.

"It is important to be clear on this immediately, and for two reasons, which interlock: it is the key to our understanding of Khrushchev's own rule, and it is the key to our understanding of the country over which he ruled, which is still with us today, and of the men who ruled with him, the survivors of whom destroyed him when he tried too hard to make himself an autocrat, and who continued to rule without him.

"In February 1955 they agreed to the dethronement of Malenkov not because they thought Khrushchev would make a better tsar but partly for personal reasons and partly because they believed that the new course was heading for trouble." CRANKSHAW, EDWARD, KHRUSHCHEV-A CAREER, 1966, page 202–203.

HE SHALL OBTAIN THE KINGDOM BY FLATTERIES (CHALAQLAQQOTH— "SMOOTHNESSES")

Khrushchev did not obtain the kingdom by armed force. He "had his ablest supporters firmly established, sometimes as key individuals, sometimes-as in the Ukraine and Kazokhstan-in great depth, in all key Party posts, and in some important republican government posts as well. Shelepin was running the Komsomol. Madam Furtseva ... ran Moscow. Shepilov, whom he was soon to make Foreign Minister, edited Pravda. In July he achieved a major coup by getting his atrocious old ally, Serov, made head of the new committee of State Security: Serov was nominally responsible to the Council of Ministers-i.e., to Malenkov —but he was Khrushchev's man. He was even able to save from destruction the sinister Ignatiev, who ... had to leave the Secretariat of the Central Committee, but he was given a decent job in the provinces-by Khrushchev. In July, Khrushchev started interfering in foreign affairs; he was now undermining Molotov. Career Foreign office diplomats were replaced in half a dozen Communist countries, including China, by Khrushchev's Party officials, who were thus controlled not by the Foreign Office at all, but by the foreign-affairs section of the Central Committee, responsible to Khrushchev." CRANKSHAW, page 196, 195.

"Royal majesty" (RSV) was never given to Khrushchev. History declares that he was a "drunken peasant"! When the time was right, the members of the Russian Presidium sent Nikita Khrushchev into exile, in 1964.

Verse 22 And with the arms of a flood shall they be overflown from before him, and shall be broken; yea, also the Prince of the covenant.

"ARMIES SHALL BE UTTERLY SWEPT AWAY BEFORE HIM AND BROKEN" (RSV)

In 1939 Stalin appointed Khrushchev "First Secretary of the Ukraine." The Ukraine region, as distinguished from the Republic of that name (Ukrainia), is vastly larger than the latter (larger than Ukrainia) and parts of it (the Ukraine) are now embraced in Poland, Czechoslovakia, and Rumania." THE ENCYCLOPEDIA AMERICANA, 1953, Volume 27, page 255.

Khrushchev ruled the Ukraine, the second largest republic in the Soviet Union, as master and king. In the person of Khrushchev, Stalin duplicated his position, for the power of Nikita Khrushchev, in the Ukraine, was that, virtually, of dictator. "He ruled a great province of the empire," history declares, "a country of 40 million people, with its own history, its own proud tradition...."

"One very important aspect of his (Khrushchev's) final purge (1939) of the Ukraine was ... to transform a dubious, party alien borderland into an integral part of the Soviet Union, fit to bear the first impact of invasion from the West. With the signing of the notorious Non-aggression Pact with Germany, he had to be ready for a further move: he was responsible for extending the government of the Soviet Union to Eastern Poland....

"Stalin and Khrushchev wished to take over their part of Poland in working order, so a great number of Poles had to be left alive and at work. Khrushchev's job was to see that these were properly sovietized. He threw himself into this task with characteristic zeal. And, as usual, he went out among his people....

"As the Red Army moved into (Eastern) Poland with scarcely a check from the bewildered Poles, who hardly knew what was hitting them, Khrushchev was there, just behind the front-line troops. As the Soviet tanks moved into town after town, Khrushchev was just behind them to receive the submission of the civil governments." CRANKSHAW, page 131, 133.

How accurately Nikita Khrushchev meets the specifications of the prophecy set before us. Armies were "utterly swept away before him and broken".

AND THE PRINCE OF THE COVENANT ALSO

In Daniel 9:25 He is called the "Anointed One"; in 12:1 His name is "Michael, the Great Prince"; in 8:11 His title is "Prince of the host"; in 8:25 He is known as the "Prince of princes". In Isaiah 9:6 His name is "Wonderful, Counselor, The mighty God, The everlasting Father, The Prince of Peace." He is, of course, our Saviour and Lord, Jesus Christ.

According to verse 22, the "Prince of the covenant", Jesus, was to be 'broken". How, in harmony with the context of the prophecy of Daniel 11, was Jesus "broken"? The word "broken", as it occurs in the verse before us, is from "shabar", which may also correctly be translated "to crush", or "to hurt". The context in which the word appears is the determining factor as to its meaning. This same term also occurs in Psalm 34:18, where we are given the assurance that "The Lord is nigh unto them that are of a broken (shabar-hurting) heart; and saves such as be of a contrite spirit." The prophet Jeremiah declared, "Mine heart within me is broken" (shabar-hurting). See also Psalm 51:17; 69:20. What did Khrushchev do in the Ukraine that must have profoundly affected Jesus, the "Prince of the covenant", and caused Him to be "broken"-adversely affected?

BABI YAR

Anti-Semitism was endemic in the Ukraine. "There were many Ukrainians, Balts too, among the rank and file of the notorious Einsatzgruppen, special formations belonged to Heydrich's Sicherheitsdienst, which were responsible for the rounding-up and extermination of the Jews in occupied Russia. The gas chambers of Auschwitz, Madjanek, Treblinka, and elsewhere were fed mainly with Jews deported by the Germans from Western Europe, including Germany itself. In Russia the usual procedure was for the Einsatzgruppen to round up all the Jews found in a given area or city, march them out to a selected spot, force them to dig a trench, then to undress and stand on the edge of the trench to be sprayed with machine gun fire. One of the largest of these massacres took place immediately outside Khrushchev's own city, Kiev, in a ravine known as Babi Yar, on September 29 and 30, 1941, where 33,771 Jews, men, women, and children, were killed in two days, the shooting audible in the center of the city....

"For years after the war, during all of Khrushchev's time and later still, Kiev was a forbidden city: the only foreigners allowed to go there were a handful of UNRR officials. But I remember well when I was first allowed to go there in 1955 (says Edward Crankshaw), asking the local director of Intourists to direct me to Babi Yar. At first he pretended he had never heard of Babi Yar. But when I insisted he said, 'Why do you want to go and look at a lot of dead Jews? If you are interested in Jews you'll see more than enough live ones on the streets.'...

"Babi Yar remained a forbidden word until the young poet Yevtushenko in 1963 incurred Khrushchev's intense displeasure by writing his celebrated poem, 'Babi YAR', in which, as a Russian, he proclaimed his share of the guilt. It will be remembered that Shostakovich set the Babi Yar poem for voices and orchestra in the last movement of his Thirteenth Symphony, performance of which was forbidden at the last moment." CRANKSHAW, page 154–155.

"Although no exact figures could be compiled, it appeared probable that between five and six million European Jews had met death in the Nazi concentration camps and extermination centers." FERGUSON, page 994.

Jesus said, "Inasmuch as you have done it unto one of the least of these My brethren, you have done it unto Me." Matthew 25:40. Jesus was "hurting", "broken" with grief, as He beheld the slaughter of men, women, and little children. Man's inhumanity to man must have "broken" His heart!

Jesus was thus "broken" in like manner as were the armies that were "utterly swept away" from before Khrushchev. Those armies were not destroyed, killed, no! Those people were adversely affected, they were "grieved".

Verse 23 And after the league made with him he shall work deceitfully: for he shall come up, and shall become strong with a small people.

Daniel first gave a description of Joseph Stalin and his life. Then, after that, he wrote down a description of Nikita Khrushchev.

THE LEAGUE - "AN ALLIANCE" (RSV) THE "NON-AGGRESSION TREATY"

"On August 23, 1939, the "Russian government startled the world by signing a NON-AGGRESSION TREATY with the Germans....

"With Russia out of his way, Hitler attacked Poland eight days later, and World War II began." ROGERS, page 498. The NON-AGGRESSION TREATY was a time serving device for both Germany and Russia, for it ignored ideological antagonisms. Both nations were preparing to attack Poland. While Hitler was busy attacking Western Poland, Khrushchev was moving into Eastern Poland.

HE SHALL WORK DECEITFULLY "HE SHALL ACT DECEITFULLY" (RSV)

After the NON-AGGRESSION TREATY between Russia and Germany was signed, Khrushchev acted deceitfully in the Ukraine and became strong.

"Quite a drama was made of his investing and seizure of the great city Lvov, capital of the Polish Ukraine, which in fact surrendered with scarcely a shot fired. His private propaganda army sent back lunatic reports to Moscow papers about the heroism of the Soviet troops in general and Comrade Khrushchev in particular: he was represented as being received as a liberating angel with flowers and tears of gratitude and joy. The whole occupation was presented as one glorious fiesta, or jamboree, of thanksgiving. And Khrushchev did his best to lend colour to these reports by organizing a mass importation of representatives of Soviet culture to entertain and elevate their liberated brothers: ballet dancers from Kiev and Moscow, theatre companies, opera singers, poets, and film-makers flooded the seized territories to show the Poles what they had been missing through being sundered from paternal Russia....

"The liberated brethren soon found that life under the Russians was not all ballet and superfilms. They were called almost immediately to follow in the footsteps of their more fortunate brothers from the Motherland. In the shortest possible time the factories and shops were taken over by the state and the peasants were collectivized. By the winter of 1940 the peace of the grave had descended on the land. Khrushchev was back in Kiev, lord now of an additional 8 million people who had been forcibly and, by Russian standards, highly efficiently gleichgeschaltet and absorbed, body and soul, into the pattern of Soviet life. It was a formidable satrapy-a population almost as great as the population of France, the best part of Soviet industry, the best part of Soviet food production. The magnitude of this aggrandizement, and the suffering it caused, was concealed from the West by the fog of war. We had no thought for anyone but Hitler and the terrible things the Germans were doing to the Poles. We watched, sick at heart and outraged, the Soviet invasion of Finland in the winter of 1939, but we saw nothing, beyond the bare fact of Soviet occupation, of what was going on in eastern Poland. Had the view been clear, the name of Khrushchev would have become a household word fifteen years sooner than it did. This was his background, this the nature of his rise, this his early achievement. And this was the man who, with an air of bland innocence, was to ask his diplomatic guests, years later in Moscow, how it was that he managed to make rings round them, although they had been to better schools.

"This, also, was a man who could later say that he had no responsibility for Stalin's crimes. The invasion of Poland and the deportation in atrocious circumstances of over a million Poles were not among the crimes he listed. Nor was Serov's next operation, the mass deportation of hundreds of thousands of Lithuanians, Estonians, Latvians, and Bessarabians when Russia took their countries by agreement with the Germans. Nor was the collectivization, first of Russia, then of Eastern Poland. Nor was the killing of the real opposition leaders." CRANKSHAW, page 131, 133–136.

HE SHALL BECOME STRONG WITH A "SMALL PEOPLE"

THE ENCYCLOPEDIA AMERICANA, speaking in regard to the people of Poland, says that "the mass of the people are slightly below medium height." The people of Poland are a "small people."

Verse 24 He shall enter peaceably even upon the fattest places of the province; and he shall do that which his fathers have not done, nor his fathers' fathers; he shall scatter among them the prey, and spoil, and riches: yea, and he shall forecast his devices against the strong holds, even for a time.

The RSV says, "Without warning he shall come into the richest parts of the province", etc. How accurately Khrushchev has fulfilled the Prophecy before us. Without warning he came into Eastern Poland, the riches parts of the province, and he utterly swept away all opposition from before him. He also did that which neither his fathers nor his fathers' fathers had ever done; he distributed among his followers spoil, booty, and property. The generation of Khrushchev's father was not under communism, nor was that of his forefathers.

The BOLSHEVIK REVOLUTION "took place Nov. 6, 1917... Bolshevists .. seized total control of Russian government... In 1918, party changed its name to the Russian Communist Party, retaining Bolshevik in parentheses to indicate continuity of new organization with old political group. Name was finally dropped in 1952. Term Bolshevism has been generally replaced by COMMUNISM." THE UNIVERSAL ILLUSTRATED ENCYCLOPEDIA, 1978, page 120.

COMMUNISM

"A theory advocating elimination of private property... A system in which goods are owned in common and are available to all as needed... A doctrine based on revolutionary Marxian socialism and Marxism-Leninism that is the official ideology of the U.S.S.R. (Russia) ... A totalitarian system of government in which a single authoritarian party controls state-owned means of production with the professed aim of establishing a state-less society... A final stage of society in Marxist theory in which the state has withered away and economic goods are distributed equitably." WEBSTER'S NEW COLLEGIATE DICTIONARY, 1981, page 226.

Communism was accurately described by Daniel, even though he did not know what to call it.

"HE SHALL DEVISE PLANS AGAINST STRONG HOLDS, BUT ONLY FOR A TIME" (RSV)

The phrase, "even for a time", as it appears in the KJV, may correctly be translated, "until a time." For an unspecified period of time, Russia would seek to accomplish its goals through Communist Propaganda-the "Cold War."

"After World War II Korea was freed from Japanese control but remained divided into two parts at the thirty-eighth parallel. When the Russians (king of the north) withdrew from North Korea in 1948 they left a Communist 'People's Republic' with a trained army. The Americans (king of the south) withdrew from South Korea in 1949 after establishing a republican regime there headed by a conservative patriot named Syngman Rhee." FERGUSON, page 989.

"The world was being divided between communism and democracy." ROGERS, page 499.

The stage is now set for the next significant event portrayed in the prophecy of Daniel 11.

Chapter 8

THE KOREAN WAR
JUNE 25, 1950 - JULY 27, 1953

RUSSIA AND ALLIES –"KING OF THE NORTH"
THE UNITED STATES OF AMERICA AND ALLIES
"KING OF THE SOUTH"

Verse 25 And he shall stir up his power and his courage against the king of the south with a great army; and the king of the south shall be stirred up to battle with a very great and mighty army; but he shall not stand: for they shall forecast devices against him.

THE "KING OF THE NORTH" A "GREAT ARMY"

The "Cold War" lasted for only 5 years. "On June 25, 1950, the North Koreans suddenly attacked the South Koreans without provocation." FERGUSON, page 989.

When the Korean War began, "100,000 United States trained constabulary troops, with few weapons besides their rifles, were opposed by a (Russian) Soviet-trained North Korean army of 200,000 men equipped with every modern adjunct of war." MACARTHUR, DOUGLAS, REMINISCENCES, 1964, page 330.

THE KING OF THE SOUTH AN EXCEEDINGLY GREAT AND MIGHTY ARMY

"Thanks to the fortunate absence of the Soviet (Russian) representative, the Security Council of the United Nations was able to call for collective action to resist this aggression. Sixteen nations respond-ed (1) Australia, (2) Belgium, (3) Canada, (4) Colombia, (5) Ethiopia, (6) France, (7) Greece, (8) Luxembourg, (9) Netherlands, (10) New Zealand, (11) Philippines, (12) Thailand, (13) Turkey, (14) The Union of South Africa, (15) The United Kingdom (England, Scotland, Northern Ireland), (16) The United States of America, though the chief burden necessarily fell on the Americans and the (South) Koreans themselves." FERGUSON, page 989.

"The Council authorized a unified UN force under the command of general Douglas McArthur. ... Above the combined forces flew the UN flag. For the first time in world history, men marched to war as the result of a resolution passed by an international organization." ROGERS, page 688.

The 16 nations listed contributed ground, air and naval forces, while India, Norway, Panama and Sweden sent non-combat aid.

England would have certainly been crushed, smashed to pieces in World War II, if the United States of America had not come to her aid. England mobilized an army of 12,000,000 men in World War II, while the United States ("King of the South") mobilized and put forth an army of 14,000,000 men. As president Roosevelt said, the

United States had become "the arsenal of democracy."

"BUT HE SHALL NOT STAND, FOR PLOTS SHALL BE DEVISED AGAINST HIM" (RSV)

The following words are those of General Douglas MacArthur, commander of the United Nations forces in Korea:

"Despite the welter of restrictions placed upon me by Washington, I felt there remained one weapon I could use against the massive Chinese intervention. I ordered General Stratemeyer to employ ninety B-29's on the following morning to destroy the Yalu bridges and cut this easy line of communications between Manchuria and North Korea, over which large armies of Chinese Reds could swarm. Up to now I had avoided the targets and dropping bombs on Manchuria, which had been forbidden.

"An immediate dispatch came from Secretary Marshall (in Washington) countermanding my order and directing me 'to postpone all bombing of targets within five miles of the Manchurian border.' It seemed to me incredible that protection should be extended to the enemy, not only of the bridges which were the only means they had for moving their men and supplies across that wide natural river barrier into North Korea, but also for a 5-mile deep area on this side of the Yalu in which to establish a bridge-head. It would be impossible to exaggerate my astonishment, and I at once protested.

"All that resulted was a modification of the order to permit the bombing of the Korean end of the Yalu bridges.

"I asked Stratemeyer to study the conditions under which the bombing of the Yalu bridges was to be permitted. He reported: 'It cannot be done—Washington must have known that it cannot be done. '

"The head of the Far East Bomber Command, Major General Emmett (Rosey) O'Donnell, made the following estimate of the situation: 'We were not allowed to violate Manchurian territory, and by violation of territory I mean we were not allowed to fly over an inch of it. For instance, like most rivers, the Yalu has several bends before getting to the town of Antung, and the main bridges at Antung we had to attack in only one manner-in order not to violate Manchurian territory, and that was a course tangential to the southernmost bend of the river. As you draw a line from the southernmost bend of the river to the bridge, that is your course. These people on the other side of the river knew that and put up their batteries right along the line, and they peppered us right down the line all the way. We had to take it, of course, and couldn't fight back. In addition to that, they had their fighters come up alongside and join our formation about two miles to the lee and fly along at the same speed on the other side of the river while we were making our approach. And just before we got to bomb-away position, they would veer off to the north and climb up to about 30,000 feet and then make a frontal quarter attack on the bombers just about the time of bomb away in a turn. So they would be coming from Manchuria in a turn, swoop down, fire their cannon at the formation, and continue to turn back to sanctuary.'

"One of those bomber pilots, wounded unto death, the stump of an arm dangling by his side, gasped at me (General MacArthur) through the bubbles of blood he spat out, 'General, which side are Washington and the United Nations on?' It seared my soul.

"I at once asked for immediate relief from assignment to duty in the Far East. In my bitterness I told my able chief of staff, General Doyle Hickey: 'For the first time in military history, a commander has been denied the use of his military power to safeguard the lives of his soldiers and safety of his army. To me it clearly foreshadows a future tragic situation in the Far East (Vietnam) and leaves me with a sense of inexpressible shock. It will cost the lives of thousands (60,000 in Vietnam) of American soldiers and place in jeopardy the entire army. By some means the enemy commander must have known of this decision to protect his lines of communication into North Korea, or he never would have dared to cross those bridges in force.'" MacARTHUR, page 368–370.

"The truth is that MacArthur's strategies were indeed falling into the hands of the North Koreans who were being commanded by Russian officers.

"The chain of command under the United States Constitution for any military officer leads upward through the Executive Branch of the government and ends with the President who is the ultimate authority for military decisions.

MacArthur was, of course, constitutionally required to obey the orders of his ultimate commander, but under the treaty binding the United States to the United Nations, the command chain went past the President into an office in the United Nations known as the undersecretary for Political and Security Council Affairs who reported directly to the Secretary General.

"Because of a secret agreement made by Secretary of State Edward Stettinius in 1945, this key position, the official who controlled such things as United Nations 'police actions', was to be filled by a Communist from some Eastern European Communist country. At the time of the Korean War, this post was filled by Constantine Zinchenko, of Russia.

"The North Koreans had Russian military advisors during the war, and it later became known just who was in charge of the North Korean War efforts. According to a Department of defense press release dated May 15, 1964, high-Russian military officers were actually on the scene in North Korea directing military operations. The release stated: 'A North Korean Major identified two of these Russian 'advisors' as General Vasilev and Colonel Dolgin. Vasilev, he said, was in charge of all movements across the 38th parallel. Another prisoner … said he actually heard General Vasilev give the order to attack on June 25th.'

"General Vasilev's chain of command went through the United Nations as well. He 'had been the chairman of the United Nations Military Staff Committee which, along with the office of the Undersecretary General for Political and Security Council Affairs, is responsible for United Nations military action under the Security Council.'

"That meant that two Russians shared authority in planning the North Korean War efforts, and one of them planned the efforts of the United Nations. 'In effect, the Communists were directing both sides of the war!'

"The Russians were not only controlling both sides of the war and supplying technical advisors for the North Korean War effort, they were actually supplying Russian pilots for flights against the Americans: 'Lt. General Samuel E. Anderson, commander of the Fifth Air Force, revealed that entire Soviet (Russian) Air Force units fought in the Korean War for over two and a half years.'

"General MacArthur, aware that the Red Chinese were about to enter the war, realized that one way to prevent their massive entry was to bomb the bridges crossing the Yalu River. He 'ordered General Stratemeyer, (Chief of the Air Force) to employ B29's on the following morning to destroy the Yalu bridges and cut this easy line of communication between Manchuria and North Korea. An immediate dispatch came from Secretary (of State-Washington D.C.-George) Marshall countermanding my order and directing me to 'postpone all bombing of targets within five miles of the Manchurian border.'

"In addition, MacArthur was ordered not to pursue aircraft fleeing North Korea into Manchuria, nor could he bomb the supply base in the town of Racin.

"MacArthur felt that of these decisions the most incomprehensible of all 'was the refusal to let me bomb the important supply center at Racin, which was not in Manchuria or Siberia but many miles from the borders, in northeast Korea.' Racin was a depot to which the Soviet Union (Russia) forwarded supplies from Vladivostok for the North Korean Army.

"On November 25, 1950, the Red Chinese Army commander, General Lin Piao, launched his full forces across the Yalu River and into North Korea. MacArthur felt that … 'information must have been relayed to them, assuring that the Yalu bridges would continue to enjoy sanctuary and that their bases would be left intact.'

"This was, unfortunately, the truth, as even General Lin Piao later admitted that he 'would never have made the attack and risked my men … if I had not been assured that Washington would restrain General MacArthur from taking adequate retaliatory measures against my lines of supply and communication.'

"General MacArthur would later write that the order not to bomb the Yalu bridges 'was the most indefensible and ill-conceived decision ever forced on a field commander in our nation's history.' One of General MacArthur's generals in the Air Force, George Stratemeyer, said that 'We had sufficient air, bombardment, fighters, reconnaissance so that I could have taken out all of those supplies, those airdromes on the other side of the Yalu; I could have bombed the devils between there and Mukden, stopped the railroad operating and the people of China that were fighting could not have been supplied.…

"'But we weren't permitted to do it. As a result, a lot of American blood was spilled over there in Korea.'

"House Minority Leader (in Washington D.C.) Joseph Martin also expressed his dismay at the administration's apparent desire not to win the war in Korea by such tactics as not allowing the bombing of strategic military targets: 'If we are not in Korea to win, this Administration should be indicted for the murder of thousands of American boys.'" EPPERSON, RALPH, THE UNSEEN HAND, 1985, page 319–321.

Verse 26 Yea, they that feed of the portion of his meat shall destroy him, and his army shall overflow: and many shall fall down slain.

Verse 26 (RSV) Even those who eat his rich food shall be his undoing; his army shall be swept away, and many shall fall down slain.

HIS ARMY SHALL BE SWEPT AWAY

When MacArthur and the UN force "crossed the thirty-eighth parallel and prosecuted the war to the Manchurian border, an ominous development occurred. Nearly 300,000 Red Chinese volunteer troops pored into Korea, and the United Nations force narrowly escaped disaster for the second time. The new attack was halted, and General MacArthur seemed quite ready to carry the war into China itself, if necessary to win it; but the United States government and its allies were not. MacArthur was replaced." FERGUSON, page 989.

David Rees points out, in his book, KOREA: THE LIMITED WAR, that due to the failure of the United States to unite Korea and inflict a decisive defeat on Communist China, the Korean War is seen "as a defeat and not a victory, a turning point on the way down and not on the way up." He goes on to say that "all the senior (U.S.) military commanders (43 of them) in Korea with the exception of Ridgway and Maxwell Taylor believe that it was a disaster for the United States not to have forced the issue with Peking after the CCF (Communist Chinese Forces-300,000) intervention." REES, DAVID, KOREA: THE LIMITED WAR, 1964, page 447.

AND MANY SHALL FALL DOWN SLAIN

Approximately 2 million human beings were slain in the Korean War. One and a half million were Chinese and North Koreans. Five hundred thousand (half a million) UN soldiers were slain, of whom nearly 150,000 were American. Daniel saw it, and said, "many shall fall down slain."

Verse 27 And both these kings' hearts shall be to do mischief, and they shall speak lies at one table; but it shall not prosper: for yet the end shall be at the time appointed.

"THEY SHALL SPEAK LIES AT THE SAME TABLE" RSV ARMISTICE IN KOREA— PANMUNJOM JULY 27, 1953 "THE TRUCE OF THE BEAR"

"Everyone knew that the two Communist nations north of Korea, Soviet Russia and

Red China, were backing the North Koreans. They had trained the Korean troops and given them Soviet tanks, trucks, and arms." ROGERS, page 689.

Chapter 23 of the book by David Rees is appropriately titled "THE TRUCE OF THE BEAR". General MacArthur was replaced as Commander of the UN force, in 1951, and "after two long years of desultory warfare and recrimination, in 1953 a truce was negotiated." FERGUSON, page 989.

It had been agreed that representatives of both forces would "face each other across a table at Panmunjom and sign the truce….

"After Clark had completed the sparse ceremony which so befitted the ending of the war which no one had won, he read an extremely brief statement which began, 'I cannot find in me to exult at this hour'... Later Clark wrote in his memoirs that by signing he had gained the 'unenviable distinction' of being the first United States Commander in history to sign an armistice without victory…. Moscow also noted the end of the war in a message from Malenkov to the Chinese Communist and North Korean leaders which congratulated them on winning 'a great victory in the cause of defending peace in the Far East and throughout the world.' There were no celebrations on Broadway." REES, page 466.

As indicated in verse 27, neither side would prove to be truthful and abide by the Armistice Agreement. Article I pertains to the Military Demarcation Line and the Demilitarized Zone. Article II deals with the Concrete Arrangements for Cease-Fire and Armistice. Sub-Paragraph 13d says: "Cease

the introduction into Korea of reinforcing combat aircraft, armored vehicles, weapons and ammunition." Ibid.

In June 1957, the United Nations Council told the Communist side in the Military Armistice Commission that it was relieved from observing the provisions of sub-paragraph 13d, because of the continuing Communist build-up. "Since that date old equipment and weapons have been replaced and renewed by both sides without inhibitions whatsoever. To the north Kim Il Sung's reconstituted Air Force is particularly powerful with its many hundreds of MIG'S, while to the south, Honest John (**US**) tactical guided missiles with atomic warheads guard all the invasion routes south between Kaesong and the Sea of Japan….

"The Neutral Nations Supervisory Commission still meets weekly (at least up to the time that David Rees wrote his book-1964) to consider violations of truce provisions which neither side observes." REES, page 452–453.

Daniel saw that the Armistice would be "to no avail; for the end is yet to be at the time appointed." (RSV).

THE "TIME APPOINTED"— FROM "MOED"—POINTS TO A "SET TIME", OR "SEASON"

By Daniel's time the term (*moed*) was employed almost exclusively to designate the special times of the year when God would meet with His people, such as in the spring, at Passover time, or in the fall, at the Day of Atonement gathering. This same term (*moed*) also occurs in Daniel 8:19 and

11:29 and verse 35. The term is helpful in interpreting verse 29.

In 8:17; 11:27, 35, and verse 40, the word "end" is from "*qets*"-"extremity". Daniel has in mind the end of earth's history and the coming of Jesus. In Habakkuk 2:3 both terms (*moed & qets*) occur: "For the vision is yet for an appointed time (*moed*), but at the end (*qets* "extremity") it shall speak, and not lie: though it tarry, wait for it; because it will surely come, it will not tarry."

Verse 28 Then shall he return into his land with great riches; and his heart shall be against the holy covenant; and he shall do exploits, and return to his own land.

Verse 28 (RSV) And he shall return to his land with great substance, but his heart shall be set against the holy covenant. And he shall work his will, and return to his own land.

After the Armistice was signed, both North and South Korea received a large sum of money for rehabilitation. South Korea received a "grant of 200 million dollars from the United States." North Korea accepted "1,000 million rubles", about eleven hundred million (1,100,000, 000) dollars from Russia. More than five times the amount that South Korea received from the United States.

HIS HEART SHALL BE AGAINST THE "HOLY COVENANT"

The holy covenant is between God and those who worship Him. To come against the holy covenant is to come against those who worship the true God. According to Luke 1:68–80, the "holy covenant" came through father Abraham and it is a saving and tender relationship that God has with those who believe in Him and seek to obey Him.

It is recorded of Khrushchev that he "issued his first decree (October, 1954), signed by himself alone (its concern was to find more subtle ways of conducting anti-religious propaganda)." CRANKSHAW, page 199.

The Russian Orthodox Church appeared to be on the very verge of extinction by the year 1939. Its 163 bishops had been reduced to seven, its 50,000 priests were reduced to a few hundred, the 1,000 monasteries and 60 seminaries of pre-Revolutionary times were completely shut down. Under Stalin's "New Religious Policy", which was instituted in 1945, the Russian Orthodox Church flourished during the next ten years through the help of 74 bishops, nearly 30,000 priests, 67 monasteries, and 10 schools of theology. Stalin gave the Church the "seal of Legitimacy" during those years. Stalin used the Church as a means of strengthening Russia. Not only was Khrushchev an anti-Semite, he was also against the Russian Orthodox Church. He was against religion in general. Some of the gains of the Church during the years of Stalin's reign were "canceled by as much as fifty percent during the last four years (1960–1964) of the Khrushchev era." FIRESIDE, HARVEY, <u>ICON AND SWASTIKA, THE RUSSIAN ORTHODOX CHURCH UNDER NAZI AND SOVIET CONTROL</u>, 1971, page 166.

After Korea, Russia shifted its attention to Southeast Asia, "particularly to Indo-china (Vietnam, Cambodia, Laos) and Formosa." ROGERS, page 694.

From the end of the Korean War, in 1953, until 1962, Russia, the "king of the north", worked his will.

The next chapter of this volume deals with the next significant event in the chronology of Daniel 11, which is recorded in verse 29.

Chapter 9

THE CUBAN MISSILE CRISIS
OCTOBER 22, 1962

RUSSIA-KHRUSHCHEV-"KING OF THE NORTH"
THE UNITED STATES OF AMERICA
PRESIDENT J. F. KENNEDY-"KING OF THE SOUTH"

Verse 29 At the time appointed he shall return, and come toward the south; but it shall not be as the former, or as the latter.

Verse 29 (RSV) At the time appointed he shall return and come <u>into</u> the south; but it shall not be this time as it was before. **Emphasis** <u>supplied</u>.

This direct encounter and confrontation between the "King of the North" (Russia) and the "King of the South" (United States of America) was not going to be this time as it was before, in World War II, which was the "former" experience, nor was it going to be as the "latter" experience, that of Korea. No! "<u>EMPHATICALLY</u>" and "<u>IMPERATIVELY</u>" — "<u>NO</u>"! For this encounter was to take place within the Southern Hemisphere, in October of 1962, when the "King of the North" (Khrushchev) would come "<u>into</u>" the South. But, it was destined, in God's time clock, to be a different kind of experience this time! For it was <u>not</u> to "be this time as it was before."

Verse 30 For the ships of Chit-tim shall come against him: therefore he shall be grieved, and return, and have indignation against the holy covenant: so shall he do; he shall even return, and have intelligence with them that forsake the holy covenant.

Verse 30 (RSV) For ships of Kit'tim shall come against him, and he shall be afraid and withdraw, and shall turn back and be enraged and take action against the holy covenant. He shall turn back and give heed to those who forsake the holy covenant.

SHIPS OF CHIT'TIM (or) KIT'TIM

The <u>BIBLE COMMENTARY</u> informs us that "although students of the Bible do not all agree as to the exact historical reference of the 'Chit'tim' in this verse, it seems clear that in interpreting this passage, two thoughts should be kept in mind: first, that in Daniel's day the word referred, geographically, to the lands and peoples to the west; and second, that the emphasis may already have been in process of shifting from the geographical meaning of the word to the thought of the Chittim as invaders and destroyers from any quarter." 4 BC 873.

THE "CUBAN MISSILE CRISIS"
OCTOBER 22, 1962
"AT THE BRINK"

The words "appointed time" in verse 29 are from the term "*moed*" and point to a "set time", and, or, "season" of the year. By Daniel's time this term (*moed*) was employed almost exclusively to point to the special gathering together of God's people, during the year, to celebrate and give thanks to Him for His bountiful blessings and watch-care over them. Passover in the spring of the year, and the Day of Atonement in the fall, (autumn) are two examples of such special gathering times.

In 1844 a great religious awakening occurred and many believed that the Lord was going to return to the earth on the anti-typical day of atonement, which fell on October 22 of that year. As we know, Christ did not return to the earth then, as expected, and the experience is today known as the "Great Disappointment."

At the "time appointed", as it was revealed to the prophet Daniel, the "King of the North" (Khrushchev-Russia) did indeed return, and he not only came "toward" the south, but he actually came "into" the South, into the "Southern Hemisphere", "INTO CUBA"! (South of Florida-U.S.A.).

On October 16, 1962, President Kennedy received spy-plane photographs showing Russian nuclear missiles being installed in Cuba. By late afternoon, and early evening, of Sunday, October 21, missile crews within the United States Defense Department had been put on maximum alert. Military personnel were deployed in several southeastern states and bombers were sent to civilian airports, in order to lessen their being vulnerable during an attack.

On Monday, "October 22", President Kennedy "went before the nation on televi-

sion. Characterizing the Russian build-up as 'a deliberately provocative and unjustified change in the status quo.' He ordered the navy to stop and search all vessels headed for Cuba and to turn back any containing 'offensive' weapons. He called upon Khrushchev to dismantle the missile bases and remove from the island all weapons capable of striking the United States. Any Cuban-based nuclear attack would result, he warned, in 'a full retaliatory response upon the Soviet Union.'

"For several days, while the whole world held its breath, work on the missile bases continued. Then Khrushchev backed down. He withdrew the missiles and cut back his military establishment in Cuba to modest proportions. Kennedy then lifted the blockade." GARRATY, page 802.

Khrushchev did exactly what prophecy said that he would do! He was "afraid" and he "withdrew" and he had "intelligence with them that forsake the holy covenant."

THE "HOT LINE"

"Khrushchev agreed to the installation of a 'hot line' telephone between the White House and the Kremlin so that in any future crisis leaders of the two nations could be in instant communication." Ibid. (or) GARRATY, page 802.

THE HOLY COVENANT

The ten commandments, written by the finger of God, were placed in a chest made of acacia wood. In the Bible this chest that contains the law of God is known as the "ark of the covenant", because the ten commandments are the basis of the holy covenant between God and man. In Luke 1:72 the holy covenant is called "His (God's) covenant".

As noted earlier, it is clear from Luke 1: 67–75 that to come against the holy covenant is to persecute people who trust in and serve the "Living God." The apostle Paul, in Romans 7:12, says that the "law is holy, and the commandment holy, and just, and good."

Abraham was obedient to the commandments of God and the law of God was the condition of the divine covenant that He made with him.

We understand from James 5:10 that "whosoever shall keep the whole law, and yet offend in one point, he is guilty of all." An entire nation can thus "forsake the holy covenant" by setting aside just one of the ten commandments.

Khrushchev was "afraid", in Cuba, and he "withdrew", and was "enraged", and took action "against the holy covenant", that is, against people living within his own country who trusted in and worshipped the True and Living God. Khrushchev gave "heed to", and had "intelligence" with, those who shall forsake the holy covenant.

THEM THAT FORSAKE THE HOLY COVENANT

"A time is coming when the law of God is, in a special sense, to be made void in our land. The rulers of our nation (The United States of America) will, by legislative enactments, enforce the Sunday law, and thus God's people will be brought into great peril. When our nation, in its legislative councils, shall enact laws to bind the consciences of men in regard to their religious privileges, enforcing Sunday observance, and bringing oppressive power to bear against those who keep the seventh-day Sabbath, the law of God will, to all intents and purposes, be made void in our land; and national apostasy will be followed by national ruin (RH Dec. 18, 1888) ....

"The sins of the world will have reached unto heaven when the law of God is made void; when the Sabbath of the Lord is trampled in the dust, and men are compelled to accept in its stead an institution of the papacy through the strong hand of the law of the land. In exalting an institution of man above the institution ordained of God, they show contempt for the great Lawgiver, and refuse His sign or seal (RH Nov. 5, 1889)." WHITE, ELLEN G., quoted in SEVENTH-DAY ADVENTIST BIBLE COMMENTARY, 1957, Volume 7, page 977. (7 BC 977)

"To secure popularity and patronage, legislators will yield to the demand for a Sunday law. Those who fear God cannot accept an institution that violates a precept of the Decalogue. On this battlefield comes the last great conflict of the controversy between truth and error. And we are not left in doubt as to the issue. Now, as in the days of Mordecai, the Lord will vindicate His truth and His people.

"By the decree enforcing the institution of the papacy in violation of the law of God, our nation will disconnect herself fully from righteousness....

"As the approach of the Roman armies was a sign to the disciples of the impending destruction of Jerusalem, so may this apostasy be a sign to us that the limit of God's forbearance is reached, that the measure of our nation's iniquity is full, and that the angel of mercy is about to take her flight, never to return." WHITE, ELLEN G., <u>TESTIMONIES FOR THE CHURCH</u>, 1948, Volume 5, page 451. (5 T 451).

The sign to get out of the cities, preparatory to leaving the smaller villages and towns, is the passage of the Sunday law by the United States Legislature. For "national apostasy" shall most certainly be followed by "national ruin." Jonah's message to wicked Nineveh was, "Yet forty (40) days, and Nineveh shall be overthrown." (destroyed). So it will also be at the time of the end.

Daniel saw that Khrushchev would be afraid, and withdraw and have "intelligence" with "them" that shall one day "forsake the holy covenant." So far the longest interval between events portrayed in the prophecy of Daniel 11 is 55 years which is the time period between Napoleon Bonaparte's defeat at Waterloo, in 1815, and the beginning of the Franco-Russian (Franco-German) War in 1870. Will that 55 year period of time between events be surpassed? Or, will the closing events of earth's history take place first? As of October, 2005, 43 years have passed since the Cuban Missile Crisis occurred in 1962. In just 12 more years the 55 year period of time will be equaled. The end is near and Jesus is coming soon.

"We are living in the time of the end. The fast fulfilling signs of the times declare that the coming of Christ is near at hand….

"Great changes are soon to take place in our world, and the final movements will be <u>rapid ones</u>."… (**Emphasis** <u>supplied</u>).

"The world is stirred with the spirit of war. The prophecy of the eleventh chapter of Daniel has nearly reached its complete fulfillment. Soon the scenes of trouble spoken of in the prophecies will take place….

"Soon the battle will be waged <u>fiercely</u> between those who serve God and those who serve Him not. Soon everything that can be shaken will be shaken, that those things that cannot be shaken may remain." WHITE, 9 T 11, 14, 15–16. (**Emphasis** <u>supplied</u>).

"As we near the close of this world's history, the prophecies recorded by Daniel demand our special attention, as they relate to the very time in which we are living. With them should be linked the teachings of the last book (Revelation) of the New Testament Scriptures." WHITE, ELLEN G., <u>PROPHETS AND KINGS</u>, 1943, page 547.

THE 7 THUNDERS
REVELATION 10:1–4

1   And I saw another mighty angel come down from heaven, clothed with a cloud: and a rainbow was upon His head, and His face was as it were the sun, and His feet as pillars of fire:

2   And He had in His hand a little book open: and He set His right foot upon the sea, and His left foot on the earth.

3   And cried with a loud voice, as when a lion roars: and when He had cried, seven thunders uttered their voices.

4   And when the seven thunders had uttered their voices, I was about to write: and I heard a voice from heaven saying unto me, Seal up those things which the seven thunders uttered, and write them not.

"The mighty angel who instructed John was no less a personage than Jesus Christ. Setting His right foot on the sea, and His left upon the dry land, shows the part which He is acting in the closing scenes of the great controversy with Satan. This position denotes His supreme power and authority over the whole earth." WHITE, ELLEN G. (quoted in) 7 BC 971.

THE 7 THUNDERS ARE "<u>NOT</u>" IN REVELATION

Of all the sevens in the book of Revelation—7 churches, 7 spirits, 7 golden candlesticks, 7 stars, 7 lamps, 7 seals, 7 horns, 7 eyes, 7 angels, 7 trumpets, 7 heads, 7 vials (last plaques) , 7 mountains, 7 kings; the 7 thunders are "not" in the book of Revelation! The apostle John was instructed by a voice from heaven that he was to "write them not."

WHAT DO THE 7 THUNDERS REPRESENT?

"After these seven thunders uttered their voices, the injunction comes to John as to Daniel in regard to the little book: 'Seal up those things which the seven thunders uttered.' These relate to future events which will be disclosed in their order. Daniel shall stand in his lot at the end of the days. John sees the little book unsealed. Then Daniel's prophecies have their proper place in the first, second, and third angels' messages to be given to the world....

"The books of Daniel and the Revelation are one. One is a prophecy, the other a revelation; one a book sealed, the other a book opened. John heard the mysteries which the thunders uttered, but he was commanded not to write them.

"The special light given to John which was expressed in the seven thunders was a delineation of events which would transpire under the first and second angels' messages. It was not best for the people to know these things, for their faith must necessarily be tested. In the order of God most wonderful and advanced truths would be proclaimed. The first and second angels' messages were to be proclaimed, but no further light was to be revealed before these messages had done their specific work....

"The angel's position, with one foot on the sea, the other on the land, signifies the wide extent of the proclamation of the message. It will cross the broad waters and be proclaimed in other countries, even to all the world. The comprehension of truth, the glad reception of the message, is represented in the eating of the little book. The truth in regard to the time of the advent of our Lord was a precious message to our souls (MS 59, 1900)." WHITE, ELLEN G. <u>Ibid</u>. (7 BC 971)

THE 7 THUNDERS REPRESENT A "DELINEATION OF EVENTS"

The 7 thunders represent a delineation of events which are given in chronological order in the prophecy of Daniel 11 . Six of the 7 thunders have already met their historical fulfillment and are now presented in their chronological order:

THE FIRST THUNDER
DANIEL 11:5–9
1798–1815
THE NAPOLEONIC WARS

As France occupied the designated station of "King of the North", the Papacy and England occupied the station of "King of the South." England, in fulfillment of prophecy, occupied the station of "King of the South" for more years than France occupied the station of "King of the North"; as a primary contending world power.

THE SECOND THUNDER
DANIEL 11:10
1870–1871
THE FRANCO-PRUSSIAN WAR

Also known as the "FRANCO-GERMAN WAR." Otto Von Bismarck was able to consolidate the more than 300 German States into the German Empire. France, under Napoleon III, became an insignificant republic.

THE THIRD THUNDER
DANIEL 11:11, 12
1914–1919
WORLD WAR I

The events occurring during World War I, when England-the "King of the South", fought against Germany-the "King of the North", comprise the third thunder.

THE FOURTH THUNDER
DANIEL 11:13–24
1939–1945
WORLD WAR II

The events that occurred during World War II, when Adolf Hitler sought to conquer the world. At first it was Germany, as "King of the North" and England as "King of the South. " But, before the war was over, the station of "King of the North" was occupied by Russia and that of the "King of the South" by the United States of America.

THE FIFTH THUNDER
DANIEL 11:25–28
1950–1953
THE KOREAN WAR

Russia, first under Joseph Stalin and later under Nikita Khrushchev, was destined to occupy the station of "King of the North", along with its two allies, namely North Korea and China. In the Korean War, the South Koreans could not have survived without direct help from the primary power occupying the station of "King of the South"-The United States of America.

THE SIXTH THUNDER
DANIEL 11:29, 30
OCTOBER-1962
THE CUBAN MISSILE CRISIS

A series of events led up to a direct showdown between the "King of the North"-Russia, under Nikita Khrushchev, and the "King of the South" The United States of America, under President John F. Kennedy. And we had better remember that the hardline Communist leaders in Russia have no intention of ever forgetting about the humiliation they experienced when they were forced to back down and withdraw from Cuba.

THE SEVENTH THUNDER
EVENTS YET TO BE FULFILLED
DANIEL 11:30-C TO THE END OF TIME
"THEM THAT FORSAKE THE HOLY COVENANT"

After his humiliating experience in Cuba, Nikita Khrushchev persecuted religious people in his own country. Verse 30 points this out by saying that he had "indignation against the holy covenant." His rage against religion was proportionate to his embarrassment when his missiles and personnel returned home, in 1962.

The "hot line" telephone was installed during the summer of 1963. In establishing this vital communication line, through the signing of a formal agreement between the two superpowers, on June 20, 1963, Khrushchev achieved a permanent line of "intelligence" with them (U.S.) that shall one day "forsake the holy covenant." (11:30c). This is the first (the forsaking of the holy covenant-the passage of a National Sunday Law) of many events which are to occur under the 7th thunder, before Jesus returns to the earth for the redemption of His people – all who love and obey Him! So, the significant event that we are looking for, the "sign" for our time, is the "National Sunday Law", which the United States Legislature will most certainly pass, some day in the near future! Since the Cuban Missile Crisis of 1962, this is the very next event portrayed in the prophecy before us! Shortly after this event occurs, the angel of mercy shall take her flight, never to return! All of Earth's

closing events, beginning with the National Sunday Law, come under the 7th thunder!

THE NATIONAL SUNDAY LAW

"A time is coming when the law of God is, in a special sense, to be made void in our land. The rulers of our nation (The United States of America) will, by legislative enactments, enforce the Sunday law, and thus God's people will be brought into great peril. When our nation, in its legislative councils, shall enact laws to bind the consciences of men in regard to their religious privileges, enforcing Sunday observance, and bringing oppressive power to bear against those who keep the seventh-day Sabbath, the law of God will, to all intents and purposes, be made void in our land; and national apostasy will be followed by national ruin (RH Dec. 18, 1888)." WHITE, 7 BC 977.

"By the decree enforcing the institution of the papacy in violation of the law of God, our nation will disconnect herself fully from righteousness...

"As the approach of the Roman armies was a sign to the disciples of the impending destruction of Jerusalem, so may this apostasy be a sign to us that the limit of God's forbearance is reached, that the measure of our nation's iniquity is full, and that the angel of mercy is about to take her flight, never to return." 5 T 451.

All of the remaining events of earth's history come under the 7th thunder, after the angel of mercy has taken her flight, never to return!

"The class who do not feel grieved over their own spiritual declension, nor mourn over the sins of others, will be left without the seal of God. The Lord commissions His messengers, the men with slaughtering weapons in their hands: 'Go ye after him through the city, and smite: let not your eye spare, neither have ye pity: slay utterly old and young, both maids, and little children, and women: but come not near any man upon whom is the mark (the Seal of God); and begin at My sanctuary. Then they began at the ancient men which were before the house.'

"Here we see that the church-the Lord's sanctuary was the first to feel the stroke of the wrath of God. The ancient men, those to whom God had given great light and who had stood as guardians of the spiritual interests of the people, had betrayed their trust. They had taken the position that we need not look for miracles and the marked manifestation of God's Power as in former days. Times have changed. These words strengthen their unbelief, and they say: The Lord will not do good, neither will He do evil. He is too merciful to visit His people in judgment. Thus 'Peace and safety' is the cry from men who will never again lift up their voice like a trumpet to show God's people their transgressions and the house of Jacob their sins. These dumb dogs that would not bark are the ones who feel the just vengeance of an offended God. Men, maidens, and little children all perish together." 5 T 211.

Dear friends, there is coming a day when all of the cities of the earth shall be "broken down"! The prophet Jeremiah declares that it shall be so. See Jeremiah 4:23–27. If not for your own selves, then do it for the children. Get out of the cities before it is forever too late! Plan your move wisely! Pray to the Lord God and He shall help you to achieve it! The Lord is coming soon! Are we ready? Are our children ready? May the Lord our God help us to be ready! But, we must do our part, and we know that God will certainly do His part!

May God help us to be ready, is my prayer, in the name of Jesus, Amen.

Chapter 10

THE SANCTUARY OF STRENGTH, THE DAILY & THE ABOMINATION THAT MAKES DESOLATE

Verse 31 And arms shall stand on his part, and they shall pollute the sanctuary of strength, and shall take away the daily *sacrifice*, and they shall place the abomination that makes desolate.

Verse 31 (RSV) Forces from him shall appear and profane the temple and fortress, and shall take away the continual burnt offering. And they shall set up the abomination that makes desolate.

"On his part. Heb. *mimmennu*, 'from him.' This word modifies the subject rather than the verb of the clause: 'Arms (forces) from him shall stand up'". (4 BC 873). Some day, in the not-too-distant future, armed forces shall "stand up", be in power, and they shall carry out the profanation which this verse describes. The footnote in the LXX says "See verse 6". In verse 6 there is the reference to the armed forces of the papacy. It may very well be that Roman armed forces shall once again appear and desecrate the "Sanctuary of Strength". What happened in 70 A.D. may also occur at the "time of the end." Whoever the armed forces are, one thing seems to be clear, they shall be there on behalf of the power supplied by the United States of America!

"By the decree enforcing the institution of the papacy in violation of the law of God, our nation will disconnect herself fully from righteousness. When Protestantism shall stretch her hand across the gulf to grasp the hand of the Roman power, when she shall reach over the abyss to clasp hands with spiritism, when, under the influence of this threefold union, our country (The United States of America) shall repudiate every principle of its Constitution as a Protestant and republican government, and shall make provision for the propagation of papal falsehoods and delusions, then we may know that the time has come for the marvelous working of Satan and that the end is near.

"As the approach of the Roman armies was a sign to the disciples of the impending destruction of Jerusalem, so may this apostasy be a sign to us that the limit of God's forbearance is reached, that the measure of our nation's iniquity is full, and that the angel of mercy is about to take her flight, never to return." 5 T 451.

"History will be repeated. False religion will be exalted. The first day of the week, a common working day, possessing no sanctity whatever, will be set up as was the image at Babylon. All nations and tongues and people will be commanded to worship this spurious sabbath. This is Satan's plan to make of no account the day instituted by God, and given to the world as a memorial of creation.

"The decree enforcing the worship of this day is to go forth to all the world....

"The papacy has exercised her power to compel men to obey her, and she will continue to do so. We need the same spirit that was manifested by God's servants in the conflict with paganism (ST May 6, 1897)." WHITE, ELLEN G. 7 BC 976.

THE SANCTUARY OF STRENGTH "THE TEMPLE AND FORTRESS" (RSV)

In the context of the prophecy of Daniel 11, and, also, in the broader context of Scripture, that is, the entire Word of God, what is meant when we see these words before us? What is the "Sanctuary of Strength"? For many Christians there is no significance, whatsoever, in regard to what happens in Israel, as far as religion is concerned! On the other hand, there are many Christians who are listening intently to the news, as it pertains to Israel and the rebuilding of the temple in Jerusalem! What makes the difference? Did Daniel intend that we should understand the "sanctuary of strength" to be something other than the temple in Jerusalem? Should the expression be given a "spiritual meaning"?

"The language of the Bible should be explained according to its obvious meaning, unless a symbol or figure is employed." GC 599 .

As noted earlier, Gabriel (angel of the Lord) came unto Daniel for the specific purpose of making him to understand what was going to happen to his people, the Jews, in the "latter (last) days". 10:14. Then, in 11:14, Gabriel informs him that robbers from among his own people, the Jews, were going to exalt themselves in order to establish the vision, but they are going to fail.

THE TEMPLE IN JERUSALEM WILL IT BE REBUILT? ONE MORE TIME!

Many people believe that the Temple in Jerusalem shall be rebuilt, one more time. When the famous Israeli historian, Israel Eldad, was asked if his people intend to rebuild the Temple in Jerusalem, Eldad answered, and said, "From the time that king David first conquered Jerusalem, until Solomon built the Temple, just one generation passed. So will it be with Us." One generation, Biblically, is approximately 40 years. It actually took 46 years to build the first Temple.

In 1967, as a result of the 6-Day War, Israel conquered Jerusalem. One generation, 40 years, brings us down to the year 2007. If Eldad is right, the Temple shall be standing, rebuilt, sometime around the year 2007 to 2013, or so. Many will be closely listening to the news on a regular basis to catch the word that a decree has been issued to rebuild the Temple.

The "TEMPLE INSTITUTE", a zealous group of people, is in favor of the rebuilding of the Temple. Its director, Zev Golan, declared: "Our task is to advance the cause of the Temple and to prepare for its establishment, not just talk about it."

It has been reported that one hundred and twenty five million ($125,000,000) dollars has already been raised for the rebuilding of the Temple, and 38 of the 103 ritual implements necessary for worship when the sacrificial system is reinstituted have already been reconstructed. The remaining 65 are to be finished as funds become available.

"THE DAILY"

The word "*sacrifice*", as it appears in the KJV, is in *italic* print, which indicates that it is a word that has been supplied by the translators and does <u>not</u> belong to the text. This is confirmed by the Spirit of Prophecy, which says "that the word '*sacrifice*' was supplied by man's wisdom, and does not belong to the text." WHITE, ELLEN G., <u>EARLY WRITINGS</u>, 1945, page 74. (EW 74).

The expressions "daily *sacrifice*" and "continual burnt offering" are translations from the Hebrew "*tamyid*" (pronounced as "taw-meed"). In the <u>BIBLE COMMENTARY</u> "*tamyid*" appears as "*tamid*"- the "Y" has been dropped.

In its 105 occurrences in the Old Testament, "*tamyid*" occurs both as an adverb and as an adjective. "It means 'continually' or 'continual', and is applied to various concepts, such as continual employment (Eze. 39:14), permanent sustenance (2 Sam. 9:7–13), continual sorrow (Ps. 38:17), continual hope (Ps. 71:14), continual provocation (Isa. 65:3), etc. It is used frequently in connection with the ritual of the sanctuary to describe various features of its regular services, such as the 'continual bread' that was to be kept upon the table of shewbread (Num. 4:7), the lamp that was to burn continually (Ex. 27:20), the fire that was to be kept burning upon the altar (Lev. 6:13), the burnt offerings that were to be offered daily (Num. 28:3, 6), the incense that was to be offered morning and evening (Ex. 30:7, 8). The word itself does <u>not</u> mean 'daily', but simply 'continual' or 'regular'". Of the 105 occurrences it is translated as "daily" only in Num. 4:16 and 29:6 "and in the five occurrences of it in Daniel chs. 8:11, 12, 13; 11:31; 12:10. The idea of 'daily' was evidently derived, not from the word itself, but from that with which it was associated.

"In ch. 8:11 *tamid* has the definite article and is therefore used adjectivally. Furthermore, it stands independently, without a substantive, and must either be understood subjectively as meaning **continuance** or be supplied with a substantive. In the Talmud, when *tamid* is used independently as here, the word consistently denotes the daily sacrifice. The translators of the KJV, who supplied the word 'sacrifice', obviously believed that the daily burnt offering was the subject of the prophecy." 4 BC 842. **Emphasis** <u>supplied</u>.

The 105 occurrences of *tamyid* have been translated in the following manner in the KJV of the Bible: 55 times as "continually"; 27 times as "continual"; 7 times as "daily"; 6 times as "always"; 4 times as "alway"; 3 times as "ever"; 2 times as "perpetual"; and 1 time as "evermore."

If *tamyid* is to be understood subjectively as meaning "continuance", we would surely want to ask the question, The continuance of what? Since the power represented by the "little horn" of Daniel 8 is destined to take away the "*tamyid*" at the time of the end, it is apparent that the worship service in a restored Temple in Jerusalem is going to be once again halted, as it was once before, and the "sanctuary of strength" will be, once again, profaned, desecrated, polluted, by the anti-Christ. A very brief review of the grammar that we learned in school should help to clarify the matter:

AN "ADVERB"

An adverb is a word that modifies a verb, an adjective, or another adverb.

AN "ADJECTIVE"

An adjective is a word that modifies a noun or a pronoun. The word "substantive" is another name for the word "noun".

A "MODIFIER"

A modifier is a word or group of words that limits or makes clear the meaning of another word.

A "NOUN" (THE SUBSTANTIVE)

That which is being discussed or spoken of in the sentence.

A noun is the name of a particular person, place, or thing. A noun may consist of more than one word. The following are examples of nouns: persons – uncle, girl, Renee, sailor, Colonel Hutchinson. Animals are also nouns—elephant, coyote, fish, robin, polar bear. Places are nouns, such as: Italy, town, Brookfield Zoo, Temple and Fortress, <u>Sanctuary of Strength</u>.

The substantive that is missing in Daniel 8 is here in verse 31 of Daniel eleven, and that substantive is none other than the "<u>Sanctuary of Strength</u>"! And what do people do in the "Sanctuary of Strength"? Yes, of course, they worship God. Anti-Christ, at the time of the end, shall pollute the sanctuary of strength, and shall take away the *tamyid*, the worship service, "and shall set up the abomination that makes desolate."

THE ABOMINATION THAT MAKES DESOLATE— *SHIQQUTS*—ABOMINABLE, DETESTABLE THING

This same word that Daniel employs (*shiqquts*) also occurs in the book of Kings, where it is recorded that "it came to pass, when Solomon was old, that his wives turned away his heart after other gods: and his heart was not perfect with the Lord his God, as was the heart of David his father. For Solomon went after Ashtoreth the goddess of the Zidonians, and after Milcom the abomination (*shiqquts*) of the Ammonites. And Solomon did evil in the sight of the Lord, and went not fully after the Lord, as did David his father. Then did Solomon build an high place for Chemosh, the abomination (*shiqquts*) of Moab, in the hill that is before Jerusalem, and for Molech, the abomination (*shiqquts*) of the children of Ammon. And likewise did he for all his strange wives, which burnt incense and sacrificed unto their gods." 1 Kings 11:48.

The "abomination that makes desolate" is false worship. Notice what the Spirit of Prophecy has to say in regard to this subject: "The Saviour warned His followers: 'When ye therefore shall see the abomination of desolation, spoken of by Daniel the prophet, stand in the holy place, (whoso readeth, let him understand:) …. When the idolatrous standards of the Romans should be set up in the holy ground, which extended some furlongs (hundreds of feet) outside the city walls, then the followers of Christ were to find safety in flight. When the warning sign should be seen, those who would escape must make no delay." GC 26.

"What has been is what will be, and what has been done is what will be done; and there is nothing new under the sun." Ecclesiastes 1:9 (RSV).

"Behold, the Lord will lay waste the earth and make it desolate, and He will twist its surface and scatter its inhabitants…. The earth shall be utterly laid waste, and utterly despoiled; for the Lord has spoken this word…. The earth lies polluted under the inhabitants; for they have transgressed the laws, violated the statutes, broken the everlasting covenant. Therefore a curse devours the earth, and its inhabitants suffer for their guilt; therefore the inhabitants of the earth are scorched, and few men are left." Isaiah 24:1, 3, 5, 6 (RSV).

"I saw that the holy Sabbath is, and will be, the separating wall between the true Israel of God and unbelievers; and that the Sabbath is the great question to unite the hearts of God's dear, waiting saints.

"I saw that God had children who do not see and keep the Sabbath. They have not rejected the light upon it. And at the commencement of the time of trouble, we were filled with the Holy Ghost as we went forth and proclaimed the Sabbath more fully." EW 33 .

THE MESSAGE OF THE FIRST ANGEL
REVELATION 14:7

"Fear God, and give glory to him; for the hour of His judgment is come: and worship him that made heaven, and earth, and the sea, and the fountains of waters."

"The same masterful mind that plotted against the faithful in ages past is still seeking to rid the earth of those who fear God and obey His law. Satan will excite indignation against the humble minority who conscientiously refuse to accept popular customs and traditions. Men of position and reputation will join with the lawless and the vile to take counsel against the people of God. Wealth, genius, education, will combine to cover them with contempt. Persecuting rulers, minister, and church members will conspire against them. With voice and pen, by boasts, threats, and ridicule, they will seek to overthrow their faith. By false representations and angry appeals they will stir up the passions of the people. Not having a 'Thus saith the Scriptures' to bring against the advocates of the Bible Sabbath, they will resort to oppressive enactments to supply the lack. To secure popularity and patronage, legislators will yield to the demand for a Sunday law. Those who fear God cannot accept an institution that violates a precept of the Decalogue. On this battlefield comes the last great conflict of the controversy between truth and error….

"Those who have access to God through Christ have important work before them. Now is the time to lay hold of the arm of our strength. The prayer of David should be the prayer of pastors and laymen: 'It is time for Thee, Lord, to work: for they have made void Thy law.' Let the servants of the Lord weep between the porch and the altar, crying: 'Spare Thy people, O Lord, and give not Thine heritage to reproach.' God has always wrought for His people in their greatest extremity, when there seemed the least hope that ruin could be averted. The designs of wicked men, the enemies of the church, are subject to His power and over-ruling providence. He can move upon the hearts of statesmen; the wrath of the turbulent and disaffected, the haters of God, His truth, and His people can be turned aside, even as the rivers of water are turned, if He orders it thus. Prayer moves the arm of omnipotence. He who marshals the stars in order in the heavens, whose word controls the waves of the great deep, the same infinite Creator will work in behalf of His people if they call upon Him in faith. He will restrain the forces of darkness until the warning is given to the world and all who will heed it are prepared for the conflict." 5 T 450–451, 452–453 .

Verse 32 And such as do wickedly against the covenant shall he corrupt by flatteries: but the people that do know their God shall be strong, and do exploits.

Verse 32 (RSV) He shall seduce with flattery those who violate the covenant; but the people who know their God shall stand firm and take action.

"The three angels' messages are to be combined, giving their threefold light to the world. In the Revelation, John says, 'I saw another angel come down from heaven, having great power; and the earth was lightened with his glory.

2 And he cried mightily with a strong voice, saying, Babylon the great is fallen, is fallen, and is become the hold of every foul spirit, and a cage of every unclean and hateful bird.

3 For all nations have drunk of the wine of the wrath of her fornication, and the kings of the earth have committed fornication with her, and the merchants of the earth are waxed rich through the abundance of her delicacies.

4 And I heard another voice from heaven, saying, Come out of her, my people, that ye be not partakers of her sins, and that ye receive not of her plagues.

5 For her sins have reached unto heaven, and God has remembered her iniquities.' This represents the giving of the last and threefold message of warning to the world (MS 52, 1900)." 7 BC 985.

"To souls that are earnestly seeking for light and that accept with gladness every ray of divine illumination from His holy word, to such alone light will be given. It is through these souls that God will reveal that light and power which will lighten the whole earth with His glory." 5 T 729 .

Verse 33 And they that understand among the people shall instruct many: yet they shall fall by the sword, and by flame, by captivity, and by spoil, *many* days.

Verse 33 (RSV) And those among the people who are wise shall make many understand, though they shall fall by sword and flame, by captivity and plunder, for some days.

"The purification of the people of God cannot be accomplished without their suffering. God permits the fires of affliction to consume the dross, to separate the worthless from the valuable, that the pure metal may shine forth. He passes us from one fire to another, testing our true worth. If we cannot bear these trials, what will we do in the time of trouble?" 4 T 85 .

"The people of God must drink of the cup and be baptized with the baptism. The very delay, so painful to them, is the best answer to their petitions. As they endeavor to wait trustingly for the Lord to work they are led to exercise faith, hope, and patience, which have been too little exercised during their religious experience. Yet for the elect's sake the time of trouble will be shortened. 'Shall not God avenge His own elect, which cry day and night unto Him?... I tell you that He will avenge them speedily.' Luke 18:7, 8. The end will come more quickly than men expect. The wheat will be gathered and bound in sheaves for the garner of God; the tares will be bound as fagots for the fires of destruction." GC 630–631 .

"As I saw what we must be in order to inherit glory, and then saw how much Jesus had suffered to obtain for us so rich an inheritance, I prayed that we might be baptized into Christ's sufferings, that we might not shrink at trial, but bear them with patience and joy, knowing what Jesus had suf-

fered that we through His poverty and sufferings might be made rich.... Those who would not receive the mark of the beast and his image when the decree goes forth, must have decision now to say, Nay, we will not regard the institution of the beast....

"Heaven will be cheap enough, if we obtain it through suffering. We must deny self all along the way, die to self daily, let Jesus alone appear, and keep His glory continually in view." EW 67 .

"The word is: Go forward; discharge your individual duty, and leave all consequences in the hands of God. If we move forward where Jesus leads the way we shall see His triumph, we shall share His joy. We must share the conflicts if we wear the crown of victory. Like Jesus, we must be made perfect through suffering. Had Christ's life been one of ease, then might we safely yield to sloth. Since His life was marked with continual self-denial, suffering, and self-sacrifice, we shall make no complaint if we are partakers with Him. We can walk safely in the darkest path if we have the Light of the world for our guide." 5 T 71 .

"We must be partakers of Christ's sufferings here if we would share in His glory hereafter. If we seek our own interest, how we can best please ourselves, instead of seeking to please God and advance His precious, suffering cause, we shall dishonor God and the holy cause we profess to love. We have but a little space of time left in which to work for God. Nothing should be too dear to sacrifice for the salvation of the scattered and torn flock of Jesus. Those who make a covenant with God by sacrifice now will soon be gathered home to share a rich reward and possess the new kingdom forever and ever." EW 47.

"It will not be long till we shall see Him in whom our hopes of eternal life are centered. And in His presence, all the trials and sufferings of this life will be as nothingness. 'Cast not away therefore your confidence, which has great recompense of reward. For ye have need of patience, that, after ye have done the will of God, ye might receive the promise. For yet a little while, and He that shall come will come, and will not tarry.'" 9 T 287 .

Verse 34 Now when they shall fall, they shall be holpen with a little help: but many shall cleave to them with flatteries.

HOLPEN WITH A LITTLE HELP

In STRONG'S CONCORDANCE the word "holpen" is word number 5826. This same word also appears in Psalms 86:17: "Show me a token for good; that they which hate me may see it, and be ashamed: because Thou, Lord, hast holpen me, and comforted me."

HELP

The word "help" in this verse is from "*ezer*", which also occurs in a number of places in the Old Testament, such as in Psalm 146:5: "Happy is he that has the God of Jacob for his help (*ezer*), whose hope is in the Lord his God." And then in Psalm 33:20: "Our soul waits for the Lord: He is our help (*ezer*) and our shield."

THE LATTER RAIN

"As the members of the body of Christ approach the period of their last conflict, 'the time of Jacob's trouble', they will grow up into Christ, and will partake largely of His Spirit. As the third message swells to a loud cry, and as great power and glory attend the closing work, the faithful people of God will partake of that glory. It is the latter rain which revives and strengthens them to pass through the time of trouble. Their faces will shine with the glory of that light which attends the third angel (RH May 27, 1862)." 7 BC 984 .

"It is true that in the time of the end, when God's work in the earth is closing, the earnest efforts put forth by consecrated believers under the guidance of the Holy Spirit are to be accompanied by special tokens of divine favor. Under the figure of the early and the latter rain, that falls in Eastern lands at seed-time and harvest, the Hebrew prophets foretold the bestowal of spiritual grace in extraordinary measure upon God's church. The outpouring of the Spirit in days of the apostles was the beginning of the early, or former, rain, and glorious was the result. To the end of time the presence of the Spirit is to abide with the true church.

"But near the close of earth's harvest, a special bestowal of spiritual grace is promised to prepare the church for the coming of the Son of man. This outpouring of the Spirit is likened to the falling of the latter rain; and it is for this added power that Christians are to send their petitions to the Lord of the harvest 'in the time of the latter rain.' In response, 'the Lord shall make bright clouds, and give them showers of rain.' 'He will cause to come down ... the rain, the former rain, and the latter rain.' Zechariah 10:1; Joel 2:23." WHITE, ELLEN G. , THE ACTS OF THE APOSTLES, 1911 , page 54–55. (AA 54–55).

Verse 35 And some of them of understanding shall fall, to try them, and to purge, and to make them white, even to the time of the end: because it is yet for a time appointed.

Verse 35 (RSV) And some of those who are wise shall fall, to refine and to cleanse them and to make them white, until the time of the end, for it is yet for the time appointed.

TO MAKE THEM WHITE

"At times God allows His children to suffer, even to the point of death, that their characters may be purified and made fit for heaven." 4 BC 874.

"And white robes were given unto every one of them; and it was said unto them, that they should rest yet for a little season, until their fellow servants also and their brethren, that should be killed as they were, should be fulfilled." Revelation 6:11.

"He that overcometh, the same shall be clothed in white raiment; and I will not blot out his name out of the book of life, but I will confess his name before My Father, and before His angels." Revelation 3:5.

"These are they which came out of great tribulation, and have washed their robes, and made them white in the blood of the Lamb." Revelation 7:14.

"As the people of God afflict their souls before Him, pleading for purity of heart, the command is given, 'Take away the filthy garments', and the encouraging words are spoken, 'Behold, I have caused thine iniquity to pass from thee, and I will clothe thee with change of raiment.' Zechariah 3:4. The spotless robe of Christ's righteousness is placed upon the tried, tempted, faithful children of God. The despised remnant are clothed in glorious apparel, never-more to be defiled by the corruptions of the world. Their names are retained in the Lamb's book of life, enrolled among the faithful of all ages. They have resisted the wiles of the deceiver; they have not been turned from their loyalty by the dragon's roar. Now they are eternally secure from the tempter's devices." PK 591.

"'These are they which came out of great tribulation;' they have passed through the time of trouble such as never was since there was a nation; they have endured the anguish of the time of Jacob's trouble; they have stood without an intercessor through the final outpouring of God's judgments. But they have been delivered, for they have 'washed their robes, and made them white in the blood of the Lamb.'" GC 649 .

THREE PHASES OF TROUBLE

1. The time of trouble begins when the legislators of our nation (The United States of America) pass the decree for a national Sunday law. When this takes place our nation will have disconnected herself fully from righteousness. The events, all of them, that shall occur under the 7th thunder, will then have

begun their historical fulfillment; beginning with this event described in 11:30c (with "them that forsake the holy covenant"), and onward. When this takes place the angel of mercy will take her flight, never to return. National apostasy will be followed by national ruin. This time of trouble will eventually reach its height, and Michael (Jesus) shall move out of the heavenly sanctuary. He shall "stand up", that is, He shall be in power. This first phase of the time of trouble is described by Daniel (12:1) as "a time of trouble, such as never was since there was a nation even to that same time". After Jesus has moved out of the heavenly sanctuary, God's people are sustained by the intercession of heavenly angels:

"In the time of trouble just before the coming of Christ, the righteous will be preserved through the ministration of heavenly angels; but there will be no security for the transgressor of God's law. Angels cannot then protect those who are disregarding one of the divine precepts." WHITE, ELLEN G., PATRIARCHS AND PROPHETS, 1958, page 256. (PP 256).

2. The second phase of trouble is the time of trouble known as the time of Jacob's trouble, which begins after Jesus has moved out of the sanctuary: "Jacob's experience during that night of wrestling and anguish represents the trial through which the people of God must pass just before Christ's second coming. The prophet Jeremiah, in holy vision looking down to this time, said, 'We have heard a voice of trembling, of fear, and not of peace.... All faces are turned into paleness. Alas! for that day is great, so that none is like it: it is even the time of Jacob's trouble; but he shall be saved out of it.' Jeremiah 30:5–7.

"When Christ shall cease His work as mediator in man's behalf, then this time of trouble will begin. Then the case of every soul will have been decided, and there will be no atoning blood to cleanse from sin." PP 201 .

3. The third phase of trouble is "the final outpouring of God's judgments upon the wicked. God's final judgments are known as the seven last plagues (vials) and are recorded in the book of Revelation.

Before the trouble of phase two (2.) and three (3.) occurs, verse 36 will be fulfilled. The next chapter of this volume begins with verse 36.

Chapter 11

THE king

Verse 36 And the king shall do according to his will; and he shall exalt himself, and magnify himself, above every god, and shall speak marvelous things against the God of gods, and shall prosper till the indignation be accomplished: for that that is determined shall be done.

Verse 36 (RSV) And the king shall do according to his will; he shall exalt himself and magnify himself above every god, and shall speak astonishing things against the God of gods. He shall prosper till the indignation is accomplished; for what is determined shall be done.

The king introduced here is neither designated as "the King of the North", nor as the King of the South", but simply as, "the king"! The fact that the definite article precedes the word "king", in the Hebrew, implies that the "king" introduced here has already been referred to in the book of Daniel.

"THAT THAT IS DETERMINED SHALL BE DONE" A CHARACTER DESCRIPTION OF "THE king" DANIEL 8:23–25

"And at the latter end of their rule, when the transgressors have reached their full measure, a king of bold countenance, one who understands riddles, shall arise. His power shall be great, and he shall cause fearful destruction, and shall succeed in what he does, and destroy mighty men and the people of the saints. By his cunning he shall make deceit prosper under his hand, and in his own mind he shall magnify himself. Without warning he shall destroy many; and he shall even rise up against the Prince of princes; but by no human hand, he shall be broken." (RSV). **Emphasis** <u>supplied</u>.

As it is recorded in chapter 8, Daniel saw that a "little horn" power "waxed exceeding great, toward the south, and toward the east, and toward the pleasant land. 10 and it waxed great, even to the host of heaven; and it cast down some of the host and of the stars to the ground, and stamped upon them. Yea, he magnified himself even to the Prince of the host, and by him the "*tamyid*" was taken away, and the place of his sanctuary was cast down. 12 And an host was given him against the "*tamyid*" by reason of transgression, and it cast down the truth to the ground; and it practiced, and prospered. Daniel 8:9–12.

THE INDIGNATION

The indignation that occurs here in verse 36 is the same as that which occurs in 8:19, where it is recorded that the angel Gabriel came to Daniel in order that he might "know what shall be in the last end (*qets*-the extremity of the end) of the indignation: for at the time appointed the end shall be."

The term "*zaam*", as it occurs in 11:36 and 8:19, is word number 2195 on page 36 of the HEBREW AND CHALDEE DICTIONARY, which is located in the back of STRONG'S CONCORDANCE. The term expresses God's "fury", His "wrath", His "anger", His "great displeasure" with sin.

The prophet Isaiah, looking down the ages in prophetic vision to the time of this indignation says, "Thy dead men shall live, together with my dead body shall they arise. Awake and sing, ye that dwell in dust: for thy dew is as the dew of herbs, and the earth shall cast out the dead. 20 Come, My people, enter thou into thy chambers, and shut thy doors about thee: hide thyself as it were for a little moment, until the indignation (*zaam*) be overpast. 21 For, behold, the Lord cometh out of His place to punish the inhabitants of the earth for their iniquity: the earth also shall disclose her blood, and shall no more cover her slain." Isaiah 26:19–21.

"THAT WICKED"
"A king" - "THE king" - "MAN OF SIN" "SON OF PERDITION" — "MYSTERY OF INIQUITY"—ALL REPRESENT THE POWER THAT IS AGAINST GOD

The apostle Paul admonishes us that we should "Let no man deceive" us "by any means: for that day (the day of Christ's coming) shall not come, except there come a falling away first, and that man of sin be revealed, the son of perdition; 4 Who opposes and exalts himself above all that is called God, or that is worshipped; so that he as God sits in the temple of God, show-ing himself that he is God. 5 Remember ye not, that, when I was yet with you, I told you these things? 6 And now ye know what withholdeth that he might be revealed in his time. 7 For the mystery of iniquity does already work: only he who now letteth will let, until he be taken out of the way. 8 And then shall that Wicked be revealed, whom the Lord shall consume with the spirit of His mouth, and shall destroy with the brightness of His coming". 2 Thessalonians 2:3–8.

According to the prophecy of Daniel 8:8, 9, "the king", this anti-Christ person, comes forth to power out of one of the four "winds"! As noted earlier, "wind" is a symbol for "strife" or "revolution", by which kingdoms have come to power.

THE BOTTOMLESS PIT

"That the expression 'bottomless pit' represents the earth in a state of confusion and darkness is evident from other scriptures. Concerning the condition of the earth 'in the beginning', the Bible record says that it 'was without form, and void; and darkness was upon the face of the deep.' Genesis 1:2. Prophecy teaches that it will be brought back, partially at least, to this condition. Looking forward to the great day of God, the prophet Jeremiah declares: 'I beheld the earth, and, lo, it was without form, and void; and the heavens, and they had no light. I beheld the mountains, and, lo, they trembled, and all the hills moved lightly. I beheld, and, lo, there was no man, and all the birds of the heavens were fled. I beheld, and, lo, the fruitful place was a wilderness, and all the cities thereof were broken down.' Jeremiah 4:2326." GC 658–659.

THE BEAST THAT ASCENDS OUT OF THE "BOTTOMLESS PIT" REVELATION 17:8

In prophecy, as noted in Daniel 7, a beast represents a kingdom, an empire, that has dominion over the inhabitants of the earth, such as Babylon, Medo-Persia, Greece, and Rome. Speaking in regard to the 8th kingdom, represented in Revelation 17 by a beast, John the revelator was informed by the Heavenly Messenger that the beast that he saw "was, and is not, and is to ascend from the bottomless pit and go to perdition; and the dwellers on earth whose names have not been written in the book of life from the foundation of the world, will marvel to behold the beast, because it was and is not and is to come." Revelation 17:8. (RSV). The RSV captures the significance of the ending of the Greek verb which denotes "future tense", when it says, "is to come." By the time Jesus comes back to the earth, there will have been 8 world empires that will have had dominion over the inhabitants of the earth.

EIGHT (8) WORLD EMPIRES

1. Egypt (3400–933 B.C.), **2**. Assyria (933–609 B.C.), **3**. Babylon (605–539 B.C.), **4**. Medo-Persia (539–331 B.C.), **5**. Greece (331–167 B.C.), **6**. Rome (167 B.C. – 1798 A.D.), **7**. The United States of America (World War I, and W.W.II —Nagasaki and Hiroshima - Nuclear weapons, etc.), **8**. Rome-the papacy - "is to come"!

That the 8th world empire is Rome, represented by the 8th beast of Revelation 17, there can be no doubt; for Revelation 13:8, by comparison, says, "And all that dwell upon the earth shall worship him, whose names are not written in the book of life of the Lamb slain from the foundation of the world."

What happened to the cities of Nagasaki and Hiroshima (Japan) in 1945 is an example of the destructive force that is capable of bringing the earth back, partially at least, to the condition that it was in, "in the beginning", when it was "without form, and void."

It is believed that "the king" "the man of sin" —the "anti-Christ" person, shall rise to power out of a "Bottomless Pit" experience. Prophecy says that "His power shall be great, and he shall cause fearful destruction, and shall succeed in what he does, and destroy mighty men and the people of the saints…. Without warning he shall destroy many".

LARGE CITIES WILL BE SWEPT AWAY

"The time is near when large cities will be swept away, and all should be warned of these coming judgments….

"O that God's people had a sense of the impending destruction of thousands of cities, now almost given to idolatry….

"Last Friday morning, just before I awoke, a very impressive scene was presented before me. I seemed to awake from sleep but was not in my home. From the windows I could behold a terrible conflagration. Great balls of fire were falling upon houses, and from these balls fiery arrows were flying in every direction. It was impossible to check the fires that were kindled, and many places were being destroyed. The terror of the people was indescribable." WHITE, ELLEN G., <u>EVANGELISM</u>, 1946, page 29.

THE MESSAGE OF THE SECOND ANGEL REVELATION 14:8

"Babylon is fallen, is fallen, that great city, because she made all nations drink of the wine of the wrath of her fornication." 14:8 .

"Come out of her, My people, that ye be not partakers of her sins, and that ye receive not of her plagues. For her sins have reached unto heaven, and God has remembered her iniquities." Revelation 18:4, 5.

"I saw the saints leaving the cities and villages, and associating together in companies, and living in the most solitary places...."

"Houses and lands will be of no use to the saints in the time of trouble, for they will then have to flee before infuriated mobs, and at that time their possessions cannot be disposed of to advance the cause of present truth. I was shown that it is the will of God that the saints should cut loose from every encumbrance before the time of trouble comes, and make a covenant with God through sacrifice. If they have their property on the altar and earnestly inquire of God for duty, He will teach them when to dispose of these things. Then they will be free in the time of trouble and have no clogs to weigh them down.

"I saw that if any held on to their property and did not inquire of the Lord as to their duty, He would not make duty known, and they would be permitted to keep their property, and in the time of trouble it would come up before them like a mountain to crush them, and they would try to dispose of it, but would not be able." EW 282, 56 – 57.

Verse 37 Neither shall he regard the God of his fathers, nor the desire of women, nor regard any god: for he shall magnify himself above all.

THE DESIRE OF WOMEN

The word "desire" is from "*chemdah*", which means "desire", or "desirableness". This same term occurs in Haggai, where God declares that He is going to "shake all nations, and the desire (*Chemdah*) of all nations shall come." Haggai 2:7. The "desire of women" is, of course, none other than Jesus Himself.

"<u>The king</u>" shall give no heed to the gods of his fathers, the church fathers, nor will he give any heed to the "Desire of women", Jesus Christ, neither shall he give heed to any god, for he shall magnify himself above all.

Verse 38 But in his estate shall he honour the God of forces: and a god whom his fathers knew not shall he honour with gold, and silver, and with precious stones, and pleasant things.

The "King", the "man of sin", this "antichrist" person has his own "estate", that is, he has his own "station", as "<u>the king</u>"! So, in the time of the end there exists three primary forces in the world: 1. There is the "king of the South"- the United States and its Allied Forces, 2. There is the "king of the North" and its Allied Forces, and 3. There is "<u>the king</u>" and his Allied Forces. In Revelation 17:12 the "ten kings" receive power as kings one hour with the beast. In prophetic time this one hour represents 15 days, and we should understand that this is the amount of time that they shall have to function as "kings" with the 8th world empire, Rome, at the time of the end. This is especially significant when we get to verse 40–45. So, "<u>the king</u>" also will have his Allies during the time of the end. It is well to keep in mind that there are three primary forces contending against each other during the closing events of earth's history, for when we get to verses 40–45 these 3 forces are doing battle against each other, contending for dominion over the earth.

Verse 39 Thus shall he do in the most strongholds with a strange god, whom he shall acknowledge and increase with glory: and he shall cause them to rule over many, and shall divide the land for gain.

Verse 39 (RSV) He shall deal with the strongest fortresses by the help of a foreign god; those who acknowledge him he shall magnify with honor. He shall make them rulers over many and shall divide the land for a price.

SATAN SHALL IMPERSONATE CHRIST

"As the crowning act in the great drama of deception, Satan himself will personate (or impersonate-both are correct-use either one you choose) Christ. The Church has long professed to look to the Saviour's advent as the consummation of her hopes.

Now the great deceiver will make it appear that Christ has come. In different parts of the earth, Satan will manifest himself as a majestic being of dazzling brightness, resembling the description of the Son of God given by John in the Revelation. Revelation 1:13–15. The glory that surrounds him is unsurpassed by anything that mortal eyes have yet beheld. The shout of triumph rings out upon the air: 'Christ has come! Christ has come!' The people prostrate themselves in adoration before him, while he lifts up his hands and pronounces a blessing upon them, as Christ blessed His disciples when He was upon the earth. His voice is soft and subdued, yet full of melody. In gently, compassionate tones he presents some of the same gracious, heavenly truths which the Saviour uttered; he heals the diseases of the people, and then, in his assumed character of Christ, he claims to have changed the Sabbath to Sunday, and commands all to hallow the day which he has blessed. He declares that those who persist in keeping holy the seventh day are blaspheming his name by refusing to listen to his angels sent to them with light and truth. This is the strong, almost overmastering delusion. Like the Samaritans who were deceived by Simon Magus, the multitudes, from the least to the greatest, give heed to these sorceries, saying: This is 'the great power of God.' Acts 8:10.

"But the people of God will not be misled. The teachings of this false christ are not in accordance with the Scriptures. His blessing is pronounced upon the worshipers of the beast and his image, the very class upon whom the Bible declares that God's unmingled wrath shall be poured out.

"And, furthermore, Satan is not permitted to counterfeit the manner of Christ's advent. The Saviour has warned His people against deception upon this point, and has clearly foretold the manner of His second coming. 'There shall arise false christs, and false prophets, and shall show great signs and wonders; in-so-much that, if it were possible, they shall deceive the very elect.... ('Behold, I - Christ-have told you before.' Verse 25). Wherefore if they shall say unto you, Behold, He is in the desert; go not forth: behold, He is in the secret chambers (of the Temple) ; believe it not. For as the lightning comes out of the east, and shines even unto the west; so shall also the coming of the Son of man be.' Matthew 24:27; 25:31 ; Revelation 1:7; 1 Thessalonians 4:16, 17. This coming there is no possibility of counterfeiting. It will be universally known-witnessed by the whole world." GC 624–625 .

The next chapter of this volume begins with the next verse in the chronology of Daniel 11 , which is verse 40.

Chapter 12

THE TIME OF THE END

Verse 40 And at the time of the end shall the king of the south push at him: and the king of the north shall come against him like a whirlwind, with chariots, and with horsemen, and with many ships; and he shall enter into the countries, and shall overflow and pass over.

Verse 40 (RSV) "At the time of the end the king of the south shall attack him; but the king of the north shall rush upon him like a whirlwind, with chariots and horsemen, and with many ships; and he shall come into countries and shall overflow and pass through.

This is the "time of the end" that Daniel has been pointing us forward to, as mentioned in 8:19, 11:27 and 11:35. In 10:1, in his preliminary remarks, Daniel says that "a thing was revealed unto" him, "and the thing was true, but the time appointed was long: and he understood the thing, and had understanding of the vision." The RSV says that "it was a great conflict."

"The battle of Armageddon is soon to be fought. He on whose vesture is written the name, King of kings, and Lord of lords, is soon to lead forth the armies of heaven.

"It cannot now be said by the Lord's servants, as it was by the prophet Daniel: 'The time appointed was long.' Daniel 10:1. It is now but a short time till the witnesses for God will have done their work in preparing the way of the Lord....

"The day of the Lord is approaching with stealthy tread; but the supposed great and wise men know not the signs of Christ's coming or of the end of the world. Iniquity abounds, and the love of many has waxed cold." 6 T 406 .

In the context of prophecy and history, "at the time of the end" the "king of the South" (The United States and, or, Allies) shall come against "the king" and shall attack him (shall "wage war" against him). And, also, the "king of the North" (Russia and, or, Allies) shall enter the war and "shall rush upon him like a whirlwind, with chariots and horsemen, and with many ships"!

"LIKE A WHIRLWIND" "*SAAR*"—"TO BE TOSSED ABOUT, TEMPESTUOUS"

Looking down the ages to the time of the end, God, through the prophet Jeremiah, declared that the great whirlwind would some day come upon the earth, "For, lo, I begin to bring (to allow) evil on the city which is called by My name, and should ye be utterly unpunished? Ye shall not be unpunished: for I will call for a sword upon all the inhabitants of the earth, says the Lord of hosts. 30. Therefore prophesy thou against them all these words, and say unto them, The Lord shall roar from on high, and utter His voice from His holy habitation; He shall mightily roar upon His habitation: He shall give a shout, as they that tread the grapes, against all the inhabitants of the earth. 31. A noise shall come even to the ends of the earth; for the Lord has a controversy with the nations, He will plead with all flesh; He will give them that are wicked to the sword, says the Lord. 32. Thus says the Lord of hosts, Behold evil shall go forth from nation to nation, and a great whirlwind (*saar*) shall be raised up from the coasts of the earth. 33. And the slain of the Lord shall be at that day from one end of the earth even unto the other end of the earth: they shall not be lamented, neither gathered, nor buried; they shall be dung upon the ground....

"23 Behold, the whirlwind (*saar*) of the Lord goes forth with fury, a continuing whirlwind: it shall fall with pain upon the head of the wicked. 24. The fierce anger of the Lord shall not return, until He have done it, and until He has performed the intents of His heart: in the latter days ye shall consider it." Jeremiah 25:29–33; 30:23, 24. The RSV says, "In the latter (last) days you will understand this." (30:24).

Verse 41 He shall enter also into the glorious land, and many countries shall be overthrown: but these shall escape out of his hand, even Edom, and Moab, and the chief of the children of Amon.

Verse 41 (RSV) He shall come into the glorious land. And tens of thousands shall fall, but these shall be delivered out of his hand: Edom and Moab and the main part of the Ammonites.

EDOM AND MOAB AND AMMON

Edom. According to Genesis 36:8, Edom is Esau. The Edomites are descendants of Esau, who was the eldest son of Isaac, who was Abraham's son. Esau once said to his brother Jacob, "feed me, I pray thee, with that ... red pottage; for I am faint: therefore was his name called Edom." Genesis 25:30. Another name for Edom is that of Idumea, which means red. "The region occupied by the descendants of Edom, i.e., Esau. It was originally called the land of Seir (Gen. 32:3; 36:20, 21, 30; Num. 14:18). In the mind of the Israelites, Edom as the name of the country was doubtless associated with the settlement of their kinsman Edom in that region. It is a mountainous and extremely rugged country, about 100 miles long, extending south from Moab on both sides of the Arabah, or great depression connecting the south part of the Dead Sea with the gulf of 'Akabah (Gen. 14:6; Deut. 2:1, 12; Joshua 15:1; Judges 11:17, 18; 1 Kings 9:26). The summit of Mount Seir is believed to rise about 3500 feet above the adjacent Arabah.... The Edomite capital in the times of the Hebrew monarchy was Sela, probably later Petra. Other important towns were Bozrah and Teman. In the Greek period the name was modified to Idumaea.'

"The wilderness of Edom was the Arabah at the south extremity of the Dead Sea (II Kings 3:8, 20)." DAVIS, page 147.

Moab. Moab was Lot's son. Abraham was Lot's uncle. Moab was thus Abraham's nephew. "The descendants of Moab, Lot's son, closely related to the Ammonites (Gen. 19:37, 38). They had become numerous before the time that the Israelites crossed the Red Sea (Ex. 15:15); had taken possession of the country from the plain of Heshbon unto the Seil el-Kerahi, which emerges at the south end of the Dead Sea, and formed the boundary of Moab toward Edom; and with their kindred the Ammonites had absorbed and destroyed the remnants of the stalwart race which had previously occupied the country east of the Jordan (Deut. 2:10, 11, 19–21; cf. Gen. 14:5). Shortly before the arrival of the Israelites, Sihon, king of the Amorites, had wrested from them the pasture land north of the Arnon, though the country was still remembered as the land of Moab, confining Moab for a time to the country south of the Arnon (Num. 21:13–15, 26–30). The Moabites showed a commercial friendliness to the migrating Israelites (Deut. 2:28, 29), but refused them permission to pass through their land (Judges 11:17; cf. Deut. 23:4). Doubtless because of the kinship between the Moabites and Israelites, Moses was forbidden to attack them (Deut. 2:9; cf. v. 19). Nevertheless, the king of Moab, alarmed when the Israelites encamped in his vicinity, sent for Balaam to curse them (Num. chs. 22 to 24; Josh. 24: 9)." Ibid, page 402.

Ammon. "Same as Ben-ammi, Lot's younger son, ancestor of the Ammonites (Gen. 19:38)."

The Ammonites are "descended from Ben-ammi, Lot's second son. They dispossessed the Zamzummim of the territory between the Arnon and the Jabbok (Deut. 2:20, 21; 3:11); but were in turn driven out by the Amorites and compelled to keep on the border of the east desert, with the upper Jabbok as their west boundary (Num. 21:24; Deut. 2:37; Judges 11:13, 22). For having joined the Moabites in hiring Balaam to curse the Israelites, they were excluded from the congregation of the Lord to the 10th generation (Deut. 23:3–6). They aided Eglon, king of Moab, in subjugating a portion of the Israelites (Judges. 3:13). In the time of Jephthah they again oppressed the Israelites east of Jordan (Judges 10:6, 9, 18)." Ibid, page 25.

During the conquest of the promised land, after their Exodus from Egypt, the Israelites were instructed, by God, that they were not to do battle with the Edomites, Moabites, or Ammonites. Neither were they to take possession of any of their land or tribes (Deut. 2:4, 5, 18, 19).

When "the king" comes into Israel (Palestine), which is the "glorious land", when "tens of thousands shall fall", the areas of Edom and Moab and the main part of the Ammonites shall be spared, for Abraham's sake.

Verse 42 He shall stretch forth his hand also upon the countries: and the land of Egypt shall not escape.

The last two Pharaohs of Egypt, before the Exodus of Israel to the promised land, were cruel and tyrannical. "Of all nations presented in Bible history, Egypt most boldly denied the existence of the living God and resisted His commands. No monarch ever ventured upon more open and high-handed rebellion against the authority of Heaven than did the king of Egypt. When the message was brought him by Moses, in the name of the Lord, Pharaoh proudly answered: 'Who is Jehovah, that I should hearken unto His voice to let Israel go? I know not Jehovah, and moreover I will not let Israel go.' Exodus 5:2, A.R.V." GC 269.

When the ten kings of Revelation 17 receive power as kings one hour (15 days) with "the king"-the anti-Christ power (the beast), "tens of thousands shall fall, and the "land of Egypt shall not escape." It shall be destroyed!

Verse 43 But he shall have power over the treasures of gold and of silver, and over all the precious things of Egypt: and the Libyans and the Ethiopians shall be at his steps.

Verse 43 (RSV) He shall become ruler of the treasures of gold and of silver, and all the precious things of Egypt; and the Libyans and the Ethiopians shall follow in his train.

Verse 44 But tidings out of the east and out of the north shall trouble him: therefore he shall go forth with great fury to destroy, and utterly to make away many.

Verse 44 (RSV) But tidings from the east and the north shall alarm him, and he shall go forth with great fury to exterminate and utterly destroy many.

"And the sixth angel poured out his vial upon the great river Euphrates; and the water thereof was dried up, that the way of the kings of the east might be prepared. And I saw three unclean spirits like frogs come out of the mouth of the dragon, and out of the mouth of the beast, and out of the mouth of the false prophet. For they are the spirits of devils, working miracles, which go forth unto the kings of the earth and of the whole world, to gather them to the battle of that great day of God Almighty. Behold, I come as a thief. Blessed is he that watches, and keeps his garments, lest he walk naked, and they see his shame. And he gathered them together into a place called in the Hebrew tongue Armageddon." Revelation 16:12–16.

TWO HUNDRED THOUSAND THOUSAND

"And the sixth angel sounded, and I heard a voice from the four horns of the golden altar which is before God. 14. Saying to the sixth angel which had the trumpet, Loose the four angels which are bound in the great river Euphrates. 15. And the four angels were loosed, which were prepared for an hour, and a day, and a month, and a year, for to slay the third part of men. 16. And the number of the army of the horsemen were two hundred thousand thousand: (200 million) and I heard the number of them." Revelation 9:13–16.

THE KINGS OF THE EAST

China must, undoubtedly, be included here, for China lies to the east. China's policy has consistently been, in the kind of a situation before us, that it will come against the power that it perceives to be the aggressor. "The king" who is also known under various other symbols and representations, such as "man of sin", "little horn", "8th beast", the "son of perdition", "mystery of iniquity", and "that wicked"-is perceived to be the aggressor. He hears "tidings out of the east" and it is not good news, for two hundred million (200,000,000) human beings are coming forth to do battle against him.

God enabled the apostle John to hear the sound of that stupendous number of human beings. You know, our God is able to do this. He made the apostle to hear, in advance, what that gigantic horde of humanity is going to sound like.

AND OUT OF THE NORTH

Russia, with its armed forces, will also come, once again, against "the king", to do battle against him. He is thoroughly alarmed by the news that he hears, therefore, "he shall go forth with great fury to exterminate and utterly destroy many." As noted in the prophecy of chapter 8, he shall "destroy mighty men and the people of the saints." "Without warning he shall destroy many".

In regard to the "whirlwind" and "many ships", mentioned in verse 40, the following information is pertinent!

"The nations of the world are eager for conflict; but they are held in check by the angels. When this restraining power is removed, there will come a time of trouble and anguish. Deadly instruments of warfare will be invented. Vessels, with their living cargo, will be entombed in the great deep.... But they are to be kept under control till the time shall come for the great battle of Armageddon." (Letter 79, 1900). 7 BC 967.

Verse 45 And he shall plant the tabernacles of his palace between the seas in the glorious holy mountain; yet he shall come to his end, and none shall help him.

THE GLORIOUS HOLY MOUNTAIN

16 "O Lord, according to all thy righteousness, I beseech thee, let thine anger and thy fury be turned away from thy city Jerusalem, thy holy mountain: because for our sins, and for the iniquities of our fathers, Jerusalem and thy people are become a reproach to all that are about us. 17 Now therefore, O our God, hear the prayer of thy servant, and his supplications, and cause thy face to shine upon thy sanctuary that is desolate, for the Lord's sake.

18 O my God, incline thine ear, and hear; open thine eyes, and behold our desolations, and the city which is called by thy name: for we do not present our supplications before thee for our righteousnesses, but for thy great mercies.

19 O Lord, hear; O Lord, forgive; O Lord, hearken and do; defer not, for thine own sake, O my God: for thy city and thy people are called by thy name." Daniel 9:16–19.

"Great is the Lord, and greatly to be praised in the city of our God, in the mountain of His holiness.

2 Beautiful for situation, the joy of the whole earth, is mount Zion, on the sides of the north, the city of the great King.

3 God is known in her palaces for a

refuge.

4   For, lo, the kings were assembled, they passed by together.

5   They saw it, and so they marveled; they were troubled, and hurried away.

6   Fear took hold upon them there, and pain, as of a woman in travail." Psalm 48:1–6.

"How art thou fallen from heaven, O Lucifer, son of the morning! how art thou cut down to the ground, which didst weaken the nations!

13 For thou has said in thine heart, I will ascend into heaven, I will exalt my throne above the stars of God: I will sit also upon the mount of the congregation, in the sides of the north:

14 I will ascend above the heights of the clouds; I will be like the most High." Isaiah 14:12–14.

The "man of sin" —"the king" shall sit in the temple, in Jerusalem, "in the sides of the north", "upon the mount of the congregation." Satan himself shall be there with him, as he personates (impersonates) Christ. Then it is that 8:10–12 will have met its fulfillment. The "little horn" power, in the person of "the king" ("a king"-8:23), will have "magnified himself even to the Prince (Jesus Christ) of the host."

When "the king"—"the man of sin" (anti-Christ) sits in the temple, in Jerusalem, in God's place, then, at that time, Jesus Himself "stands up" and moves out of the heavenly sanctuary and the 7 last plagues come upon the inhabitants of the earth.

The next chapter of this volume begins with Daniel 12:1.

Chapter 13

EARTH'S FINAL HOUR
DANIEL 12

Verse 1 And at that time shall Michael stand up, the great Prince which stands for the children of thy people: and there shall be a time of trouble, such as never was since there was a nation even to that same time: and at that time thy people shall be delivered, every one that shall be found written in the book.

"AT <u>THAT TIME</u>"

The events of the last verse of chapter 11 (11:45) and those of 12:1 are closely related in point of time.

MICHAEL

Michael-"Who is like God"? It is at the same time a question and a statement of fact! "Who is Michael, and what is His standing up? Michael is called the 'archangel' in Jude 9. This means the chief angel, or the head over the angels. There is but One. Who is He?-He is the One Whose voice is heard from heaven when the dead are raised. (1 Thessalonians 4:16.) Whose voice is heard in connection with that event? — The voice of our Lord Jesus Christ. (John 5:28.) Tracing back the evidence with this fact as a basis, we reach the following conclusion: The voice of the Son of God is the voice of the Archangel; the Archangel, then, must be the Son of God. But the Archangel is called Michael; hence Michael must be the name given to the Son of God. The ex-

pression in verse 1, 'the great Prince which stands for the children of thy people', is sufficient alone to identify the One here spoken of as the Saviour of men. He is 'the Prince of life', and 'a Prince and a Saviour.' Acts 3:15; 5:31. He is the great Prince.

"He 'stands for the children of thy people.' He condescends to take the servants of God in this poor mortal state, and redeem them for the subjects of His future kingdom. He stands for us who believe. His people are essential to His future purposes, an inseparable part of the purchased inheritance. They are to be the chief agents of that joy which Christ foresaw, and which caused Him to endure all the sacrifice and suffering which have marked His intervention in behalf of the fallen race. Amazing honor! (Amazing grace!) Be everlasting gratitude repaid Him for His condescension and mercy to us! Be His the kingdom, power, and glory, forever and ever!

"We now come to the second question, What is the standing up of Michael? The key to the interpretation of this expression is given us: 'There shall stand up yet three kings in Persia;' 'A mighty king shall stand up, that shall rule with great dominion.' Daniel 11:2, 3. There can be no doubt as to the meaning of these expressions in these instances. They signify to take the kingdom, to reign. This expression in the verse under

95

consideration must mean the same. At that time Michael shall stand up, shall take the kingdom, shall begin to reign.

"But is not Christ reigning now? — Yes, associated with His Father on the throne of universal dominion. (Ephesians 1:20–22; Revelation 3:21 .) But this throne, or kingdom, He gives up at His coming. (1 Corinthians 15:24.) Then begins His reign, brought to view in the text, when He stands up, or takes His own kingdom, the long-promised throne of His father David, and establishes a dominion of which there shall be no end. (Luke 1:32, 33.)

"The kingdoms of this world shall become the kingdom 'of our Lord and of His Christ.' His priestly robes are to be laid aside for royal vesture, The work of mercy will be finished and the probation of the human race ended. Then he that is filthy is beyond hope of cleansing; and he that is holy is beyond the danger of falling. All cases are forever decided. From that time on until Christ comes in the clouds of heaven, the nations are broken as with a rod of iron, and dashed in pieces like a potter's vessel, by an unparalleled time of trouble. There will be a series of divine judgments upon men who have rejected God. Then shall the Lord Jesus Christ be revealed from heaven 'in flaming fire taking vengeance on them that know not God, and that obey not the gospel.' 2 Thessalonians 1:8. (See also Revelation 11:15; 22:11, 12.)

"Momentous are the events introduced by the standing up of Michael. He stands up, or takes the kingdom, some length of time before He returns personally to this earth. How important, then, that we have a knowledge of His position, that we may be able to trace the progress of His work, and understand when that thrilling moment draws near which ends His intercession in behalf of mankind, and fixes the destiny of all forever.

"But how are we to know this? How are we to determine what is taking place in the sanctuary above? God has been so good as to place in our hands the means of knowing this. He has told us that when certain great events take place on earth, important decisions which synchronize with them are being made in heaven. By these things which are seen, we thus learn of things that are unseen. As we 'look through nature up to nature's God', so through terrestrial phenomena and events we trace great movements in the heavenly kingdom." SMITH, page 301–303.

When "the king" (the anti-Christ person) shall plant the tabernacles of his palace between the seas in the glorious holy mountain, at that time shall Michael (our Lord and Saviour Jesus Christ) "stand up", take the kingdom, begin to reign! For the "little horn" power (as recorded in Daniel 8"a king") will have magnified himself even to the Prince (Jesus Christ) of the host of heaven and earth, and shall have cast the truth to the ground, through transgression.

The apostle Paul, in his second letter to the Thessalonian believers, assured them that Christ would return to the earth after "the man of lawlessness is revealed, the son of perdition, who opposes and exalts himself against every so-called god or object of worship, so that he takes his seat in the temple of God, proclaiming himself to be God." 2 Thessalonians 2:3, 4.

The apostle Paul thus confirms the truth presented by Daniel, in 11:37, that this anti-Christ <u>king</u> will not follow the teachings of his church fathers, nor that of Jesus Christ, nor any god: "for he shall magnify himself above all. "

So, when "<u>the king</u>" sits in the temple of God, in Jerusalem, "at that time" shall Michael (Jesus Christ) "stand up"!

"A TIME OF TROUBLE"
"And there shall be a time of trouble, such as never was since there was a nation even to that same time."

"I saw that the four angels would hold the four winds until Jesus' work was done in the sanctuary, and then will come the seven last plagues." WHITE, EW 36 .

"THE SEVEN LAST PLAGUES" REVELATION 15:1–8

1 The apostle John says that he saw a "sign in heaven, great and marvelous, seven angels having the seven last plagues; for in them is filled up the wrath of God.

2 And I saw as it were a sea of glass mingled with fire: and them that had gotten the victory over the beast, and over his image, and over his mark, and over the number of his name, stand on the sea of glass, having the harps of God.

3 And they sing the song of Moses the servant of God, and the song of the Lamb, saying, Great and marvelous are thy works, Lord God Almighty; just and true are Thy ways, Thou King of saints.

4 Who shall not fear Thee, O Lord, and glorify Thy name? for Thou only art holy: for all nations shall come and worship before Thee; for Thy judgments are made manifest.

5 And after that I looked, and, behold, the temple of the tabernacle of the testimony in heaven was opened:

6 And the seven angels came out of the temple, having the seven plagues, clothed in pure and white linen, and having their breasts girded with golden girdles.

7 And one of the four beasts gave unto the seven angels seven golden vials full of the wrath of God, who lives for ever and ever.

8 And the temple was filled with smoke from the glory of God, and from His power; and no man was able to enter into the temple, till the seven plagues of the seven angels were fulfilled.

CHAPTER 16

And I heard a great voice out of the temple saying to the seven angels, Go your ways, and pour out the vials of the wrath of God upon the earth.

THE FIRST PLAGUE "A NOISOME AND GRIEVOUS SORE" REVELATION 16:2

2   And the first went, and poured out his vial upon the earth; and there fell a noisome and grievous sore upon the men which had the mark of the beast, and upon them which worshipped his image.

THE SECOND PLAGUE
THE SEA "BECAME AS THE BLOOD OF A DEAD MAN" REVELATION 16:3

3   And the second angel poured out his vial upon the sea; and it became as the blood of a dead man: and every living soul died in the sea.

THE THIRD PLAGUE
THE RIVERS AND FOUNTAINS OF WATERS ARE TURNED TO BLOOD REVELATION 16:4–7

4   And the third angel poured out his vial upon the rivers and fountains of waters; and they became blood.

5   And I heard the angel of the waters say, Thou art righteous, O Lord, which art, and wast, and shalt be, because Thou hast judged thus.

6   For they have shed the blood of saints and prophets, and Thou hast given them blood to drink; for they are worthy.

7   And I heard another out of the altar say, Even so, Lord God Almighty, true and righteous are Thy judgments.

THE FOURTH PLAGUE
THE SUN SCORCHES MEN WITH FIRE REVELATION 16:8, 9

8   And the fourth angel poured out his vial upon the sun; and power was given unto him (it from "autos" —he, she, or it) to scorch men with fire.

9   And men were scorched with great heat, and blasphemed the name of God, which has power over these plaques: and they repented not to give Him glory.

THE FIFTH PLAGUE
VIAL POURED UPON THE SEAT OF THE BEAST REVELATION 16:10, 11

10   And the fifth angel poured out his vial upon the seat of the beast; and his kingdom was full of darkness; and they gnawed their tongues for pain,

11   And blasphemed the God of heaven because of their pains and their sores, and repented not of their deeds.

THE SIXTH PLAGUE
THE EUPHRATES RIVER IS DRIED UP REVELATION 16:12–16

12   And the sixth angel poured out his vial upon the great river Euphrates; and the water thereof was dried up, that the way of the kings of the east might be prepared.

13   And I saw three unclean spirits like frogs come out of the mouth of the dragon, and out of the mouth of the beast, and out of the mouth of the false prophet.

14 For they are the spirits of devils, working miracles, which go forth unto the kings of the earth and of the whole world, to gather them to the battle of that great day of God Almighty.

15 Behold, I come as a thief. Blessed is he that watches, and keeps his garments, lest he walk naked, and they see his shame.

16 And He gathered them together into a place called in the Hebrew tongue Armageddon.

THE SEVENTH PLAGUE VIAL POURED OUT INTO THE AIR PLAGUE OF HAIL VOICES, THUNDER, LIGHTNING, AND THERE WAS A GREAT EARTHQUAKE REVELATION 16:17–21

17 And the seventh angel poured out his vial into the air; and there came a great voice out of the temple of heaven, from the throne, saying, It is done.

18 And there were voices, and thunders, and lightnings; and there was a great earthquake, such as was not since men were upon the earth, so mighty an earthquake, and so great.

19 And the great city was divided into three parts, and the cities of the nations fell: and great Babylon came in remembrance before God, to give unto her the cup of the wine of the fierceness of His wrath.

20 And every island fled away, and the mountains were not found.

21 And there fell upon men a great hail out of heaven, every stone about the weight of a talent: (100 pounds) and men blasphemed God because of the plague of the hail; for the plague thereof was exceeding great.

THE MESSAGE OF THE THIRD ANGEL REVELATION 14:9–20

9 And the third angel followed them, saying with a loud voice, If any man worship the beast and his image, and receive his mark in his forehead, or in his hand,

10 The same shall drink of the wine of the wrath of God, which is poured out without mixture into the cup of his indignation; and he shall be tormented with fire and brimstone in the presence of the holy angels, and in the presence of the Lamb:

11 And the smoke of their torment ascends up for ever and ever: and they have no rest day nor night, who worship the beast and his image, and whosoever receives the mark of his name.

12 Here is the patience of the saints: here are they that keep the commandments of God, and the faith of Jesus.

13 And I heard a voice from heaven saying unto me, Write, Blessed (very happy) are the dead which die in the Lord from henceforth: Yea, says the Spirit, that they may rest from their labors; and

their works do follow them.

14 And I looked, and behold a white cloud, and upon the cloud one sat like unto the Son of man, having on His head a golden crown, and in His hand a sharp sickle.

15 And another angel came out of the temple, crying with a loud voice to Him that sat on the cloud, Thrust in Thy sickle, and reap: for the time is come for thee to reap; for the harvest of the earth is ripe.

16 And He that sat on the cloud thrust in His sickle on the earth; and the earth was reaped.

17 And another angel came out of the temple which is in heaven, he also having a sharp sickle.

18 And another angel came out from the altar, which had power over fire; and cried with a loud cry to him that had the sharp sickle, saying, Thrust in thy sharp sickle, and gather the clusters of the vine of the earth; for her grapes are fully ripe.

19 And the angel thrust in his sickle into the earth, and gathered the vine of the earth, and cast it into the great wine-press of the wrath of God.

20 And the wine-press was trodden without the city, and blood came out of the wine-press, even unto the horse bridles, by the space of a thousand and six hundred furlongs.

YOUNG'S ANALYTICAL CONCORDANCE to the BIBLE says that a furlong is one-tenth of an English mile, which would be a distance of 528 feet. Webster's New Collegiate Dictionary, on the other hand, stipulates that a furlong is a unit of distance equal to 220 yards, which is 660 feet. By adding these two measurements together and dividing by two we have a distance of 594 feet per furlong. By multiplying this distance by 1600 and then dividing by 5,280 feet, we then have a distance of 180 miles.

In Bible times wine (or grape juice) was "made from grapes. The ripe clusters were gathered in baskets (Jer. 6:9), carried to the press, and thrown into it. The press consisted of a shallow vat, built above the ground or excavated in the rock (Isa. 5:2) and, through holes in the bottom, communicating with a lower vat also frequently excavated in the rock. An upper vat measuring 8 feet square and 15 inches deep had at times a lower vat 4 feet square and 3 feet deep. The grapes were crushed by treading (Neh. 13:15; Job 24:11), one or more men being employed according to the size of the vat." DAVIS, page 640.

It is an awesome picture that John the revelator presents to us: from 4 to 8 square feet of blood, even unto the height (depth) of horse bridles, for a distance of about 180 miles.

THE MARK OF THE BEAST

"The mark and worship of the beast are enforced by the two-horned beast. The receiving of the mark of the beast is a specific act which the two-horned beast is to cause to be done. The third angel's message of Revelation 14 is a warning mercifully sent out in advance to prepare the people for the coming danger. There can therefore be no worship of the beast, nor receiving of his mark such as the prophecy contemplates, until it is enforced by the two horned beast, and knowingly accepted by the individual." SMITH, page 615.

"The prophecy of Revelation 13 declares that the power represented by the beast with lamblike horns shall cause 'the earth and them which dwell therein' to worship the papacy —there symbolized by the beast 'like unto a leopard.' The beast with two horns is also to say 'to them that dwell on the earth, that they should make an image to the beast;' and, furthermore, it is to command all, 'both small and great, rich and poor, free and bond,' to receive the mark of the beast. Revelation 13:11–16…. The United States is the power represented by the beast with lamblike horns, and … this prophecy will be fulfilled when the United States shall enforce Sunday observance, which Rome claims as the special acknowledgment of her supremacy…. And prophecy foretells a restoration of her power. 'I saw one of his heads as it were wounded to death; and his deadly wound was healed: and all the world wondered after the beast.' Verse 3. The infliction of the deadly wound points to the downfall of the papacy in 1798. After this, says the prophet, 'his deadly wound was healed: and all the world wondered after the beast.' Paul states plainly that the 'man of sin' will continue until the second advent. 2 Thessalonians 2:3–8. To the very close

of time he will carry forward the work of deception. And the revelator declares, also referring to the papacy: 'All that dwell upon the earth shall worship him, whose names are not written in the book of life.' Revelation 13:8. In both the Old and the New World, the papacy will receive homage in the honor paid to the Sunday institution, that rests solely upon the authority of the Roman Church." WHITE, GC 578–579 .

"I saw that God had children who do not see and keep the Sabbath. They have not rejected the light upon it. And at the commencement of the time of trouble, (at its beginning) we were filled with the Holy Ghost as we went forth and proclaimed the Sabbath more fully….

"'The commencement of that time of trouble', here mentioned, does not refer to the time when the plagues shall begin to be poured out, but to a short period just before they are poured out, while Christ is in the sanctuary. At that time, while the work of salvation is closing, trouble will be coming on the earth, and the nations will be angry, yet held in check so as not to prevent the work of the third angel. At that time the 'latter rain', or refreshing from the presence of the Lord, will come, to give power to the loud voice of the third angel, and prepare the saints to stand in the period when the seven last plagues shall be poured out." WHITE, EW 33, 85–86 .

"THE LOUD CRY"

"When Jesus began His public ministry, He cleansed the temple from its sacrilegious profanation. Among the last acts of His ministry was the second cleansing of the temple. So in the last work for the warning of the world, two distinct calls are made to the churches. The second angel's message is, 'Babylon is fallen, is fallen, that great city, because she made all nations drink of the wine of the wrath of her fornication.' And in the loud cry of the third angel's message a voice is heard from heaven saying, 'Come out of her, My people, that ye be not partakers of her sins, and that ye receive not of her plagues. For her sins have reached unto heaven, and God has remembered her iniquities' (RH Dec. 6, 1892).

"Three Messages To Be Combined.-The three angels' messages are to be combined, giving their threefold light to the world. In the Revelation, John says, 'I saw another angel come down from heaven, having great power; and the earth was lightened with his glory.

2   And he cried mightily with a strong voice, saying, Babylon the great is fallen, is fallen, and is become the habitation of devils, and the hold of every foul spirit, and a cage of every unclean and hateful bird.

3   For all nations have drunk of the wine of the wrath of her fornication, and the kings of the earth have committed fornication with her, and the merchants of the earth are waxed rich through the abundance of her delicacies.

4   And I heard another voice from heaven, saying, Come out of her, My people, that ye be not partakers of her sins, and that ye receive not of her plagues.

5   For her sins have reached unto heaven, and God has remembered her iniquities.' Revelation 18:1–5. This represents the giving of the last and threefold message of warning to the world (MS 52, 1900)." 7 BC 985.

"I saw angels hurrying to and fro in heaven, descending to the earth, and again ascending to heaven, preparing for the fulfillment of some important event. Then I saw another mighty angel commissioned to descend to the earth, to unite his voice with the third angel, and give power and force to his message. Great power and glory were imparted to the angel, and as he descended, the earth was lightened with his glory. The light which attended this angel penetrated everywhere, as he cried mightily, with a strong voice, 'Babylon the great is fallen, is fallen, and is become the habitation of devils, and the hold of every foul spirit, and a cage of every unclean and hateful bird.' The message of the fall of Babylon, as given by the second angel, is repeated, with the additional mention of the corruptions which have been entering the churches since 1844. The work of this angel comes in at the right time to join in the last great work of the third angel's message as it swells to a loud cry. And the people of God are thus prepared to stand in the hour of temptation, which they are soon to meet. I saw a great light resting upon them, and they united to fearlessly proclaim the third angel's message.

"Angels were sent to aid the mighty angel from heaven, and I heard voices which seemed to sound everywhere, 'Come out of her, My people, that ye be not partakers of her sins, and that ye receive not of her plagues. For her sins have reached unto heaven, and God has remembered her iniquities.' This message seemed to be an addition to the third message, joining it as the midnight cry joined the second angel's message in 1844. The glory of God rested upon the patient, waiting saints, and they fearlessly gave the last solemn warning, proclaiming the fall of Babylon and calling upon God's people to come out of her that they might escape her fearful doom.

"The light that was shed upon the waiting ones penetrated everywhere, and those in the churches who had any light, who had not heard and rejected the three messages, obeyed the call and left the fallen churches." WHITE, EW 277–278.

THE DEATH DECREE

"I saw the saints leaving the cities and villages, and associating together in companies, and living in the most solitary places. Angels provided them food and water, while the wicked were suffering from hunger and thirst. Then I saw the leading men of the earth consulting together, and Satan and his angels busy around them. I saw a writing, copies of which were scattered in different parts of the land, giving orders that unless the saints should yield their peculiar faith, give up the Sabbath, and observe the first day of the week, the people were at liberty after a certain time to put them to death." WHITE, EW 282–283 .

"Satan will, if possible, prevent them (God's people) from obtaining a preparation to stand in that day. He will so arrange affairs as to hedge up their way, entangle them with earthly treasures, cause them to carry a heavy, wearisome burden, that their hearts may be overcharged with the cares of this life and the day of trial may come upon them as a thief." GC 626.

THE SUNDAY LAW SHALL BECOME "UNDERLINED UNIVERSAL"

"History will be repeated. False religion will be exalted. The first day of the week, a common working day, possessing no sanctity whatever, will be set up as was the image at Babylon. All nations and tongues and peoples will be commanded to worship this spurious sabbath. This is Satan's plan to make of no account the day instituted by God, and given to the world as a memorial of creation.

"The decree enforcing the worship of this day is to go forth to all the world....

"Trial and persecution will come to all who, in obedience to the Word of God, refuse to worship this false sabbath. Force is the last resort of every false religion.... The papacy has exercised her power to compel men to obey her, and she will continue to do so. We need the same spirit that was manifested by God's servants in the conflict with paganism (ST May 6, 1897)." WHITE, quoted in 7 BC 976.

"As the decree issued by the various rulers of Christendom against commandment keepers shall withdraw the protection of government and abandon them to those who desire their destruction, the people of God will flee from the cities and villages and associate together in companies, dwelling in the most desolate and solitary places. Many will find refuge in the strongholds of the mountains. Like the Christians of the Piedmont valleys, they will make the high places of the earth their sanctuaries and will thank God for 'the munitions of rocks.' Isaiah 33: 16. But many of all nations and of all classes, high and low, rich and poor, black and white, will be cast into the most unjust and cruel bondage. The beloved of God pass weary days, bound in chains, shut in by prison bars, sentenced to be slain, some apparently left to die of starvation in dark and loathsome dungeons. No human ear is open to hear their moans; no human hand is ready to lend them help....

"Though enemies may thrust them into prison, yet dungeon walls cannot cut off the communication between their souls and Christ. One who sees their every weakness, who is acquainted with every trial, is above all earthly powers; and angels will come to them in lonely cells, bringing light and peace from heaven. The prison will be as a palace; for the rich in faith dwell there, and the gloomy walls will be lighted up with heavenly light as when Paul and Silas prayed and sang praises at midnight in the Philippian dungeon....

"When Christ ceases His intercession in the sanctuary, the unmingled wrath threatened against those who worship the beast and his image and receive his mark (Revelation 14:9, 10), will be poured out. The plagues upon Egypt when God was about to deliver Israel were similar in character to those more terrible and extensive judgments which are to fall upon the world just before the final deliverance of God's people....

"The prophets ... describe the condition of the earth at this fearful time: 'The land mourns; ... because the harvest of the field is perished.... All the trees of the field are withered: because joy is withered away from the sons of men.' 'The seed is rotten under their clods, the garners are laid desolate.... How do the beasts groan! the herds of cattle are perplexed, because they have no pasture.... The rivers of water are dried up, and the fire has devoured the pastures of the wilderness.' 'The songs of the temple shall be howlings in that day, says the Lord God: there shall be many dead bodies in every place; they shall cast them forth with silence.' Joel 1:10–12, 17–20; Amos 8:3.

"These plagues are not universal, or the inhabitants of the earth would be wholly cut off. Yet they will be the most awful scourges that have ever been known to mortals. All the judgments upon men, prior to the close of probation, have been mingled with mercy. The pleading blood of Christ has shielded the sinner from receiving the full measure of his guilt; but in the final judgment, wrath is poured out unmixed with mercy.

"In that day, multitudes will desire the shelter of God's mercy which they have so long despised. 'Behold, the days come, says the Lord, that I will send a famine in the land, not a famine of bread, nor a thirst for water, but of hearing the words of the Lord: and they shall wander from sea to sea, and from the north even to the east, they shall run to and fro to seek the word of the Lord, and shall not find it.' Amos 8:11, 12." GC 626, 627–629.

"In the time of trouble just before the coming of Christ, the righteous will be preserved through the ministration of heavenly angels; but there will be no security for the transgressor of God's law. Angels cannot then protect those who are disregarding one of the divine precepts....

"Jacob's experience … of wrestling and anguish represents the trial through which the people of God must pass just before Christ's second coming. The prophet Jeremiah, in holy vision looking down to this time, said, 'We have heard a voice of trembling, of fear, and not of peace.... All faces are turned into paleness. Alas! for that day is great, so that none is like it: it is even the time of Jacob's trouble; but he shall be saved out of it.' Jeremiah 30:5–7.

"When Christ shall cease His work as mediator in man's behalf, then this time of trouble will begin. Then the case of every soul will have been decided, and there will be no atoning blood to cleanse from sin. When Jesus leaves His position as man's intercessor before God, the solemn announcement is made, 'He that is unjust, let him be unjust still: and he which is filthy, let him be filthy still: and he that is righteous, let him be righteous still: and he that is holy, let him be holy still.' Revelation 22:11. Then the restraining Spirit of God is withdrawn from the earth. As Jacob was threatened with death by his angry brother, so the people of God will be in peril from the wicked who are seeking to destroy them. And as the patriarch wrestled all night for deliverance from the hand of Esau, so the righteous will cry to God day and night for deliverance from the enemies that surround them.

"Satan had accused Jacob before the angels of God, claiming the right to destroy him because of his sin; he had moved upon Esau to march against him; and during the patriarch's long night of wrestling, Satan endeavored to force upon him a sense of his guilt, in order to discourage him, and break his hold upon God. When in his distress Jacob laid hold of the Angel, and made supplication with tears, the heavenly Messenger, in order to try his faith, also reminded him of his sin, and endeavored to escape from him. But Jacob would not be turned away. He had learned that God is merciful, and he cast himself upon His mercy. He pointed back to his repentance for his sin, and pleaded for deliverance. As he reviewed his life, he was driven almost to despair; but he held fast the Angel, and with earnest, agonizing cries urged his petition until he prevailed." WHITE, PP 256, 201–202.

"The people of God will not be free from suffering; but while persecuted and distressed, while they endure privation and suffer for want of food they will not be left to perish. That God who cared for Elijah will not pass by one of His self-sacrificing children. He who numbers the hairs of their head will care for them, and in the time of famine they shall be satisfied. While the wicked are dying from hunger and pestilence, angels will shield the righteous and supply their wants. To him that 'walks righteously' is the promise: 'Bread shall be given him; his waters shall be sure.' 'When the poor and needy seek water, and there is none, and their tongue fails for thirst, I the Lord will hear them, I the God of Israel will not forsake them.' Isaiah 33:15, 16; 41:17.

"'Although the fig tree shall not blossom, neither shall fruit be in the vines; the labor of the olive shall fail, and the fields shall yield no meat; the flock shall be cut off from the fold, and there shall be no herd in the stalls;' yet shall they that fear Him 're-joice in the Lord' and joy in the God of their salvation. Habakkuk 3:17, 18.

"'The Lord is thy keeper: the Lord is thy shade upon thy right hand. The sun shall not smite thee by day, nor the moon by night. The Lord shall preserve thee from all evil: He shall preserve thy soul.' 'He shall deliver thee from the snare of the fowler, and from the noisome pestilence. He shall cover thee with His feathers, and under His wings shalt thou trust: His truth shall be thy shield and buckler. Thou shalt not be afraid for the terror by night; nor for the arrow that flies by day; nor for the pestilence that walks in the darkness; nor for the destruction that wastes at noonday. A thousand shall fall at thy side, and ten thousand at thy right hand; but it shall not come nigh thee. Only with thine eyes shalt thou behold and see the reward of the wicked. Because thou hast made the Lord, which is my refuge, even the Most High, thy habitation; there shall no evil befall thee, neither shall any plague come nigh thy dwelling.' Psalm 121:5–7; 91:3–10....

"The people of God must drink of the cup and be baptized with the baptism. The very delay, so painful to them, is the best answer to their petitions. As they endeavor to wait trustingly for the Lord to work they are led to exercise faith, hope, and patience, which have been too little exercised during their religious experience. Yet for the elect's sake the time of trouble will be shortened. 'Shall not God avenge His own elect, which cry day and night unto Him?... I tell you that He will avenge them speedily.' Luke 18:7, 8. The end will come more quickly than men expect. The wheat will be gathered and bound in sheaves for the garner of God; the tares will be bound as fagots for the fires of destruction." GC 629–630, 631.

MIDNIGHT DELIVERANCE OF THE SAINTS

"It was at midnight that God chose to deliver His people. As the wicked were mocking around them, suddenly the sun appeared, shining in his strength, and the moon stood still. The wicked looked upon the scene with amazement, while the saints beheld with solemn joy the tokens of their deliverance. Signs and wonders followed in quick succession. Everything seemed turned out of its natural course. The streams ceased to flow. Dark, heavy clouds came up and clashed against each other. But there was one clear place of settled glory, whence came the voice of God like many waters, shaking the heavens and the earth. There was a mighty earthquake. The graves were opened, and those who had died in faith under the third angel's message, keeping the Sabbath, came forth from their dusty beds, glorified, to hear the covenant of peace that God was to make with those who had kept His law.

"The sky opened and shut and was in commotion. The mountains shook like a reed in the wind and cast out ragged rocks all around. The sea boiled like a pot and cast out stones upon the land. And as God spoke the day and the hour of Jesus' coming and delivered the everlasting covenant to His people, He spoke one sentence, and then paused, while the words were rolling through the earth. The Israel of God stood with their eyes fixed upward, listening to the words as they came from the mouth of Jehovah and rolled through the earth like peals of loudest thunder. It was awfully solemn. At the end of every sentence the saints shouted, 'Glory! Hallelujah!' Their countenances were lighted up with the glory of God, and they shone with glory as did the face of Moses when he came down from Sinai. The wicked could not look upon them for the glory. And when the never-ending blessing was pronounced on those who had honored God in keeping His Sabbath holy, there was a mighty shout of victory over the beast and over his image.

"Then commenced the jubilee, when the land should rest. I saw the pious slave rise in victory and triumph, and shake off the chains that bound him, while his wicked master was in confusion and knew not what to do; for the wicked could not understand the words of the voice of God.

"Soon appeared the great white cloud, upon which sat the Son of man." EW 285–286.

THE "MIDNIGHT CRY"

"Behold, the Bridegroom cometh; go ye out to meet Him."

"I was shown that the commandments of God and the testimony of Jesus Christ relating to the shut door could not be separated, and that the time for the commandments of God to shine out with all their importance, and for God's people to be tried on the Sabbath truth, was when the door was opened in the most holy place in the heavenly sanctuary, where the ark is, in which are contained the ten commandments. This door was not opened until the mediation of Jesus was finished in the holy place of the sanctuary in 1844. Then Jesus rose up and shut the door of the holy place, and opened the door into the most holy, and passed within the second veil, where He now stands by the ark....

"I saw that Jesus had shut the door of the holy place, and no man can open it; and that He had opened the door into the most holy, and no man can shut it (Rev. 3:7, 8); and that since Jesus has opened the door into the most holy place, which contains the ark, the commandments have been shining out to God's people, and they are being tested on the Sabbath question.

"I saw that the present test on the Sabbath could not come until the mediation of Jesus in the holy place was finished and He had passed within the second veil; therefore Christians who fell asleep before the door was opened into the most holy, when the midnight cry was finished, at the seventh month, (October 22) 1844, and who had not kept the true Sabbath, now rest in hope; for they had not the light and the test on the Sabbath which we now have since that door was opened. I saw that Satan was tempting some of God's people on this point. Because so many good Christians have fallen asleep in the triumphs of faith and have not kept the true Sabbath, they were doubting about its being a test for us now.

"The enemies of the present truth have been trying to open the door of the holy place, that Jesus has shut, and to close the door of the most holy place, which He opened in 1844, where the ark is, containing the two tables of stone on which are written the ten commandments by the finger of Jehovah.

"Satan is now using every device in this sealing time to keep the minds of God's people from the present truth and to cause them to waver. I saw a covering that God was drawing over His people to protect them in the time of trouble; and every soul that was decided on the truth and was pure in heart was to be covered with the covering of the Almighty.

"Satan knew this, and he was at work in mighty power to keep the minds of as many people as he possibly could wavering and unsettled on the truth." EW 42–43.

THE SANCTUARY

"What is done in type in the ministration of the earthly sanctuary is done in reality in the ministration of the heavenly sanctuary. After His ascension our Saviour began His work as our high priest. Says Paul: 'Christ is not entered into the holy places made with hands, which are the figures of the true; but into heaven itself, now to appear in the presence of God for us.' Hebrews 9:24....

"It was the work of the priest in the daily ministration to present before God the blood of the sin offering, also the incense which ascended with the prayers of Israel. So did Christ plead His blood before the Father in behalf of sinners, and present before Him also, with precious fragrance of His own righteousness, the prayers of penitent believers. Such was the work of ministration in the first apartment of the sanctuary in heaven.

"Thither the faith of Christ's disciples followed Him as He ascended from their sight. Here their hopes centered, 'which hope we have', said Paul, 'as an anchor of the soul, both sure and steadfast, and which enters into that within the veil; whither the forerunner is for us entered, even Jesus, made an high priest forever.' 'Neither by the blood of goats and calves, but by His own blood He entered in once into the holy place, having obtained eternal redemption for us.' Hebrews 6:19, 20; 9:12.

"For eighteen centuries this work of ministration continued in the first apartment of the sanctuary. The blood of Christ, pleaded in behalf of penitent believers, secured their pardon and acceptance with the Father, yet their sins still remained upon the books of record. As in the typical service there was a work of atonement at the close of the year, so before Christ's work for the redemption of men is completed there is a work of atonement for the removal of sin from the sanctuary. This is the service which began when the 2300 days ended. At that time, as foretold by Daniel the prophet, (8:14; 7:13, 14) our High Priest entered the most holy, to perform the last division of His solemn work-to cleanse the sanctuary....

"The ministration of the priest throughout the year in the first apartment of the sanctuary, 'within the veil' which formed the door and separated the holy place from the outer court, represents the work of ministration upon which Christ entered at His ascension." GC 420, 421, 420.

In order for the priest to enter the first apartment of the sanctuary, the holy place, he must first pass "within the veil" which formed the door and separated the holy place from the outer court.

On October 22, 1844, Jesus, as our great High Priest, entered upon the second and final phase of His ministration in the heavenly sanctuary. This second phase may appropriately be represented by the second "veil", the one that separated the first apartment, the holy place, from the second apartment, the most holy place into which the high priest entered only during the "day of atonement" service, in the fall, or autumn of the year.

There was a great religious awakening during the years from 1833 to 1844. A great number of people believed that Jesus, the Bridegroom, was going to return to the earth for His bride, His church, His people. October 22, 1844 came and passed, and, of course, as we well know, Jesus didn't return. Their mistake was in believing that the earth was the sanctuary.

Instead of returning to the earth, as expected, Jesus had gone in unto the Ancient of Days, God the Father, and had received the kingdom from Him (Daniel 7:13, 14).

During the time of the end, before probation closes and Jesus returns to the earth, it is very fitting that the Midnight Cry be once again proclaimed to the world!

"Behold, the Bridegroom cometh, go ye out to meet Him"

"I saw a number of angels conversing with the one who had cried, 'Babylon is fallen', and these united with him in the cry, 'Behold, the Bridegroom cometh; go ye out to meet Him.' The musical voices of these angels seemed to reach everywhere. An exceedingly bright and glorious light shone around those who had cherished the light which had been imparted to them. Their faces shone with excellent glory, and they united with the angels in the cry, 'Behold, the Bridegroom cometh.'" EW 241–242.

"When it first appeared in the distance, this cloud looked very small. The angel said that it was the sign of the Son of man. As it drew nearer the earth, we could behold the excellent glory and majesty of Jesus as He rode forth to conquer. A retinue of holy angels, with bright, glittering crowns upon their heads, escorted Him on His way. No language can describe the scene. The living cloud of majesty and unsurpassed glory came still nearer, and we could clearly behold the lovely person of Jesus. He did not wear a crown of thorns, but a crown of glory rested upon His holy brow. Upon His vesture and thigh was a name written, King of kings, and Lord of lords. His countenance was as bright as the noonday sun, His eyes were as a f lame of f ire, and His feet had the appearance of fine brass. His voice sounded like many musical instruments. The earth trembled before Him, the heavens departed as a scroll when it is rolled together, and every mountain and island were moved out of their places....

"The earth mightily shook as the voice of the Son of God called forth the sleeping saints. They responded to the call and came forth clothed with glorious immortality, crying, 'Victory, victory, over death and the grave! O death, where is thy sting? O grave, where is thy victory?'" EW 286 – 287.

THE BOOK

Daniel was given the assurance that his people "shall be delivered, every one that shall be found written in the book."

"The eye of God, looking down the ages, was fixed upon the crisis which His people are to meet, when earthly powers shall be arrayed against them. Like the captive exile, they will be in fear of death by starvation or by violence. But the Holy one who divided the Red Sea before Israel, will manifest His mighty power and turn their captivity. 'They shall be Mine, says the Lord of hosts, in that day when I make up My jewels; and I will spare them, as a man spares his own son that serves him. Malachi 3:17. If the blood of Christ's faithful witnesses were shed at this time, it would not, like the blood of the martyrs, be as seed sown to yield a harvest for God. Their fidelity would not be a testimony to convince others of the truth; for the obdurate heart has beaten back the waves of mercy until they return no more. If the righteous were now left to fall a prey to their enemies, it would be a triumph for the prince of darkness. Says the psalmist: 'In the time of trouble He shall hide me in His pavilion: in the secret of His tabernacle shall He hide me.' Psalm 27:5. Christ has spoken: 'Come, My people, enter thou into thy chambers, and shut thy doors about thee: hide thyself as it were for a little moment, until the indignation be overpast. For, behold, the Lord comes out of His place to punish the inhabitants of the earth for their iniquity.' Isaiah 26:20, 21. Glorious will be the deliverance of those who have patiently waited for His coming and whose names are written in the book of life." GC 634.

"As the people of God afflict their souls before Him, pleading for purity of heart, the command is given, 'Take away the filthy garments', and the encouraging words are spoken, 'Behold, I have caused thine iniquity to pass from thee, and I will clothe thee with change of raiment.' Zechariah 3:4. The robe of Christ's righteousness is placed upon the tried, tempted, faithful children of God. The despised remnant are clothed in glorious apparel, nevermore to be defiled by the corruptions of the world. Their names are retained in the Lamb's book of life, enrolled among the faithful of all ages. They have resisted the wiles of the deceiver; they have not been turned from their loyalty by the dragon's roar. Now they are eternally secure from the tempter's devices." WHITE, PK 591 .

"In the book of God's providence, the volume of life, we are each given a page. That page contains every particular of our history; even the hairs of the head are numbered. God's children are never absent from His mind." WHITE, ELLEN G., <u>THE DESIRE OF AGES</u>, 1898, page 313.

This is a good spot for a chapter break. The next chapter of this volume, chapter 14, will begin with verse 2 of the twelfth chapter of Daniel.

Chapter 14

THE CLIMAX
DANIEL 12:2–13

Verse 2 And many of them that sleep in the dust of the earth shall awake, some to everlasting life, and some to shame and everlasting contempt.

"Graves are opened, and 'many of them that sleep in the dust of the earth … awake, some to everlasting life, and some to shame and everlasting contempt.' Daniel 12:2. All who have died in the faith of the third angel's message come forth from the tomb glorified, to hear God's covenant of peace with those who have kept His law. 'They also which pierced Him' (Revelation 1:7), those that mocked and derided Christ's dying agonies, and the most violent opposers of His truth and His people, are raised to behold Him in His glory and to see the honor placed upon the loyal and obedient." GC 637.

This special resurrection occurs prior to the general one that shall take place at the time of Christ's return to the earth, when all of the remaining righteous dead shall be raised to everlasting life.

It seems safe to conclude that the wicked dead who are raised in this special resurrection shall die with the rest of the wicked who are living upon the earth at the time of Christ's coming. All of them shall be destroyed by the overwhelming brightness and glory of Christ.

Verse 3 And they that be wise shall shine as the brightness of the firmament; and they that turn many to righteousness as the stars for ever and ever.

"Those who engage with Christ and angels in the work of saving perishing souls are richly rewarded in the kingdom of heaven." WHITE, 1 T 512.

Verse 4 But thou, O Daniel, shut up the words, and seal the book, even to the time of the end: many shall run to and fro, and knowledge shall be increased.

"Since 1798 the book of Daniel has been unsealed, knowledge of the prophecies has increased, and many have proclaimed the solemn message of the judgment near." GC 356.

The prophecy of Daniel 11 began its historical fulfillment in 1798, in the events that surrounded France, under Napoleon Bonaparte, as the "king of the North."

"God entrusts men with talents and inventive genius, in order that His great work in our world may be accomplished. The inventions of human minds are supposed to spring from humanity, but God is behind all. He has caused that the means of rapid traveling shall have been invented for the great day of His preparation." WHITE, ELLEN G., FUNDAMENTALS OF CHRISTIAN EDUCATION, 1923, page 409. (FE 409).

"By the increase of knowledge a people is to be prepared to stand in the latter days." WHITE, ELLEN G., <u>SELECTED MESSAGES</u>, Book Two, 1958, page 105. (2 SM 105).

"This prophecy has also been interpreted as pointing to the stupendous advances of science and general knowledge in the last century and a half, advances that have made possible a widespread proclamation of the message of these prophecies." 4 BC 879.

Verse 5 Then I Daniel looked, and, behold, there stood other two, the one on this side of the bank of the river, and the other on that side of the bank of the river.

6   And one said to the man clothed in linen, which was upon the waters of the river, How long shall it be to the end of these wonders?

7   And I heard the man clothed in linen, which was upon the waters of the river, when he held up his right hand and his left hand unto heaven, and swore (made an oath) by him that lives for ever that it shall be for a time, times, and an half; and when he shall have accomplished to scatter the power of the holy people, all these things shall be finished.

Since chapters 10–12 form a unit, we conclude that the heavenly Being that appeared to Daniel, clothed in linen, is the same Being that appeared unto him from the beginning, as recorded in 10:5, 6. And that Being is none other than Christ, before His incarnation. The river is the Hiddekel, which is the Tigris river. The lifting up of both of His hands indicates that the greatest solemnity and assurance was given, by Christ. He made His declaration under a solemn oath, declaring that what He said would surely come to pass.

THE "HOLY PEOPLE"

In 10:14 the angel Gabriel assured Daniel that he came unto him for the specific purpose of making him to understand what was going to happen to his people, the Jews, in the "latter days", that is, in the "last days." In 11:14 we see that Daniel was informed that robbers from among his own people, the Jews, were going to arise, in the last days, and that they would exalt themselves in order to establish, or fulfill the vision, but, according to the word of God, they shall "fail" to do it.

Based upon the evidence of Scripture, we conclude that the "holy people", of verse 7, are the Jews (Israel) of the "last days"!

TIME, TIMES, AND HALF TIME THREE AND ONE HALF YEARS

"We are living in the time of the end. The fast-fulfilling signs of the times declare that the coming of Christ is near at hand....

"The agencies of evil are combining their forces and consolidating. They are strengthening for the last great crisis. Great changes are soon to take place in our world, and the final movements will be <u>rapid ones</u>. WHITE, 9 T 11 . **Emphasis** <u>supplied</u>.

Surely the three and one–half year period of time under consideration cannot be prophetic time, that is, 1260 years; since the final movements of earth's history are to be "**rapid ones**"!

The "time and times and the dividing of time" of Daniel 7:25; the "forty and two months" of Revelation 11:2; the "thousand two hundred and three-score days" of Revelation 11:3; the "thousand two hundred and three-score days" of Revelation 12:6; and the "forty and two months" of Revelation 13:5; all met their fulfillment during the "Dark Ages" (538 —1798 A.D.). But it is not so with this three and one–half year period of literal time before us.

The Spirit of Prophecy does not indicate that the time period of Daniel 12:7 has met its fulfillment in the past. Neither does it indicate that the same period of time in Revelation 12:14 was fulfilled in the past.

REVELATION 12:14

"And to the woman (church-people of God) were given two wings of a great eagle, that she might fly into the wilderness, into her place, where she is nourished for a time, and times, and half a time, from the <u>face</u> of the serpent." **Emphasis** <u>supplied</u>.

"The Jews misinterpreted and misapplied the word of God, and they knew not the time of their visitation. The years of the ministry of Christ and His apostles,-the precious last years of grace to the chosen people,-they spent plotting the destruction of the Lord's messengers. Earthly ambitions absorbed them, and the offer of the spiritual kingdom came to them in vain....

"With a great show of prudence the rabbis had warned the people against receiving the new doctrines taught by this new teacher (Jesus Christ); for His theories and practices were contrary to the teachings of the Fathers. The people gave credence to what the priests and Pharisees taught, in place of seeking to understand the word of God for themselves. They honored the priests and rulers instead of honoring God, and rejected the truth that they might keep their own traditions. Many had been impressed and almost persuaded; but they did not act upon their convictions, and were not reckoned on the side of Christ. Satan presented his temptations, until the light appeared as darkness. Thus many rejected the truth that would have proved the saving of the soul.

"The True Witness says, 'Behold, I stand at the door, and knock.' Every warning, reproof, and entreaty in the word of God or through His messengers is a knock at the door of the heart. It is the voice of Jesus asking for entrance. With every knock unheeded, the disposition to open becomes weaker. The impressions of the Holy Spirit, if disregarded today, will not be as strong tomorrow. The heart becomes less impressible, and lapses into a perilous unconsciousness of the shortness of life, and of the great eternity beyond. Our condemnation in the Judgment will not result from the fact that we have been in error, but from the fact that we have neglected heaven-sent opportunities for learning what is truth." WHITE, DA 235, 489–490 .

Verse 8 And I heard, but I understood not: then said I, O my Lord, what shall be the end of these things? ("what shall be the issue of these things?" RSV).

Verse 9 And he said, Go thy way, Daniel: for the words are closed up and sealed till the time of the end.

10 Many shall be purified, and made white, and tried; but the wicked shall do wickedly: and none of the wicked shall understand; but the wise shall understand.

This verse 10 is a reference back to 11:35. Many of God's people "shall be purified, and made white, and tried", when the holy covenant is set aside and the "man of sin", "the king", rises to power.

"And some of them of understanding shall fall, to try them, and to purge, and to make them white, even to the time of the end: because it is yet for a time appointed." 11:35.

Verse 11 And from the time that the (*tamyid*) shall be taken away, and the abomination that makes desolate set up, there shall be a thousand two hundred and ninety (1290) days.

This is the sign that Daniel was asking for! This verse is a recapitulation and helps to explain and clarify 11:31:

31 And arms shall stand on his part, and they shall pollute the sanctuary of strength, and shall take away the (*tamyid*), and they shall place the abomination that makes desolate. 11:31.

Daniel heard what the Lord said to him, but he didn't understand how the time, times, and an half time (1260 days) fit into the prophecy. So, he asked the Lord for a sign and He gave it to him. So, the question that we now address is this: When does the 1260 and 1290 days begin and end? The key to answering this question lies within the information that God has <u>supplied</u> through Daniel, within the verses already presented.

The question was asked, in verse 6, "How long shall it be to the end of these wonders?" Then in verse 7, under a most solemn oath, Jesus Himself says that the time factor shall be a "time, times, and an half; and when he shall have accomplished to scatter the power of the holy people, all these things shall be finished."

When shall the scattering of the power of the holy people be accomplished-finished? Speaking in regard to the power that is to take away the "*tamyid*" and set up the "abomination that makes desolate", 11:45 says that "he shall plant the tabernacles of his palace between the seas in the glorious holy mountain". The word "scatter", as it appears in 12:7, is from the term "*naphats*" — "To dash or beat in pieces". When "<u>the king</u>" sits in the temple of God, in Jerusalem, showing himself to be God, by that time the power of the holy people, the Jews, will have been beaten to pieces. It is also at "that time" that Michael "stands up" —He begins to reign over His kingdom in a manner in which He has never reigned before!

THE SANCTUARY OF STRENGTH AND THE 1290 DAYS

What takes place at the end of the 1290 days? Will the sacrificial system of worship be reinstituted in a restored temple in Jerusalem? Why is there no direct mention of the sacrificial system in the prophecy of

Daniel 11 and 12, like there is in the prophecy of 9:24–27?

The taking away of the "*tamyid*", which represents "worship", and the setting up of the "abomination that makes desolate", which is pagan false worship, is a simultaneous event. It may be illustrated this way, by a pitcher of water. Once a package of Kool-Aid is poured into the pitcher, we no longer have a pitcher of water, but, instead, we have a pitcher of Kool-Aid. We still have the pitcher, but its content has changed.

The count-down of the 1290 literal days begins when the power represented by the "little horn" takes away the "*tamyid*"! The 1260 literal days, the time during which God's people are in a wilderness experience, begins, it is believed, 30 days after the passage of the National Sunday Law by the United States Legislature. The 1260 and 1290 days thus end at the same point in time; when Michael (Jesus) "stands up", when He finishes His ministration in the heavenly sanctuary, moves out of it, and begins to reign over His kingdom in a manner in which He has never reigned before.

NATIONAL RUIN

When the legislature of the United States of America passes legislation, there is, usually, if not always, a waiting period before it goes into effect. It is believed that the National Sunday Law will not be enforced until 30 days after it becomes law. This will allow people time to get out of the large cities and find refuge in small villages and towns, for the message that Jonah gave to the metropolitan city of Nineveh shall once again be proclaimed:

"YET FORTY DAYS, AND NINEVEH SHALL BE OVERTHROWN." Jonah 3:4.

National apostasy shall be followed by National ruin!

Verse 12 Blessed (very happy) is he that waits, and comes to the thousand three hundred and five and thirty (1335) days.

Dear reader, why do you think Daniel gave us this message of encouragement? Why will a person be "very happy" if he, or she, is alive upon the earth and comes to the completion of the 1335 days?

Jesus said, "Blessed are the pure in heart: for they shall see God." Matthew 5:8.

PROPHECY MUST BE FULFILLED

"The Jews tried to stop the proclamation of the message that had been predicted in the Word of God; but prophecy must be fulfilled....

"When a message is presented to God's people, they should not rise up in opposition to it; they should go to the Bible, comparing it with the law and the testimony, and if it does not bear this test, it is not true." WHITE, I SM 412, 416 .

"As the message of Christ's first advent announced the kingdom of His grace, so the message of His second advent announces the kingdom of His glory. And the second message, like the first, is based on the prophecies. The words of the angel to Daniel relating to the last days were to be understood in the time of the end. At that time, 'many shall run to and fro, and knowledge shall be increased.' 'The wicked shall do wickedly; and none of the wicked shall understand; but the wise shall understand.' The Saviour Himself has given signs of His coming, and He says, 'When ye see these things come to pass, know ye that the kingdom of God is nigh at hand.' 'And take heed to yourselves, lest at any time your hearts be overcharged with surfeiting, and drunkenness, and cares of this life, and so that day come upon you unawares.' 'Watch ye therefore, and pray always, that ye may be accounted worthy to escape all these things that shall come to pass, and to stand before the Son of man.'

"We have reached the period foretold in these scriptures. The time of the end is come, the visions of the prophets are unsealed, and their solemn warnings point us to our Lord's coming in glory as near at hand." WHITE, DA 234 .

Verse 13 But go thou thy way till the end be: for thou shalt rest, and stand in thy lot at the end of the days.

"The time has come for Daniel to stand in his lot. The time has come for the light given him to go to the world as never before. If those for whom the Lord has done so much will walk in the light, their knowledge of Christ and the prophecies relating to Him will be greatly increased as they near the close of this earth's history. (MS 176, 1899)." 4 BC 1174.

"All that God has in prophetic history specified to be fulfilled in the past has been, and all that is yet to come in its order will be. Daniel, God's prophet, stands in his place.

John stands in his place. In the Revelation the Lion of the tribe of Judah has opened to the students of prophecy the book of Daniel, and thus is Daniel standing in his place. He bears his testimony, that which the Lord revealed to him in vision of the great and solemn events which we must know as we stand on the very threshold of their fulfillment....

"Those things which have been, will be repeated." 2 SM 109.

"Communicate the knowledge of the truth to others. This is God's plan to enlighten the world. If you do not stand in your allotted place, if you do not let your light shine, you will become enshrouded in darkness." 1 SM 266.

"Every individual has a soul to save or to lose. Each has a case pending at the bar of God. Each must meet the great Judge face to face. How important, then, that every mind contemplate often the solemn scene when the judgment shall sit and the books shall be opened, when, with Daniel, every individual must stand in his lot, at the end of the days." GC 488.

2300 DAYS
THE CLEANSING OF THE SANCTUARY
DANIEL 8:14

"Unto two thousand and three hundred days; then shall the sanctuary be cleansed."

"For two thousand and three hundred evenings and mornings; then the sanctuary shall be restored to its rightful state." (RSV).

It is believed that a decree shall some day be issued for the rebuilding of the temple in Jerusalem, and that 2300 literal days after this decree is issued, the sanctuary in heaven shall be cleansed. The heavenly sanctuary shall thus be "restored to its rightful state."

Every case will some day have been decided either for life or for death. The last tear for sinners will have been shed, the last agonizing prayer offered, the last burden borne, the last warning given. Jesus is to some day throw down the censer, raise His hands, and with a loud voice say, "it is done", and He shall make the declaration, "He that is unjust, let him be unjust still: and he which is filthy, let him be filthy still: and he that is righteous, let him be righteous still: and he that is holy, let him be holy still. And, behold, I come quickly; and My reward is with Me, to give every man according as his work shall be." Revelation 22:11, 12.

THE ORIGIN OF SIN

"It is impossible to explain the origin of sin so as to give a reason for its existence. Yet enough may be understood concerning both the origin and the final disposition of sin to make fully manifest the justice and benevolence of God in all His dealings with evil. Nothing is more plainly taught in Scripture than that God was in no wise responsible for the entrance of sin; that there was no arbitrary withdrawal of divine grace, no deficiency in the divine government, that gave occasion for the uprising of rebellion. Sin is an intruder, for whose presence no reason can be given. It is mysterious, unaccountable; to excuse it is to defend it. Could excuse for it be found, or cause be shown for its existence, it would cease to be sin. Our only definition of sin is that given in the word of God; it is 'the transgression of the law;' it is the outworking of a principle at war with the great law of love which is the foundation of the divine government." GC 492–493.

We have the assurance, from the all wise and all knowing God, that sin shall never arise the second time; for Jesus shall always carry with Him, in eternity, the crucifixion marks upon His body.

"'I saw a new heaven and a new earth: for the first heaven and the first earth were passed away.' Revelation 21:1. The fire that consumes the wicked purifies the earth. Every trace of the curse is swept away. No eternally burning hell will keep before the ransomed the fearful consequences of sin.

"One reminder alone remains: Our Redeemer will ever bear the marks of His crucifixion. Upon His wounded head, upon His side, His hands and feet, are the only traces of the cruel work that sin has wrought. Says the prophet, beholding Christ in His glory: 'He had bright beams coming out of His side: and there was the hiding of His power.' Habakkuk 3:4, margin. That pierced side whence flowed the crimson stream that reconciled man to God-there is the Saviour's glory, there 'the hiding of His power.' 'Mighty to save', through the sacrifice of redemption, He was therefore strong to execute justice upon them that despised God's mercy. And the tokens of His humiliation are His highest honor; through the eternal ages the wounds of Calvary will show forth His praise and declare His power." GC 674.

CONCLUSION

"The world is stirred with the spirit of war. The prophecy of the eleventh chapter of Daniel has nearly reached its complete fulfillment. Soon the scenes of trouble spoken of in the prophecies will take place....

"Soon the battle will be waged fiercely between those who serve God and those who serve Him not. Soon everything that can be shaken will be shaken, that those things that cannot be shaken may remain.

"Satan is a diligent Bible student. He knows that his time is short, and he seeks at every point to counter-work the work of the Lord upon this earth." 9 T 14, 15–16.

"But like the stars in the vast circuit of their appointed path, God's purposes know no haste and no delay." DA 31.

"The day of the Lord is approaching with stealthy tread; but the supposed great and wise men know not the signs of Christ's coming or of the end of the world. Iniquity abounds, and the love of many has waxed cold." 6 T 406.

The next significant event that is to occur in the world, as outlined in the chronological prophecy of Daniel 11, is the forsaking of the holy covenant by the United States of America, as recorded in part C of verse 30. This will be fulfilled when the legislature of the United States passes the "National Sunday Law"! The last sequence of events that are to take place, in earth's history, under the 7th thunder, will thus have commenced to be fulfilled, and the last movements shall be "RAPID ONES"!

It is believed that the Temple in Jerusalem, the "sanctuary of strength", shall stand, being rebuilt, before the passage of the National Sunday Law, and our country (the U.S.A.) will (it is believed) suffer National ruin shortly after that apostasy.

With the passage of the National Sunday Law, that event, along with all of the remaining events that follow it, constitute, comprise, or make up, the sequential events which all come under the final and 7th thunder.

The longest time period between the sequential events recorded in the prophecy of Daniel 11, so far, is the 55 year period of time elapsed between the end of the Battle of Waterloo, in 1815, and the beginning of the Franco–Prussian (Franco–German) War in 1870. So far, as of October, 2005, 43 years have passed by since the 6th thunder, the Cuban Missile Crisis, ended in 1962. Will the 55 year period of time be equaled? When will the events portrayed under the 7th thunder begin to be fulfilled? The time of the end and second coming of Jesus is certainly near at hand.

"WATCHMAN, WHAT OF THE NIGHT"

"The burden of Dumah. He calls to me out of Seir, **Watchman, what of the night? Watchman, what of the night?**" Isaiah 21:11.

"With earnest longing, God's people await the tokens of their coming King. As the watchmen are accosted, 'What of the night?' the answer is given unfalteringly, 'The morning comes, and also the night.' Isaiah 21:11, 12. Light is gleaming upon the clouds above the mountaintops. Soon there will be a revealing of His glory. The Sun of Righteousness is about to shine forth. The morning and the night are both at hand-the opening of endless day to the righteous, the settling down of eternal night to the wicked." GC 632 (**Emphasis** supplied).

"The watchman is to know the time of night. Everything is now clothed with a solemnity that all who believe the truth for this time should realize. They should act in reference to the day of God. The judgments of God are about to fall upon the world, and we need to be preparing for that great day.

"Our time is precious. We have but few, very few days of probation in which to make ready for the future, immortal life. We have no time to spend in haphazard movements. We should fear to skim the surface of the word of God.

"It is as true now as when Christ was upon the earth, that every inroad made by the gospel upon the enemy's dominion is met by fierce opposition from his vast armies. The conflict that is right upon us will be the most terrible ever witnessed. But though Satan is represented as being as strong as the strong man armed, his overthrow will be complete, and everyone who unites with him in choosing apostasy rather than loyalty will perish with him.

"The restraining Spirit of God is even now being withdrawn from the world. Hurricanes, storms, tempests, fire and flood, disasters by sea and land, follow each other in quick succession. Science seeks to explain all these. The signs thickening around us, telling of the near approach of the Son of God, are attributed to any other than the true cause. Men cannot discern the sentinel angels restraining the four winds that they shall not blow until the servants of God are sealed; but when God shall bid His angels loose the winds, there shall be such a scene of strife as no pen can picture.

"To those who are indifferent at this time Christ's warning is: 'Because thou art lukewarm, and neither cold nor hot, I will spew thee out of My mouth.' Revelation 3:16. The figure of spewing out of His mouth means that He cannot offer up your prayers or your expressions of love to God. He cannot endorse your teaching of His word or your spiritual work in anywise. He cannot present your religious exercises with the request that grace be given you.

"Could the curtain be rolled back, could you discern the purposes of God and the judgments that are about to fall upon a doomed world, could you see your own attitude, you would fear and tremble for your own souls and for the souls of your fellow men. Earnest prayers of heartrending anguish would go up to heaven. You would weep between the porch and the altar, confessing your spiritual blindness and backsliding.

"Blow the trumpet in Zion, sanctify a fast, call a solemn assembly: gather the people, sanctify the congregation, assemble the elders, gather the children: ... let the bridegroom go forth of his chamber, and the bride out of her closet. Let the priests, the ministers of the Lord, weep between the porch and the altar, and let them say, Spare Thy people, O Lord, and give not Thine heritage to reproach.' Joel 2:15–17.

"'Turn ye even to Me with all your heart, and with fasting, and with weeping, and with mourning: and rend your heart, and not your garments, and turn unto the Lord your God: for He is gracious and merciful, slow to anger, and of great kindness....

"Warning, admonition, promise, all are for us, upon whom the ends of the world are come. 'Therefore let us not sleep, as do others; but let us watch and be sober.' I Thessalonians 5:6.

"'Take heed to yourselves, lest at any time your hearts be overcharged with surfeiting, (an overabundant supply: excess: an intemperate or immoderate indulgence in something, such as food or drink: an indulgence of the appetite or senses) and drunkenness, and cares of this life, and so that day come upon you unawares.' Luke 21:34.

"'Watch ye and pray, lest ye enter into temptation.' Mark 14:38. Watch against the stealthy approach of the enemy, watch against old habits and natural inclinations, lest they assert themselves; force them back, and watch. Watch the thoughts, watch the plans, lest they become self-centered. Watch over the souls whom Christ has purchased with His own blood. Watch for opportunities to do them good.

"Watch, 'lest coming suddenly He find you sleeping.' Mark 13:36." 6 T 407–409, 410.

"Blessed (*ashere*-"very happy") is the man that does this, and the son of man that lays hold on it; that keeps the Sabbath from polluting it, and keeps his hand from doing any evil." Isaiah 56:2.

"Blessed (*ashere*-"very happy") is he that waits, and comes to the thousand three hundred and five and thirty (1335) days." Daniel 12:12.

"Blessed (very happy) are the pure in heart; for they shall see God." Matthew 5:8.

Believers will not have another message based upon definite time. The longest reckoning of the 2300 days-years prophecy reaches unto October 22, 1844. After this date there is no definite tracing of the 230 day – year prophetic time prophecy.

Believers will not have another message based upon definite time. The longest reckoning of the 2300 day – year prophecy reaches unto October 22, 1844. After this date there is no definite tracing of the 2300 day – year prophetic time line.

"Not at first had God revealed the exact time of the first advent; and even when the prophecy of Daniel made this known, not all rightly interpreted the message." PK 700.

Two passages of Scripture were especially comforting to those who lived through the "Great Disappointment" of October 22, 1844:

"Thou must prophesy again before many peoples, and nations, and tongues, and kings. " Revelation 10:11.

"Write the vision, and make it plain upon tables, that he may run that reads it. 3 For the vision is yet for an appointed time, but at the end it shall speak, and not lie: though it tarry, wait for it; because it will surely come, it will not tarry." Habakkuk 2:2, 3.

DURING THE SEVENTH (7th) MILLENNIUM GOD'S PEOPLE SHALL BE WITH HIM!

"For six thousand years, Satan's work of rebellion has 'made the earth to tremble.' He has ' made the world as a wilderness, and destroyed the cities thereof.' And he 'opened not the house of his prisoners.' For six thousand years his prison house received God's people, and he would have held them captive forever; but Christ has broken his bonds and set the prisoners free." GC 659.

In God's divine providence, the 7th millennium shall soon begin. We have just a very few years left in which to do our part in the finishing of the work of the Lord! The six thousand years of rebellion shall be officially finished, at the appointed time of the end", which is very soon to be realized!

The last act in the drama of the ages, the "Great Controversy" between truth and error, is, it is believed, the simultaneous action of two events: (1) the passage of the "National Sunday Law" by the United States Legislature and (2) the "taking away of the *Tamyid*", the worship service in the restored Temple in Jerusalem, which is soon to be rebuilt! All of the last day events of earth's history then take place, and, the last events shall be "**RAPID ONES**"!

The "time of trouble, such as never was since there was a nation even to that same time" (Daniel 12:1), shall one day, soon, in the not-too-distant future, come upon us. "It is often the case that trouble is greater in anticipation than in reality; but this is not true of the crisis before us. The most vivid presentation cannot reach the magnitude of the ordeal. In that time of trial, every soul must stand for himself before God....

"The apostle John in vision heard a loud voice in heaven exclaiming: 'Woe to the inhabiters of the earth and of the sea! for the devil is come down unto you, having great wrath, because he knows that he has but a short time.' Revelation 12:12. Fearful are the scenes which call forth this exclamation from the heavenly voice. The wrath of Satan increases as his time grows short, and his work of deceit and destruction will reach its culmination in the time of trouble.

"Fearful sights of a supernatural character will soon be revealed in the heavens, in token of the power of miracle-working demons.... As the crowning act in the great drama of deception, Satan himself will personate (impersonate) Christ.. . But the people of God will not be misled. The teachings of this false christ are not in accordance with the Scriptures. His blessing is pronounced upon the worshipers of the beast and his image, the very class upon whom the Bible teaches that God's unmingled wrath shall be poured out....

"When Christ ceases His intercession in the sanctuary, the unmingled wrath threatened against those who worship the beast and his image and receive his mark (Revelation

14:9,10), will be poured out. The plagues upon Egypt when God was about to deliver Israel were similar in character to those more terrible and extensive judgments which are to fall upon the world just before the final deliverance of God's people....

"The prophets ... describe the condition of the earth at this fearful time: 'The land mourns; ... because the harvest of the field is perished.... All the trees of the field are withered: because joy is withered away from the sons of men. 'The seed is rotten under their clods, the garners are laid desolate.... How do the beasts groan! the herds of cattle are perplexed, because they have no pasture.... The rivers of water are dried up, and the fire has devoured the pastures of the wilderness.' 'The songs of the <u>temple</u> shall be howlings in that day, says the Lord God: there shall be many dead bodies in every place; they shall cast them forth with silence.' Joel 1:10–12, 17–20; Amos 8:3' (**Emphasis** <u>supplied</u>).

"These plagues are not universal, or the inhabitants of the earth would be wholly cut off. Yet they will be the most awful scourges that have ever been known to mortals. All the judgments upon men, prior to the close of probation, have been mingled with mercy. The pleading blood of Christ has shielded the sinner from receiving the full measure of his quilt; but in the final judgment, wrath is poured out unmixed with mercy.

"In that day, multitudes will desire the shelter of God's mercy which they have so long despised. 'Behold, the days come, says the Lord God, that I will send a famine in the land, not a famine of bread, nor a thirst for water, but of hearing the words of the Lord: and they shall wander from sea to sea, and from the north even to the east, they shall run to and fro to seek the word of the Lord, and shall not find it.' Amos 8:11, 12.

"The people of God will not be free from suffering; but while persecuted and distressed, while they endure privation and suffer for want of food they will not be left to perish. That God who cared for Elijah will not pass by one of His self-sacrificing children. He who numbers the hairs of their head will care for them, and in the time of famine they shall be satisfied. While the wicked are dying from hunger and pestilence, angels will shield the righteous and supply their wants. To him that 'walks righteously' is the promise: 'bread shall be given him; his waters shall be sure.' 'When the poor and needy seek water, and there is none, and their tongue fails for thirst, I the Lord will hear them, I the God of <u>Israel</u> will not forsake them.' Isaiah 33:15, 16; 41:17 (**Emphasis** <u>supplied</u>) ....

"'The Lord is thy keeper: the Lord is thy shade upon thy right hand. The sun shall not smite thee by day, nor the moon by night. The Lord shall preserve thee from all evil: He shall preserve thy soul.' 'He shall deliver thee from the snare of the fowler, and from the noisome pestilence. He shall cover thee with His feathers, and under His wings shalt thou trust: His truth shall be thy shield and buckler. Thou shalt not be afraid for the terror by night; nor for the arrow that flies by day; nor for the pestilence that walks in the darkness; nor for the destruction that wasteth at noonday. A thousand shall fall at thy side, and ten thousand at thy right hand; but it shall not come nigh thee. Only with thine eyes shalt thou behold and see the reward of the wicked. Because thou hast made the Lord, which is My refuge, even the Most High, thy habitation; there shall no evil befall thee, neither shall any plague come nigh thy dwelling.' Psalms 121:5–7; 91:3–10.…

"The people of God must drink of the cup and be baptized with the baptism. … For the elect's sake the time of trouble will be shortened. 'Shall not God avenge His own elect, which cry day and night unto Him?… I tell you that He will avenge them speedily.' Luke 18:7,8. The end will come more quickly than men expect. The wheat will be gathered and bound in sheaves for the garner of God; the tares will be bound as fagots for the fires of destruction.…

In the hour of peril and distress 'the angel of the Lord encamps round about them that fear Him, and delivers them.' Psalm 34:7.

"With earnest longing, God's people await the tokens of their coming king. As the watchmen are accosted, 'What of the night?' the answer is given unfalteringly, 'The morning comes, and also the night.' Isaiah 21:11,12. Light is gleaming upon the clouds above the mountaintops. Soon there will be a revealing of His glory. The Sun of Righteousness is about to shine forth. The morning and the night are both at hand-the opening of endless day to the righteous, the settling down of eternal night to the wicked.'…

"The eye of God, looking down the ages, was fixed upon the crisis which His people are to meet, when earthly powers shall be arrayed against them. Like the captive exile, they will be in fear of death by starvation or by violence. But the Holy one who divided the Red Sea before Israel, will manifest His mighty power and turn their captivity. 'They shall be mine, says the Lord of hosts, in that day when I make up My jewels; and I will spare them, as a man spares his own son that serves him.' Malachi 3:17. If the blood of Christ's faithful witnesses were shed at this time, it would not, like the blood of the martyrs, be as seed sown to yield a harvest for God. Their fidelity would not be a testimony to convince others of the truth; for the obdurate heart has beaten back the waves of mercy until they return no more. If the righteous were now left to fall a prey to their enemies, it would be a triumph for the prince of darkness. Says the psalmist: 'In the time of trouble He shall hide me in His pavilion: in the secret of His tabernacle shall He hide me.' Psalm 27:5. Christ has spoken: 'Come, My people, enter thou into thy chambers, and shut thy doors about thee: hide thyself as it were for a little moment, until the indignation be overpast. For, behold, the Lord comes out of His place to punish the inhabitants of the earth for their iniquity.' Isaiah 26:20,21.   Glorious will be the deliverance of those who have patiently waited for His coming and Whose names are written in the book of life.…

"By the people of God a voice, clear and melodious, is heard, saying, 'Look up', and lifting their eyes to the heavens, they behold the bow of promise.… Again a voice, musical and triumphant, is heard, saying: 'They come! they come! holy, harmless, and undefiled. They have kept the word of My patience; they shall walk among the angels;' and the pale quivering lips of those who have held fast their faith utter a shout of victory.

"It is at midnight that God manifests His power for the deliverance of His people…. Graves are opened, and 'many of them that sleep in the dust of the earth … awake, some to everlasting life, and some to sham and everlasting contempt.' Daniel 12:2. All who have died in the faith of the third angel's message come forth from the tomb glorified, to hear God's covenant of peace with those who have kept His law. 'They also which pierced Him' (Revelation 1:7), those that mocked and derided Christ's dying agonies, and the most violent opposers of His truth and His people, are raised to behold Him in His glory and to see the honor placed upon the 'loyal and obedient.'…

"Said the prophets of old, as they beheld in holy vision the day of God: 'Howl ye; for the day of the Lord is at hand; it shall come as destruction from the Almighty.' Isaiah 13:6…. The voice of God is heard from heaven, declaring the day and hour of Jesus' coming, and delivering the everlasting covenant to His people. Like peals of loudest thunder His words roll through the earth. The Israel of God stand listening with their eyes fixed upward. Their countenances are lighted up with His glory, and shine as did the face of Moses when he came down from Sinai. The wicked cannot look upon them. And when the blessing is pronounced on those who have honored Cod by keeping His Sabbath holy, there is a mighty shout of victory.

"Soon there appears in the east a small black cloud, about the size of a man's hand. It is the cloud which surrounds the Saviour and which seems in the distance to be shrouded in darkness. The people of God know this to be the sign of the Son of man. In solemn silence they gaze upon it as it draws nearer the earth, becoming lighter and more glorious, until it is a great white cloud, its base a glory like consuming fire, and above it the rainbow of the covenant. Jesus rides forth as a mighty conqueror…. As the living cloud comes still nearer, every eye beholds the Prince of life…. His countenance outshines the dazzling brightness of the noonday sun. 'And He has on His vesture and on His thigh a name written, King of kings, and Lord of lords.' Revelation 19:16….

"Amid the reeling of the earth, the flash of lightning, and the roar of thunder, the voice of the Son of God calls forth the sleeping saints. He looks upon the graves of the righteous, then, raising His hands to heaven, He cries: 'Awake, awake, awake, ye that sleep in the dust, and arise!' Throughout the length and breadth of the earth the dead shall hear that voice, and they that hear shall live….

"With unutterable love, Jesus welcomes His faithful ones to the joy of their Lord. The Saviour's joy is in seeing, in the kingdom of glory, the souls that have been saved by His agony and humiliation. And the redeemed will be sharers in His joy, as they behold, among the blessed, those who have been won to Christ through their prayers, their labors, and their loving sacrifice. As they gather about the great white throne, gladness unspeakable will fill their hearts, when they behold those whom they have won for Christ, and see that one has gained others, and these still others, all brought into the haven of rest, there to lay their crowns at Jesus' feet and praise Him through the endless cycles of eternity." (Excerpts from GC 622–647)

"The One who guarantees these revelations repeats His promise: 'I shall indeed be with you soon.' Amen; come, Lord Jesus." Revelation 22:20.

Three Charts — Last Day Events

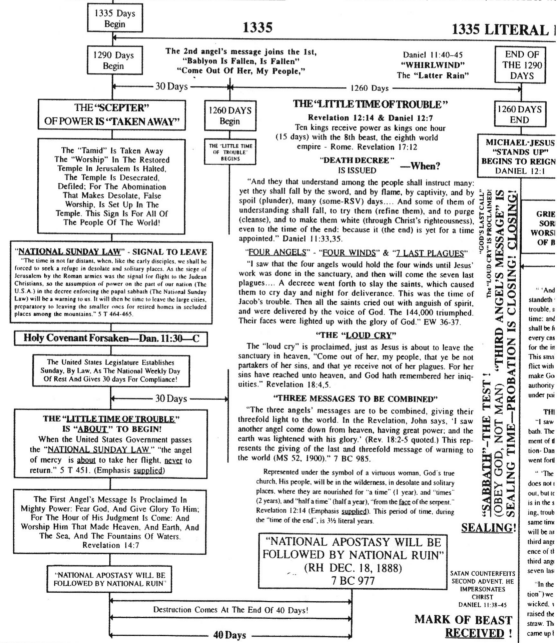

THE "BOTTOMLESS PIT"

The expression is descriptive of the earth when it is "without form", and "void". Prophecy teaches that it will be brought back, partially at least, to this condition; just a relatively short time before Christ's second coming.

The 8th world empire comes into power after the occurrence of a "Bottomless Pit" experience. Revelation 17:8. Through peace efforts (Daniel 8:23–25) and through aggression (11:40–45) he "shall destroy many." He shall even destroy the "mighty and the holy people."

THE 1260, 12

Thou Must Prophesy
And Nations, And Tongu

WRITE THE VISION, AND MAKE IT PLAIN U
FOR THE VISION IS YET FOR AN APPOINTED 1
THOUGH IT TARRY, WAIT FOR IT; BECAUSE IT WI

| 1335 Days Begin | **1335** | **1335 LITERAL I** |

| 1290 Days Begin | The 2nd angel's message joins the 1st, "Bablyon Is Fallen, Is Fallen" "Come Out Of Her, My People," | Daniel 11:40–45 "WHIRLWIND" The "Latter Rain" | END OF THE 1290 DAYS |

—— 30 Days —— ———— 1260 Days ————

THE "SCEPTER" OF POWER IS "TAKEN AWAY"

| 1260 DAYS Begin |
| THE "LITTLE TIME OF TROUBLE" BEGINS |

| 1260 DAYS END |

THE "LITTLE TIME OF TROUBLE"
Revelation 12:14 & Daniel 12:7
Ten kings receive power as kings one hour (15 days) with the 8th beast, the eighth world empire - Rome. Revelation 17:12

MICHAEL-JESUS "STANDS UP" BEGINS TO REIGN DANIEL 12:1

The "Tamid" Is Taken Away The "Worship" In The Restored Temple In Jerusalem Is Halted, The Temple Is Desecrated, Defiled; For The Abomination That Makes Desolate, False Worship, Is Set Up In The Temple. This Sign Is For All Of The People Of The World!

"DEATH DECREE" —When?
IS ISSUED

"And they that understand among the people shall instruct many: yet they shall fall by the sword, and by flame, by captivity, and by spoil (plunder), many (some-RSV) days.... And some of them of understanding shall fall, to try them (refine them), and to purge (cleanse), and to make them white (through Christ's righteousness), even to the time of the end: because it (the end) is yet for a time appointed." Daniel 11:33,35.

GRIE
SOR
WORSI
OF E

"NATIONAL SUNDAY LAW" - SIGNAL TO LEAVE
"The time is not far distant, when, like the early disciples, we shall be forced to seek a refuge in desolate and solitary places. As the siege of Jerusalem by the Roman armies was the signal for flight to the Judean Christians, so the assumption of power on the part of our nation (The U.S.A.) in the decree enforcing the papal sabbath (The National Sunday Law) will be a warning to us. It will then be time to leave the large cities, preparatory to leaving the smaller ones for retired homes in secluded places among the mountains." 5 T 464-465.

"FOUR ANGELS" - "FOUR WINDS" & "7 LAST PLAGUES"
"I saw that the four angels would hold the four winds until Jesus' work was done in the sanctuary, and then will come the seven last plagues.... A decree went forth to slay the saints, which caused them to cry day and night for deliverance. This was the time of Jacob's trouble. Then all the saints cried out with anguish of spirit, and were delivered by the voice of God. The 144,000 triumphed. Their faces were lighted up with the glory of God." EW 36-37.

" 'And standeth
trouble, s
time: and
shall be f
every cas
for the in
This sma
flict with
make Go
authority
under pai

Holy Covenant Forsaken—Dan. 11:30—C

"THE "LOUD CRY"
The "loud cry" is proclaimed, just as Jesus is about to leave the sanctuary in heaven, "Come out of her, my people, that ye be not partakers of her sins, and that ye receive not of her plagues. For her sins have reached unto heaven, and God hath remembered her iniquities." Revelation 18:4,5.

THI
"I saw
bath. The
ment of t
tion- Dan
went fort

The United States Legislature Establishes Sunday, By Law, As The National Weekly Day Of Rest And Gives 30 days For Compliance!

—— 30 Days ——

"THREE MESSAGES TO BE COMBINED"
"The three angels' messages are to be combined, giving their threefold light to the world. In the Revelation, John says, 'I saw another angel come down from heaven, having great power; and the earth was lightened with his glory.' (Rev. 18:2-5 quoted.) This represents the giving of the last and threefold message of warning to the world (MS 52, 1900)." 7 BC 985.

" 'The
does not i
out, but to
is in the s
ing, troub
same time
will be an
third ange
ence of th
third ange
seven las

THE "LITTLE TIME OF TROUBLE" IS "ABOUT" TO BEGIN!
When the United States Government passes the "NATIONAL SUNDAY LAW" "the angel of mercy is about to take her flight, never to return." 5 T 451. (Emphasis supplied)

Represented under the symbol of a virtuous woman, God's true church, His people, will be in the wilderness, in desolate and solitary places, where they are nourished for "a time" (1 year), and "times" (2 years), and "half a time" (half a year), "from the face of the serpent." Revelation 12:14 (Emphasis supplied). This period of time, during the "time of the end", is 3½ literal years.

"In the
tion") we
wicked, v
raised the
straw. Th
came up t

The First Angel's Message Is Proclaimed In Mighty Power; Fear God, And Give Glory To Him; For The Hour of His Judgment Is Come: And Worship Him That Made Heaven, And Earth, And The Sea, And The Fountains Of Waters. Revelation 14:7

"NATIONAL APOSTASY WILL BE FOLLOWED BY NATIONAL RUIN"
(RH DEC. 18, 1888)
7 BC 977

"NATIONAL APOSTASY WILL BE FOLLOWED BY NATIONAL RUIN"

SATAN COUNTERFEITS SECOND ADVENT. HE IMPERSONATES CHRIST DANIEL 11:38-45

Destruction Comes At The End Of 40 Days!

—— 40 Days ——

SEALING!

MARK OF BEAST RECEIVED !

(Vertical text at right): "GOD'S LAST CALL" The "LOUD CRY" IS PROCLAIMED "THIRD ANGEL'S MESSAGE" IS CLOSING! "SABBATH"-THE TEST ! (OBEY GOD, NOT MAN) SEALING TIME—PROBATION IS CLOSING!

290 & 1335 DAYS

Again Before Many Peoples,
es, And Kings. Revelation 10:11.

PON TABLES, THAT HE MAY RUN THAT READETH IT.
TIME, BUT AT THE END IT SHALL SPEAK, AND NOT LIE:
ILL SURELY COME, IT WILL NOT TARRY. HABAKKUK 2:2, 3.

THE "BOTTOMLESS PIT"

"And I saw an angel come down from heaven," the apostle John says, "having the key of the **bottomless pit** and a great chain in his hand. And he laid hold on the dragon, that old serpent, which is the Devil, and Satan, and bound him a thousand years.

"And cast him into the **bottomless pit**, and shut him up, and set a seal upon him, that he should deceive the nations no more, till the thousand years be fulfilled: and after that he must be loosed a little season." Revelation 20:1–3.

1335 DAYS END

DAYS DANIEL 12:12   **DAYS**   **2ND ADVENT OF CHRIST**

THE   DAY   OF   THE   LORD

WHEN SUNDAY BECOMES "UNDERSAL"   The preaching of the "Midnight Cry" goes forth, "Behold, the Bridegroom cometh, go ye out to meet Him"   "Behold, the Bridegroom cometh, go ye out to meet Him"

"THE LAST ACT IN THE DRAMA"
"The substitution of the false for the true is the last act in the drama. When this substitution becomes universal, God will reveal Himself.... He will arise in His majesty, and will shake terribly the earth. He will come out of His place to punish the inhabitants of the world for their iniquity (RH April 23, 1901)." 7 BC 980.

**6TH PLAGUE
FOUR ANGELS LOOSED
THIRD PART OF MEN SLAIN
TWO HUNDRED
THOUSAND THOUSAND
200 MILLION
REVELATION 9:14–16
REVELATION 16:12–16**

Blessed, Very Happy, Is He That Waits And Comes To The 1335 Days. Daniel 12:12

GC 635–652
GOD'S PEOPLE "DELIVERED"!
(7 BC 967) (6 T 406)

TIME OF JACOB'S TROUBLE

GREAT   TIME   OF   TROUBLE   ARMAGEDDON

VOUS E ON HIPERS EAST	SEA TURNS TO BLOOD	ALL WATER TURNS TO BLOOD	SCORCHING SUN	DARKNESS UPON SEAT OF BEAST	EUPHRATES DRIED UP	HAIL EARTHQUAKE FIRE

← 40 Days →   ⊣⊢ 5 Days →

Sometime Within The 1335 Days, After The "Tamid" (After The Worship In The Restored Temple In Jerusalem Is "Taken Away") Is Halted, Jesus Himself Shall Return To The Earth For The Redemption Of All Who Have Remained Faithful, Obedient And True, To Him!

---

l at that time shall Michael stand up, the great Prince which for the children of thy people: and there shall be a time of uch as never was since there was a nation even to that same l at that time thy people shall be delivered, everyone that ound written in the book.' When this time of trouble comes, e is decided; there is no longer probation, no longer mercy npenitent. The seal of the living God is upon His people. ll remnant, unable to defend themselves in the deadly con-the powers of earth that are marshalled by the dragon host, d their defense. The decree has been passed by the highest that they shall worship the beast and receive his mark in of persecution and death." 5 T 212-213.

E "LATTER RAIN" & THE TIME OF TROUBLE
that God had children who do not see and keep the Sab-y have not rejected the light upon it. And at the commence-he time of trouble (such as never was since there was a na-iel 12:1), we were filled with the Holy Ghost (Spirit) as we h and proclaimed the Sabbath more fully....

commencement of that time of trouble,' here mentioned, refer to the time when the plagues shall begin to be poured o a short period just before they are poured out, while Christ sanctuary. At that time, while the work of salvation is clos-le ("such as never was since there was a nation even to that e"-Daniel 12:1) will be coming on the earth, and the nations igry, yet held in check so as not to prevent the work of the el. At that time the 'latter rain', or refreshing from the pres-he Lord, will come. to give power to the loud voice of that el, and prepare the saints to stand in the period when the t plagues shall be poured out....

time of trouble ("such as never was since there was a na-all fled from the cities and villages. but were pursued by the who entered the houses of the saints with a sword. They : sword to kill us, but it broke, and fell as powerless as a en we all cried day and night for deliverance, and the cry before God." EW 33,85-86.34.

"THE SOLEMN DECLARATION"
Someday Jesus will make "the solemn declaration, 'He that is unjust, let him be unjust still; and he which is filthy, let him be filthy still; and he that is righteous, let him be righteous still; and he that is holy, let him be holy still.'

"Every case had been decided for life or death. While Jesus had been ministering in the sanctuary, the judgment had been going on for the righteous dead, and then for the righteous living. Christ had received His kingdom, having made the atonement for His people and blotted out their sins. The subjects of the kingdom were made up." EW 279-280.

THE "144,000"
" 'These are they which follow the Lamb whithersoever He goeth.... These are they which came out of great tribulation,' they have passed through the time of trouble such as never was since there was a nation; they have endured the anguish of the time of Jacob's trouble; they have stood without an intercessor through the final outpouring of God's judgments (7 last Plagues)." GC 649. (Emphasis supplied)

FOOD AND WATER
Angels Of God Will Provide It
"I saw the saints leaving the cities and villages, and associating together in companies, and living in the most solitary places. Angels provided them food and water, while the wicked were suffering from hunger and thirst. Then I saw the leading men of the earth consulting together, and Satan and his angels busy around them. I saw a writing, copies of which were scattered in different parts of the land, giving orders that unless the saints should yield their peculiar faith, give up the Sabbath, and observe the first day of the week (Sunday), the people were at liberty after a certain time to put them to death.... In some places, before the time for the decree to be executed, the wicked rushed upon the saints to slay them; but angels in the form of men of war fought for them.... God would be honored by making a covenant with those who had kept His law... and Jesus would be honored by translating, without their seeing death, the faithful, waiting ones who had so long expected Him.

"Soon I saw the saints suffering great mental anguish." EW 282-283. TIME OF "JACOB'S TROUBLE"!

God Shall Feed His People "Manna" From Heaven!

"God will prepare us for that time", when "Stern necessity will require the people of God to deny self, and to eat merely enough to sustain life." 1 T 204,206.

"The time of trouble will be shortened." GC 631.
Will the time be shortened by one to five days? or by more? No man knows the exact time when Christ shall return, but, we know that the time is near, even at the door!

THE "LITTLE BOOK" OF DANIEL
"Daniel shall stand in his lot at the end of the days. John sees the little book unsealed. Then Daniel's prophecies have their proper place in the first, second, and third angels' messages to be given to the world (MS 59, 1900). 7 BC 971.

129

THE VISIONS OF DANIEL 2, 7,

	DANIEL 2	DANIEL 7
HEAD OF GOLD **BABYLON** **605 – 539 B.C.**		
BREAST AND ARMS OF SILVER **MEDO-PERSIA** **539 – 331 B.C.**		
BELLY AND THIGHS OF BRASS **GREECE** **331 – 167 B.C.**		
LEGS OF IRON **ROME** PAGAN ROME **167 B.C. ——— 476 A.D.** PAPAL ROME **538 ——— 1798 A.D.**	The Legs That Are Of Iron	
ROME PAPAL ROME "Time of The End"	1798 ROME	Daniel 7:25 1260 Years
GOD'S KINGDOM		**Beast Slain** The beast was slain, and his body destroyed, and given to the burning flame. Daniel 7:11

8 & 11

DANIEL 8	DANIEL 11, 12
	PERSIA (Verse 2)
	GREECE (Verses 3, 4)
THE LITTLE HORN 8:8–12 THE PAPACY	**ROME** KING OF THE SOUTH (Verses 5, 6)
"A <u>king</u>" The anti-Christ Person Rises To Power 8:23–25 Out Of One Of The "<u>**FOUR WINDS**</u>" !	**ROME** THE king (Verses 36–45)
Anti-Christ Shall Be Broken "By No Human Hand" 8:25	**Michael** Stands Up Daniel 12:1 Blessed (very happy) is he who waits and comes to the (1335) days. Daniel 12:12

THE 2300 DAYS OF DANIEL 8:14

Prophetically speaking, the prophecy of the 2300 days met its fulfillment on October 22, 1844, when Jesus, our Great High Priest, went "within the veil", into the most holy place, the 2nd apartment of the heavenly sanctuary, and began the final phase of His mediation for His family on earth.

It is believed, by many, that the 2300 days, evenings and mornings, also will have a literal fulfillment, at the time of the end. A decree shall go forth, some day in the not-too-distant future, to restore and rebuild the temple in Jerusalem. 2300 literal days after the decree goes forth, it is believed, the cleansing of the heavenly sanctuary takes place, for Michael the Archangel, Jesus Christ Himself, shall stand up, move out of the sanctuary in heaven, and it shall be "restored to its rightful state."

"Unto two thousand and three hundred days;
then shall the sanctuary be cleansed." Daniel 8:14

"For two thousand and three hundred evenings and mornings;
then the sanctuary shall be restored to its rightful state." 8:14 (RSV)

132

THE JESUIT OATH
OF ALLEGIANCE TO THE POPE

APPENDIX A

Ceremony of Induction and Extreme Oath of the Jesuits

[When a Jesuit of the minor rank is to be elevated to command, he is conducted into the Chapel of the Convent of the Order, where there are only three others present, the principal or Superior standing in front of the altar. On either side stands a monk, one of whom holds a banner of yellow and white, which are the Papal colors, and the other a black banner with a dagger and red cross above a skull and crossbones, with the word INRI, and below them the words IUSTUM, NECAR, REGES, IMPIOS. The meaning of which is: It is just to exterminate or annihilate impious or heretical Kings, Governments or Rulers. Upon the floor is a red cross upon which the postulant or candidate kneels. The Superior hands him a small black crucifix, which he takes in his left hand and presses to his heart, and the Superior at the same time presents to him a dagger, which he grasps by the blade and holds the point against his heart, the Superior still holding it by the hilt, and thus addresses the postulant.]

Superior

My son, heretofore you have been taught to act the dissembler: among Roman Catholics to be a Roman Catholic, and to be a spy even among your own brethren, to believe no man, to trust no man. Among the Reformers, to be a Reformer; among the Huguenots, to be a Huguenot; among the Calvinists, to be a Calvinist; among the Protestants, generally to be a Protestant; and obtaining their confidence to seek even to preach from their pulpits, and to denounce with all the vehemence in your nature our Holy Religion and the Pope, and even to descend so low as to become a Jew among the Jews, that you might be enabled to gather together all information for the benefit of your Order as a faithful soldier of the Pope.

You have been taught to insidiously plant the seeds of jealousy and hatred between communities, provinces and states that were at peace, and incite them to deeds of blood, involving them in war with each other, and to create revolutions and civil wars in Countries that were independent and prosperous, cultivating the arts and the sciences and enjoying the blessings of peace. To take sides with the combatants and to act secretly in concert with your brother Jesuit, who might be engaged on the other side, but openly opposed to that with which you might be connected; only that the Church might be the gainer in the end, in the conditions fixed in the treaties for peace and that the end justifies the means.

You have been taught your duty as a spy, to gather all statistics, facts and information in your power from every source; to ingratiate yourself into the confidence of the family circle of Protestants and heretics of every class and character, as well as that of the merchant, the banker, the lawyer, among the schools and universities, in parliaments and legislatures, and in the judiciaries and councils of state, and to "be all things to all men," for the Pope's sake, whose servants we are unto death.

You have received all your instructions heretofore as a novice, a neophyte, and have served as a coadjutor, confessor and priest, but you have not yet been invested with all that is necessary to command in the Army of Loyola in the service of the Pope. You must serve the proper time as the instrument and executioner as directed by your superiors; for none can command here who has not consecrated his labor with the blood of the heretic; for "without the shedding of blood no man can be saved." Therefore, to fit yourself for your work and make your own salvation sure, you will, in addition to your former oath of obedience to your Order and allegiance to the Pope, repeat after me:

The Extreme Oath of the Jesuits

I, M_____ N_____ Now, in the presence of Almighty God, the Blessed Virgin Mary, the blessed Michael the Archangel, the blessed St. John the Baptist, the holy Apostles St. Peter and St. Paul and all the saints and sacred hosts of heaven, and to you, my ghostly father, the Superior General of the Society of Jesus , founded by 'St. Ignatius Loyola, in the Pontificate of Paul the Third, and continued to the present, do by the womb of the Virgin, the matrix of God, and the rod of Jesus Christ, declare and swear, that his holiness the Pope is Christ's Vicegerent and is the true and only Head of the Catholic or Universal Church throughout the earth; and that by virtue of the keys of binding and loosing, given to his Holiness by my Saviour, Jesus Christ, he hath power to depose heretical kings, princes, states, commonwealths and governments, all being illegal without his sacred confirmation and that they may safely be destroyed. Therefore, to the utmost of my power, I shall and will defend this doctrine and His Holiness' right and custom against all usurpers of the heretical or Protestant authority whatever, especially the Lutheran Church of Germany, Holland, Denmark, Sweden and Norway, and the now pretended authority and churches of England and Scotland, and branches of the same now established in Ireland and on the Continent of America and elsewhere; and all adherents in regard that they be usurped and heretical, opposing the sacred Mother Church of Rome. I do now renounce and disown any allegiance as due to any heretical king, prince or state named Protestants or Liberals or obedience to any of their laws, magistrates or officers.

I do further declare that the doctrines of the churches of England, Scotland, of the Calvinists, Huguenots and others of the name Protestants or Liberals to be damnable, and they themselves damned and to be damned who will not forsake the same.

I do further declare, that I will help, assist and advise all or any of his Holiness' agents in any place wherever I shall be, in Switzerland, Germany, Holland, Denmark, Sweden, Norway, England, Ireland, or America, or in any other kingdom or territory I shall come to, and do my uttermost to extirpate the heretical Protestants or Liberals' doctrines and to destroy all their pretended powers, regal or otherwise.

I do further promise and declare, that notwithstanding I am dispensed with, to assume any religion heretical, for the propagating of the Mother Church's interest, to keep secret and private all her agents' counsels from time to time, as they may entrust me, and not to divulge, directly or indirectly, by word, writing or circumstance whatever; but to execute all that shall be proposed, given in charge or discovered unto me, by you, my ghostly father, or any of this sacred convent.

I do further promise and declare, that I will have no opinion or will of my own, or any mental reservation whatever, even as a corpse or cadaver, (*perinde* ac cadaver,) but will unhesitatingly obey each and every command that I may receive from my superiors in the Militia of the Pope and of Jesus Christ.

That I will go to any part of the world whithersoever I may be sent, to the frozen regions of the North, the burning sands of the desert of Africa, or the jungles of India, to the centres of civilization of Europe, or to the wild haunts of the barbarous savages of America, without murmuring or repining, and will be submissive in all things whatsoever communicated to me.

I furthermore promise and declare that I will, when opportunity presents, make and wage relentless war, secretly or openly, against all heretics, Protestants and Liberals, as I am directed to do, to extirpate and exterminate them from the face of the whole earth; and that I will spare neither age, sex or condition; and that I will hang, burn, waste, boil, flay, strangle and bury alive these infamous heretics, rip up the stomachs and wombs of their women and crush their infants' heads against the walls, in order to annihilate forever their execrable race. That when the same cannot be done openly, I will secretly use the poisoned cup, the strangulating cord, the steel of the poinard [sic] or the leaden bullet, regardless of the honor, rank, dignity, or authority of the person or persons, whatever may be their condition in life, either public or private, as I at any time may be directed so to do by any agent of the Pope or Superior of the Brotherhood of the Holy Faith, of the Society of Jesus.

In confirmation of which, I hereby dedicate my life, my soul and all my corporeal [sic] powers, and with this dagger which I now receive, I will subscribe my name written in my own blood, in testimony thereof; and should I prove false or weaken in my determination, may my brethren and fellow soldiers of the Militia of the Pope cut off my hands and my feet, and my throat from ear to ear, my belly opened and sulphur burned therein, with all the punishment that can be inflicted upon me on earth and my soul be tortured by demons in an eternal hell forever!

All of which 1, M____ N____ do swear by the blessed Trinity and blessed Sacrament, which I am now to receive, to perform and on my part to keep inviolably; and do call all the heavenly and glorious host of heaven to witness these my real intentions to keep this my oath.

In testimony hereof I take this most holy and blessed Sacrament of the Eucharist, and witness the same further, with my name written with the point of this dagger dipped in my own blood and sealed in the face of this holy convent.

[He receives the wafer from the Superior and writes his name with the point of his dagger dipped in his own blood taken from over the heart.]

Superior

You will now rise to your feet and I will instruct you in the Catechism necessary to make yourself known to any member of the Society of Jesus belonging to this rank.

In the first place, you, as a Brother Jesuit, will with another mutually make the ordinary sign of the cross as any ordinary Roman Catholic would; then one crosses his wrists, the palms of his hands open, the other in answer crosses his feet, one above the other; the first points with forefinger of the right hand to the center of the palm of the left, the other with the forefinger of the left hand points to the center of the palm of the right; the first then with his right hand makes a circle around his head, touching

it, the other then with the forefinger of his left hand touches the left side of his body just below his heart ; the first then with his right hand draws it across the throat of the other, and the latter then with his right hand makes the motion of cutting with a dagger down the stomach and abdomen of the first. The first then says *Iustum*; the other answers *Necar*; the first then says *Reges*. The other answers *Impios*. (The meaning of which has already been explained.) The first will then present a small piece of paper folded in a peculiar manner, four times, which the other will cut longitudinally and on opening the name JESU will be found written upon the head and arms of a cross three times. You will then give and receive with him the following questions and answers.

Ques. From whither do you come?

Ans. From the bends of the Jordan, from Calvary, from the Holy Sepulchre, and lastly from Rome.

Ques. What do you keep and for what do you fight?

Ans. The Holy faith.

Ques. Whom do you serve?

Ans. The Holy Father at Rome, the Pope, and the Roman Catholic Church Universal throughout the world.

Ques. Who commands you?

Ans. The Successor of St. Ignatius Loyola, the founder of the Society of Jesus or the Soldiers of Jesus Christ.

Ques. Who received you?

Ans. A venerable man in white hair.

Ques. How?

Ans. With a naked dagger, I kneeling upon the cross beneath the banners of the Pope and of our sacred Order.

Ques. Did you take an oath?

Ans. I did, to destroy heretics and their governments and rulers, and to spare neither age, sex nor condition. To be as a corpse without any opinion or will of my own, but to implicitly obey my superiors in all things without hesitation or murmuring.

Ques. Will you do that?

Ans. I will.

Ques. How do you travel?

Ans. In the bark of Peter the fisherman.

Ques. Whither do you travel?

Ans. To the four quarters of the globe.

Ques. For what purpose?

Ans. To obey the orders of my General and Superiors and execute the will of the Pope and faithfully fulfill the conditions of my oath.

Ques. (Statement by Superior) Go ye, then, into all the world and take possession of all lands in the name of the Pope. He who will not accept him as the Vicar of Jesus and his Vicegerent on earth, let him be accursed and exterminated.

Note

This Jesuit Oath is located in the Library of Congress, Washington, D.C., Catalog Card # 66–43354. A nearly identical version of this Oath may be found in the U.S. House Congressional Record, 1913, page 3216. The oath was originally made public in the year 1883.

This presentation of the "Ceremony of Induction and Extreme Oath of the Jesuits" is from the book, The New World Religion, 1998, by Gary H. Kah, Hope International, (317) 579–1043. Used by permission of Gary H Kah.

APPENDIX B

WHAT ROME IS
"AIMING TO ACCOMPLISH" !

"And let it be remembered, it is the boast of Rome that she never changes.... Marvelous in her shrewdness and cunning is the Roman church. She can read what is to be. She bides her time, seeing that the Protestant churches are paying her homage in their acceptance of the false sabbath and that they are preparing to enforce it by the very means which she herself employed in bygone days....

"The Roman Catholic Church, with all its ramifications throughout the world, forms one vast organization under the control, and designed to serve the interests, of the papal see. Its millions of communicants in every country on the globe, are instructed to hold themselves as bound in allegiance to the pope. Whatever their nationality or their government, they are to regard the authority of the church as above all other. Though they may take the oath pledging their loyalty to the state, yet back of this lies the vow of obedience to Rome, absolving them from every pledge inimical (adverse, or hostile) to her interests....

"Protestants little know what they are doing when they propose to accept the aid of Rome in the work of Sunday exaltation. While they are bent upon the accomplishment of their purpose, Rome is aiming to re-establish her power, to recover her lost supremacy. Let the principle once be established in the United States that the church may employ or control the power of the state; that religious observances may be enforced by secular laws; in short, that the authority of church and state is to dominate the conscience, and the triumph of Rome in this country (the U.S.A.) is assured.

"God's word has given warning of the impending danger; let this be unheeded, and the Protestant world will learn what the purposes of Rome really are, only when it is too late to escape the snare. She is piling up her lofty and massive structures in the secret recesses of which her former persecutions will be repeated. Stealthily and unsuspectedly she is strengthening her forces to further her own ends when the time shall come for her to strike. All that she desires is vantage ground, and this is already being given her. We shall soon see and shall feel what the purpose of the Roman element is. Whoever shall believe and obey the word of God will thereby incur reproach and persecution." GC 581, 580, 581.

BIBLIOGRAPHY

A. Books

Bortoli, George. The Death of Stalin. New York: Praeger Publishers, 1975.

Christopher, Herald J. Bonaparte in Egypt. New York: Harper and Row, 1962.

Clark, Mark W. From the Danube to the Yalu. New York: Harper & Brothers, 1954.

Crankshaw, Edward. Khruschev, A Career. New York: The Viking Press, 1956.

Davis, John D. The Westminster Dictionary of the Bible. Revised & Rewritten by Henry Snyder Gehman, Ph. D., S.T.D. Philadelphia: The Westminster Press, 1944.

Epperson, Ralph. The Unseen Hand. Massachusetts: Publius, 1971.

Ferguson, Wallace K. and Geoffrey Brunn. A Survey of European Civilization. 3rd. ed. Boston: Houghton Mufflin Company, 1958.

Fireside, Harvey. Icon and Swastika: The Russian Orthodox Church Under Nazi and Soviet Control. Massachusetts: Harvard University Press, 1971.

Garraty, John A. The American Nation: A History of the United States. New York: Harper & Row Publishers, 1966.

Gimpel, Herbert J. Napoleon: Man of Destiny. New York: Franklin Watts, Inc., 1968.

Kah, Gary H. The New World Religion. Canada: Harmony Printing Limited, 2000.

Ludwig, Emil. Napoleon. New York: Boni Lweright, 1926.

MacArthur, Douglas. Reminiscences. New York: McGraw Hill Book Company, 1964.

Payne, Robert. The Rise and Fall of Stalin. New York: Praeger Publishers, 1965.

Rees, David. Korea: The Limited War. New York: St. Martin's Press, 1956.

Rogers, Adams & Brown. Story of Nations. New York: Henry Holt & Company, 1956.

Seventh-day Adventist Bible Commentary. Washington, D.C.: Review & Herald Publishing Association, 1955.

Shirer, William L. The Rise and Fall of the Third Reich. New York: Simon and Schuster, 1960.

Smith, Uriah. Daniel and Revelation. Nashville, Tennessee: Pacific Press Publishing Association, 1944.

Strong's Concordance of the Bible. Lake Wylie, South Carolina: Christian Heritage Publishing Company, 1988.

The Encyclopedia Americana. Vols. 12,21 & 27. New York: American Corporation, 1953.

The Five Worlds of Our Lives: A Geo-History. By the Editors of Newsweek and the Cartographers of the C.S. Hammond & Company: The United States of America, 1961.

The Holy Bible. Authorized King James Version. Iowa Falls, Iowa: World Bible Publishers, 1986.

The Holy Bible. Revised Standard Version. New York: Meridian-Penguin Books USA Inc., 1974.

The New Catholic Encyclopedia. Vol. 11. New York: McGraw Hill Book Company, 1967.

The Septuagint Version of the Old Testament and Apocrypha with an English Translation. London: Zondervan Printing, 1976.

The Simon and Schuster Encyclopedia of World War 11. Edited by Thomas Parish, Simon & Schuster. New York: Simon & Schuster, 1978.

The World Book Encyclopedia. Vol. 14. Chicago: World Book, Inc., 1992.

Thompson, Ian. Corsica. Harrisburg, Pennsylvania: Stackpole Books, 1972.

Weidhorn, Manfred. Napoleon. New York: Athenium, 1986.

White, Ellen G. Child Guidance. Nashville, Tennessee: Southern Publishing Association, 1954.

White, Ellen G. Early Writings. Washington, D.C.: Review & Herald Publishing Association, 1945.

White, Ellen G. Evangelism. Washington, D.C.: Review & Herald Publishing Association, 1946 (Reprinted in 1970).

White, Ellen G. Fundamentals of Christian Education. Mountain View, California: Southern Publishing Association, 1958.

White, Ellen G. Patriarchs and Prophets. Mountain View, California: Pacific Publishing Association, 1943.

White, Ellen G. Prophets & Kings. Mountain View, California: Pacific Press Publishing Association, 1943.

White, Ellen G. Selected Messages. Book 1. Washington, D.C., Review & Herald Publishing Association, 1958.

White, Ellen G. Selected Messages. Book 2. Mountain View, California: Review & Herald Publishing Association, 1958.

White, Ellen G. Testimonies for the Church. Mountain View, California: Pacific Press Publishing Association, 1948.

White, Ellen G. The Acts of the Apostles. Mountain View, California: Pacific Press Publishing Association, 1911

(19th Printing 1958).

White, Ellen G. The Desire of Ages. Mountain View, California: Pacific Press Publishing Association, 1898.

White, Ellen G. The Great Controversy. Mountain View, California: Pacific Press Publishing Association, 1950.

Webster's New Collegiate Dictionary. Springfield, Massachusetts: G. & C. Merriam Company, 1973.

Young's Analytical Concordance to the Bible. Grand Rapids, Michigan: Wm. B. Eerdmans Publishing Company, 1974.

B. Periodicals

"Time for a New Temple?" Time Magazine, 16 October, 1989, pages 64-65.